"ARE WE GONNA BE SAFE?" I ASKED.

"What you mean, girl?" Dizzle said with an attitude. His jaw locked tight. He ain't never have no attitude with me before.

"Where we all gonna sleep?" I asked. And just like that Dizzle slapped me across my mouth. He did it so fast that I had to blink away the hurt. I heard Nausy suck in air, cuz she was shocked, too.

"Shut the f— up! I ain't bring you all the way out here for you to think you can start disrespecting me. I don't see you paying for shit."

I sucked my lips, hoping the sting of his words and my mouth would stop hurting. A tear rolled down my cheek.

"Get in there and lay the f— down until I tell you to come out," he said, like he was trying to calm hisself down. "I'm so f—ing pissed off at you right now. Questioning me and shit."

More tears fell from my eyes. I couldn't believe he hit me. Him and Nausy both walked out of the trailer, the weak door snatching shut behind them...

PRAISE FOR KIA DuPREE'S NOVELS

silenced

"Its inner city realism compares favorably with Sister Souljah's *The Coldest Winter Ever* and Sapphire's *Push*. This is easily one of my top-five fiction books of the year."   —*Library Journal* (starred review)

"DuPree's knack for dialogue and her insight and compassion for her characters inspire the reader's empathy—an outstanding achievement."   —*Publishers Weekly*

"Shockingly provocative and earnestly raw...DuPree holds nothing back, but explores the poverty, pain, and hopelessness of the slums with absolute openness...Her writing is vibrant, descriptive, and full of flavor."
                                        —*Decatur Daily*

"Powerful...emotionally wringing...a raw deep look at surviving the mean streets...provides profound insight into the other side of living in D.C."
                                        —*Midwest Book Review*

"Honest and heartbreakingly intense...DuPree scores another win in the urban realism department...Every page of this novel is intriguing and entertaining... It has the ability to make us look at one another similarly, and maybe, even for a brief amount of time, allow us to see past cultural differences and try to understand and change the flaws that plague our society... together."

—*SUAVV* magazine

damaged

"A knockout of a story... raw, gritty, uncompromising realism, telling like it is honestly and well. DuPree is an author to watch."   —*Library Journal*

"An unvarnished look at the troubled, violence-filled lives of inner-city youth in Washington, D.C.... DuPree displays an excellent ear for the dialogue, thinking, music, and worldviews of her young characters and a talent for setting: The grimy streets, rundown hotels, beat-up houses, sweaty house parties, and clubs feel real and far above standard street lit."   —*Publishers Weekly*

"Riveting."   —*Gazette*

"Kia DuPree's literary voice sings in this beautifully written story of a young lady's tumultuous life. Easily the best book I've read this year!"

—Tracy Brown, *Essence* bestselling author of *Twisted*

SHATTERED

OTHER NOVELS BY KIA DuPREE

Damaged
Silenced

SHATTERED

A NOVEL

KIA DuPREE

GRAND CENTRAL
PUBLISHING

NEW YORK   BOSTON

Copyright © 2012 by Kia DuPree

Grand Central Publishing
Hachette Book Group
237 Park Avenue
New York, NY 10017

www.HachetteBookGroup.com

Printed in the United States of America
RRD-C

First Edition: October 2012

10 9 8 7 6 5 4 3 2 1

Grand Central Publishing is a division of Hachette Book Group, Inc. The Grand Central Publishing name and logo is a trademark of Hachette Book Group, Inc.

The Hachette Speakers Bureau provides a wide range of authors for speaking events. To find out more, go to www.hachettespeakersbureau.com or call (866) 376-6591.

The publisher is not responsible for websites (or their content) that are not owned by the publisher.

Library of Congress Cataloging-in-Publication Data
DuPree, Kia.
Shattered / Kia DuPree. — 1st ed.
     p. cm.
Sequel to: Damaged.
ISBN 978-0-446-54777-2
1. African Americans—Fiction. 2. Washington (D.C.) —Fiction. 3. Urban fiction. I. Title.
PS3604.U68S53 2012
813'.6—dc23
                                        2011052226

Dedicated to Sherry C. Oden for staring adversity in the face at every turn and giving that wench a run for her money. Your strength through recent trials inspires me.

This book is also for victims of sexual abuse and to the millions of lost girls everywhere.

ACKNOWLEDGMENTS

Extra-special thanks goes to Wilfrance Lominy for constantly staying on me to chase my dreams and giving me the support I need to get there. You're the best. To Darlene Backstrom, what would I do without you in my life? Thank you so much for being on my team, rallying behind me, and helping me when I feel like I'm losing my way. Thanks, Marcha Dyer, for your early critiques and for pushing this story. Many thanks go to Ms. Gail Elliot for all the wonderful educational and character building gifts you bestow on my son Izaiah.

Latoya C. Smith, your imagination is impressive. Thank you for your creative sparks that made this novel better than I expected it could be. Thank you to my fabulous agent, Victoria Sanders, who continues to believe in me, and to all the book clubs and readers who continue to support my work.

Also, many thanks go to my friends and family, especially Cynthia D. Dawkins; John DuPree; John Antwan; Jonathan; Douglas Omar; Doug Jamar; Michael; Timothy; Deanna; Janai; my husband, Donnell; and son, Izaiah, for your love and encouragement.

SHATTERED

What I am is what I am.

—Lauryn Hill, "A Rose Is Still a Rose"
from Edie Brickell & New Bohemians

PROLOGUE

November 2011
Washington, D.C.

Life is funny. One minute you think you got everything figured out. Then just like that, something random happens to make you question it all. I felt like that a month ago when somebody I ain't seen in forever bumped my shoulder hard as I stood in line at Nordstrom. Just when I was about to curse a bitch out, I heard, "KiKi! Oh my God, I knew that was you!" I blinked hard when I heard Nausy's voice screaming. She hugged me tight before I totally realized it was her. I couldn't believe how beautiful she looked and so different from what I remembered when I met her over ten years ago.

Nausy used to be big and chocolate with plump lips that matched her oversized attitude. The first day we met at Ms. Val's foster house on South Dakota Avenue, she sounded out every single syllable in her whole name. "It's Nau-sy-ni-ka and get it right," she had told me, her neck snapping left to right for each syllable. We was kids then, but wow—look at her now.

"How you been, girl?" she asked, squeezing me close again.

"I been good. Look at you!" I said, looking her over. Her chocolate skin was flawless; her dark eyebrows arched to perfection; her slim, curvy shape wearing the gray wrap dress like it was tailor-made. "You look really good."

"You do, too! Girl, give me your number. I came in here to grab some shoes to match a dress I'm wearing to this gala tonight, but I still gotta get my hair done," she said while taking her phone out of her handbag. "We gotta catch up, and I'm serious!"

It didn't take us long to exchange numbers, say we'd call each other, and give another round of hugs before we went our separate ways. It felt good as hell to see her. Even if she ain't never call me, I was happy to know she was doing good after all we had been through together. A lot had happened since the last time I saw her.

The next morning when Nausy called, talking about her new life and the YELL Foundation she worked for as a fund-raising associate for at-risk youth, I was shocked for more reasons than one. I thought her job was a nice fit for her considering she was once a part of that same group of teens growing up. Nausy sounded like she had her head on straight and like none of the stuff we faced back in the day had scarred her in the least. She seemed more outgoing than I remembered her, like a light radiated inside. Something about her made me want to lift my chin up and sit up straighter, too. I smiled listening to the excitement in her voice.

We planned to meet up for brunch at Front Page, a nice restaurant near Dupont Circle. A couple hours later, we was laughing and crying, talking about how life used to be for both of us, how she graduated from American University two years ago and the nonprofit organization she interned with since her junior year. She seemed so happy. And then...I told her about what happened during the years after I moved back home.

Even though Nausy was different, I could tell she was still the same girl who I used to tell all my secrets to. She was listening to my every word and not waiting for a break in our conversation to tell me more about her wonderful new life. I could tell she really wanted to know what happened to me. I thought about all the good, the bad, and the worst. When she asked me, "Ow haga ave haga ou yaga eally raga een baga?" in the same broken pig latin we used to talk back in the day, I smiled remembering her teaching it to me.

"How have you really been?" I repeated to see if I still understood it.

"You remember?" she said, smiling hard.

I thought about the question for a moment, took a sip of my pomegranate mimosa, then began pouring my heart out to her. Before long, only she cried. My own words had numbed me as I sat staring at my glass. Nausy reached across the table, breaking my concentration. Her hands rested on mine when she said, "You know you gotta tell my girls, right?"

I didn't understand, and I guess my face showed that I didn't cuz Nausy said, "They gotta hear your story and know they will be okay, too."

"What you mean?" I said after taking another sip from my glass. I ain't have nothing to say to them kids. Wasn't like I was a college graduate or had some big career I could brag about like her. What was I gonna tell them? I sold my body for more than half my life?

"Look at you now. You still here," she said matter-of-factly. "Somebody told me once that some people gotta take the rough and muddy road in life."

I rolled my eyes and looked over Nausy's shoulder at a waiter refreshing a customer's glass.

"You know why?" Nausy asked, her eyes penetrating me.

I shook my head. Hell, I ain't never heard no shit like that.

"The easy road is a setup," Nausy said before frowning up her face. "You can't see snakes and wolves lurking in the woods like you do on a muddy road. Plus, with every long stride you take, digging your heels in and pulling them out, over and over again, you're building your strength for whatever's ahead of you."

Maybe she was right. I swallowed the last of my drink and considered Nausy's words.

TWO YEARS EARLIER...

2009

1

Th-thump, th-thump, th-thump. That loud bass beat knocked me back to reality. The walls and ceiling shook so hard the wood paneling covering the basement vibrated. For real, for real, I forgot where I was until I noticed the tacky, sky-blue bedsheet covering the patio window. Then I remembered Meeka dragged me out to some stupid house party all the way out Riggs Park that I already knew was suspect as soon as we walked up the sidewalk. Nothing but broke niggas grinning from ear to ear. Meeka said she promised somebody she knew she'd make it out, so I just kept my mouth shut, except for the drinks. Now my head felt like it weighed a ton. Had to be the cloudy haze hanging in the air.

Whoever Big Cuz was, he sleeping all up on my shoulder like he knew me. Dude must be insane. What I look like? A bed? He slid off easy when I sat up, but his hand still managed to stay on my thigh. *Oh, hell no.* I stood and pulled my skirt down. Where was Meeka at? It was hard to see in the room slightly lit by the glow from the huge fish tank spread across the far wall. Some people was hugged up on couches, dancing in corners, but there was no sign of Meeka's chunky, milk chocolate ass in that pink halter. I stepped across legs and limbs and made my way up the stairs. I excused my way past a crowd. Oh, hell no. There she was. "Meeka! Get your ass down!"

I rushed over to the coffee table where she danced naked for some knotty-headed dudes. This heifer even had a Heineken bottle stuck in between her body glitter–covered thighs, twirking her hips to the same *th-thump, th-thump, th-thump* that woke me from my sleep. Her rose tattoo, painted on her upper thigh, popped in and out to the conga beat.

"Move!" I pushed past the swarm of niggas panting over her.

"Hold up, slim," somebody said, shifting my elbow over.

"Excuse me!" I snapped at the troll who had touched me and snatched my arm away. He threw his hands up like he knew I wasn't playing. "Meeka, come on, girl! Let's go!"

"What, KiKi?" She giggled and flashed her silver peg tongue ring, the whole time still twirking. The ripples on her sweaty, thick thighs moved in waves.

A tall dude threw some ones at Meeka as he video-taped her on his cell phone. She was pudgy cuz she was short, and she had an unusually flat stomach to have such chunky arms and thighs. Most niggas loved her shape. I know Meeka did, and she carried herself like she was the best-looking thing on the planet, even if she could stand to lose a few pounds.

"This shit ain't even fucking worth it. Come on!" I yanked her arm to the boos rising from the hungry audience behind me.

"Nah, shawty, let her go," the tall dude said.

"I'm just having fun," she hollered.

"Meeka!" I yelled again, this time with even more attitude. She knew I was her ride, and if she ain't wanna get left, she'd better pay me some attention.

"Hold up, let me just get my money." Meeka put the beer bottle down and scraped up the handful of dollars on the table before she climbed down.

"Whoa!," "Don't stop!," "Where you going, thick youngin'?" filled the room. I shook my head. After all this time, you'd think she'd know better than to dance for damn near free for some broke-ass niggas in the hood.

"What?" Meeka asked with her corny-ass Kool-Aid smile, counting her money.

"How much is it? Fifteen dollars?" I pressed my lips to the side.

"Stop hating, KiKi. I was just having some fun."

I helped her find her clothes as the crowd scattered. Some bitches rolled their eyes at us as we walked to the door.

"The fuck you looking at?" Meeka shouted in their direction. "Can't stand jealous bitches!"

"Come on, Meeka!" I snatched her arm and pulled her out the door. "That ain't even necessary."

"You kill me, KiKi," Meeka said as we jumped in my Acura. "Like you so innocent."

She and I both knew that was hardly the case. I'm just saying if you gon' do it, make some money doing it. Meeka probably had only earned about forty dollars. What the hell she gon' buy with that? A SmarTrip card for the Metro? "Unless you counted more than five hundred dollars, your ass stupid."

"Yeah, okay." She recounted her money in her lap. "You hungry?"

"A little bit."

"Let's go to IHOP. My treat," she said, smiling again and waving her ones like she had a big stack.

I shook my head and drove toward Bladensburg Road. I knew Meeka since I was little. We grew up on Fourth and W Streets, but we ain't start getting close until I ran into her at Everest College. She was taking classes to be a medical assistant, too. I liked her cuz she was cool as hell. Plus, she was almost finished with her program and she was giving me all her old tests and textbooks. She already knew about my hustle and didn't hate in the slightest cuz she was about making money, too. Meeka was willing to do just about anything to close the gaps between Temporary Assistance for Needy Families and child support checks from Quentin's father.

When we got to IHOP, the restaurant was practically empty except two other tables. I ordered pancakes, eggs, and bacon. She got coffee, waffles, and sausage.

"You talk to 'Reem lately?" Meeka asked, raking her fingers through her long extensions.

"Psst. Last time I talked to him, he talking about his name Hamza."

"What?" she asked, twisting her face up, confused. "Huum-zaah?"

"Yep. Hamza," I repeated. "Just cuz somebody done gave him a Malcolm X book, I'm supposed to call him that now."

"Oh no. Not another one of *them*," she said sipping her coffee.

"Yes, one of *them*. I'm sorry, but I can't do it. I'm not *that* in love. Forget what you heard. Me wearing scarves over my precious face? Picture that."

She laughed. "No, I can't picture that. Ain't Kareem a Muslim name anyway?"

"Exactly."

The waitress brought over our food, and we both attacked it, though my mind was still on Kareem. Maybe because he was the only real boyfriend I ever had. But that's the thing about Kareem, he's such a follower. Always trying to do what the next man do cuz the next man says he's supposed to do it. Such a turnoff. Weak and whack don't mix. That's how he got caught up breaking into that music studio on Georgia Avenue. Trying to steal some equipment with his dumb-ass friends. 'Til this day, I still can't figure out how he's the only one that got locked up behind that. It had to be a setup. Now he sitting up in jail, putting Allah's name in every other sentence. Talking 'bout things gon' be different when he get out. *Tssk.* I don't know about all that. "If I get one more picture in the mail of him wearing a kufi with that thick 'fro around his chin, I'ma scream!"

Meeka cracked up, laughing. "How long he been in there?"

"It'll be fourteen months next week."

"He's still your baby."

I rolled my eyes. I'm not gon' lie, Kareem held me down at first. I ain't have to work the streets no more. I had a place to stay. Even had a job washing hair at Peaches's salon in Lanham, but when Kareem got locked up, the bills piled up. One after the other. Pepco, WASA, Comcast, Sprint, State Farm. I sure as hell wasn't gon' lose the apartment. Hell nah. Not when I had a bank in between my thighs.

"Baby? I guess that's what he thinks." I took another bite and looked over her shoulder where a couple seemed too in love to notice nothing else happening in the room. That used to be us. But not no more. Kareem promised I wasn't gonna ever have to do what I used to do to eat. As far as I was concerned, his D.C. jail phone calls was just a way to pass the time when I was bored. "He'd be so blown if he knew what was really real for me right now."

Meeka nodded. She knew exactly what I was talking about.

"And I'm sure his Imam won't think I'm wifey material no way."

"You ain't never lied," she said smirking before scooping up another bite.

Wifey material? Would I ever be somebody's wifey material? Me and Meeka probably wasn't ever gonna wear that title. I ain't know what it was Kareem ever saw in me in the first place. I tried to hide my life from him in the beginning, but it ain't take him long to figure out that I had a lot of shit with me. Hell, I was never available when he wanted to go out. I was always tired or in the middle of doing something when he called. For a long time, Kareem actually thought me and my girls worked the bar at the Pearl on Ninth Street. Since he only went to Go Gos, he never knew no different. I was a bartender, not a ho. That was until the day Nut caught me sitting in Kareem's car in front of my apartment building.

I swear I can still remember it just like it happened yesterday. Nut had rolled up and double-parked beside Kareem's Magnum, blocking him in. As soon as I saw that silver Excursion in the corner of my eye, my heart damn near jumped out my chest cuz I thought Nut's crazy ass and my cousin Marcha had went to Myrtle Beach for Bike Week.

"You look like you just seen the devil. You all right?" Kareem had asked me.

I nodded, but the whole time I was thinking what the hell was I gonna do next. I watched Nut go inside his tiny apartment building I shared with all of his girls. Wasn't nobody there cuz Trina Boo and Camille had both went to get their hair done in Southwest, and Marcha was *supposed* to be with him. If he saw me, Nut was gonna go the fuck off. I was breaking a rule. As long as he took care of me, I wasn't supposed to be in no nigga's face unless they paid Nut to have my undivided attention. Camille warned me about sneaking around with Kareem and told me that this day was gonna come sooner than later, but I ain't wanna listen.

"You all right? You shaking and shit," Kareem said, placing his wide hand on my thigh.

I nodded again and tried blocking my face, hoping Nut wouldn't notice me through Kareem's tinted windows whenever he finally came back out.

"My ex-boyfriend just went in there," I whispered. "I really don't want him to see me. He's crazy."

"Who? That bama smoking right there?" said Kareem, mean-mugging Nut. His pretty-boy face tensed, and his jaws locked tight.

I didn't want to turn and see for myself, but if Nut was smoking in front of my building, that meant he already knew something was up and he was just waiting for the chance to call me out. Before I could think of something to say, Kareem rolled down my passenger window. Shit.

"Hey, Moe. I need you to let me out," Kareem shouted to Nut, his hand possessively tight on my thigh. This was not the time to try and flex. If he knew just how crazy that sicko was, Kareem would have never made that stupid move.

"Nah, son. You got my girl in the car," Nut said, puffing his cigarillo. "And I know you ain't have no appointment cuz I ain't see no money yet."

Kareem looked confused. I sat speechless.

"Ain't that right, KiKi?" Nut said puffing calmly. "You got some money for me, girl?"

The hurt in Kareem's eyes as Nut's words sank in was something I ain't ever wanna see again. He had been treating me like a queen, taking me here and there, buying me this and that for the past two months, and I ain't even fuck him yet, only for him to find out that I wasn't the kind of girl he thought I was. A foul look swelled his face. He shook his head and unlocked my door without even looking at me.

"Bye, Kareem," I managed to mumble as I climbed out.

Nut laughed, then pushed me into the building like

I was a piece of shit before he went to move his car. Later on, Nut punched me in my face so hard, I fell and chipped one of my teeth. I cried all night, not because of Nut, but cuz I knew something real that I had was now over. Except Kareem surprised me. Like two weeks later, he called and told me if I really wanted to change my life that he would be there for me. And little by little he was.

Meeka said something about the waitress being slow that snapped me out of my thoughts. I laughed, pretending I was listening, then toyed with my food for a second before she threw cash on the table.

"Fuck it. Let's go," Meeka said, standing up.

As soon as we walked out of IHOP, I lit a cigarette. Meeka did, too.

"If it wasn't for Kareem, I probably would've never got my GED," I said as I unlocked the car. "Hell, he got me this Ac' just cuz I ain't stop going to school."

"Told you, he still your baby."

She was right. Kareem ain't give up on me.

After I dropped Meeka off at her grandmother's house on Upshur Street, I headed home to my apartment on R Street. It wasn't the best place to live, but it was a long way from that hole-in-the-wall, roach-infested apartment I used to live in on Nineteenth Street. Sometimes I missed that old apartment, the neighborhood that never seemed to sleep, and my girls who shared the four-unit building with me. Meeka's little stunt tonight made me remember Trina Boo and how crazy she was. My girl was never scared to take risks or drop it like it was hot for an opportunity. Just like when she up and left us to roll to New York with a megaproducer. Now she's one of the top video models, making crazy money and dating big-name rappers like T'yahze and Spider Black.

I miss my bestie Camille, too. She was the one who first made me get on my paper game. Because of her, I charged niggas double cuz that's what she was getting away with. Now her smart-ass at Norfolk State in Virginia working on her degree. Camille opened my eyes. She made me realize I had to start thinking about what else I was gonna do with my life. When she went to night school, I finally did, too. Watching Meeka shaking her ass on that coffee table for a group of no-nothing-ass niggas just for a lousy couple dollars was like I was taking a step back, too. That girl's goals was limited.

I backed into a parking spot two doors down from my building, then reached in the backseat to grab my handbag. As soon as I took my keys out of the ignition and climbed out of the car, I heard a voice behind me whisper, "You might as well hand them over."

I turned around and couldn't believe it. Some boy with a black mask covering half his face was pointing a gun at me. Was this shit for real?

"I said gimme the keys," he said so smoothly I thought I was being punk'd.

"You gon' steal my car?" I asked, more blown than anything.

His bushy eyebrows raised, and then he snatched the keys right out of my hand.

"I cannot believe this." My fucking blade was in my bag, but then again, what was a blade to a gun?

"Just call your insurance company. You'll be straight," he said, starting my car like it had been his all along.

If only it was that simple. I stopped paying that bill four months ago. I watched that little young mother-fucker back out and pull off in the only thing Kareem left me out here with besides the apartment with rent more expensive than my shampooing gig with Peaches could ever cover.

"Man, fuck!" I screamed. I had to be the only person out on the block. It was so quiet besides a few cars driving down North Capitol Street. Thank God I still had my handbag, which meant I had my cell phone.

The next day I went to Mommy's house around Fourth and W Streets. I had to catch the damn bus, which I hadn't done in at least three years. I forgot how claustrophobic that shit was. People all up on you, little kids crying and fussing, niggas joning, and bitches running their mouths on the phone, bums sleeping and stinking up the spot. Uggh. I got chills just thinking about it. The fucked-up thing was when the police showed up about my car, they asked me for my insurance card. I was so shocked cuz I thought they was just gonna ask for my license. I faked like it was in my wallet for a while before I told them I ain't have it with me. Do you know these niggas gave me a fucking ticket for not having it? Then they had the nerve to tell me that it was a fine, like a hundred dollars a day for each day my car wasn't insured. That'll be like five thousand dollars! All I wanted was for those motherfuckers to find my goddamn car. Now, I'm gon' be in debt for that shit? Nah, fuck that. Whoever got it can keep it now.

The last time I was here, Mommy got pissed at me for not giving her fifty dollars to play Powerball, but oh well, she'd get over it. I would not see my hard-earned money being gambled away. The days of just handing over my money to people was over anyway. Mother or not.

I opened her refrigerator and took out the leftover pork chops she cooked for dinner. She walked in the kitchen with half her head braided.

"Oh, 'Kirwuh, I ain't know you wuz here."

I put the food in the microwave and waited for it to be done while she washed the dishes. Mommy was legally deaf. She could hear some, but she was an expert at reading lips. When we was young, I used to be embarrassed by her, especially when she used to scream our names through the window. "Torah, Rain, Yoti, and Shakirwuh!" she'd be yelling instead of Toya, Ryan, Yodi, and Shakira. Her words was choppy and slurred. All the kids from school thought she was an alchy until they saw us using our hands to talk to her sometimes. Mommy always made sure she looked good, though. Pretty bright skin and big hazel eyes like all her girls. No matter how poor we was, she made sure her nails, her eyebrows, and her hair stayed done. It was almost like she was trying not to give people more to talk about since she was already different.

Daddy was just thirty-seven when he died in a freak accident at his job with the National Park Service. He was trying to cut down a tree that had collapsed in Rock Creek Park and was laying stretched across Beach Drive, blocking traffic. A thick limb snapped unexpectedly and pinned him underneath. Mommy ain't seem right for a long time after he died, especially since Yodi was only one when it happened.

A couple years later, Mommy started dating again. But it wasn't easy, cuz it seemed like men kept trying to take advantage of her cuz she was partially deaf. She did try to keep a man in her life, though. One of them trifling-ass niggas was the reason we all got split up when I was eight. A bag of crack fell out of Yodi's diaper bag at her day care and that was all she wrote. Ryan was ten, Toya was eleven, and Yodi was just three when Child Protective Services stepped in, leaving Mommy no time to explain how it had got there. They ain't wanna hear nothing about it being a stupid accident, cuz they called it child endangerment. We couldn't even go to my aunt's cuz she had five kids and no room for us. For years, I ain't know where none of my family was at.

I wouldn't wish what happened to us on my worst enemy. How could they split us up after we had just lost our father? Then they took Mommy away when she was doing the best she could to take care of us. We ain't have nobody. All of us split up all over the city during a time that was already confusing for us cuz we was kids and we ain't understand much about life, let alone about why we couldn't be with Mommy no more. We ain't even know *who* to blame. My family still fucked up behind that shit. Toya stay having a nasty attitude with everybody, Ryan don't trust nobody and barely speaks, and Yodi act like she scared to leave the damn house. Mommy, well, she overcompensates for everything cuz she feel so guilty about what happened. She makes excuses for everybody and turn a blind eye to shit she know ain't right cuz she wants us to forgive her for what happened to us. In my heart, I know it's not her fault.

2

Mommy never used hearing aids when she was in the house. She said it irritated her the way an artificial limb would probably feel to me, so we always signed or talked looking at her since she needed to see our lips. Once she caught her man Londell having a full-fledged convo with another chick right in her face. That nigga had to bounce after that. But Mommy's men wasn't the only people who tried to take advantage of her. We all did in a way. It was how I stayed out for weekends and then school nights when I was in middle school cuz I faked like I ain't understand what she said or I snuck in and out cuz I knew she'd never know. Hell, we all did our dirt. Being apart from Mommy all that time in foster care left each one of us with different scars that needed to heal. And that's exactly why Yodi got two kids and she only seventeen, why Ryan been acting like a strange hermit since he was twelve, and why I ended up dropping out of school in the eighth grade, moving out when I was fourteen to live with Nut and the other girls that worked the streets with me.

Toya's the only one Mommy ain't have nothing bad to say about. She always act so proud of her firstborn since she was the only one to graduate from high school, giving Mommy the only chance to see one of her children walk across McKinley's stage. Forget that I got my GED. For real, I can't stand Toya's ass. She so busy making it her job to point out how fucked up everybody else's life is compared to hers. Her grouchy ass think I ain't know she been jealous of me ever since we was young. Calling me Project Barbie every chance she get. It sure as hell ain't my fault that she ain't never do nothing with herself or that she can't keep a man. All she had going for her was that stupid-ass government job that had her working a thousand hours a week, even when she slept. Mommy could brag all she wanted to about Toya's selfish ass and that high-paying job that owned her.

Mommy wasn't a perfect mother, either. I mean, I loved her, but there was plenty of days when I had to find a way to make sure I had the clothes and shoes I needed for school cuz she couldn't afford to get it for me. Shit, if it meant I had to hit a dude up for money so I could have what I needed, then I ain't care. Even exchange. So what, Toya got her own car and an apartment uptown. She can't hardly function without a bottle of Moscato. Bet Mommy don't know that foul shit.

"Hurry up, Mommy," I signed.

"Okay, 'Kirwuh!" she yelled. "I coming. Comb down!"

Don't be telling me to calm down. I'ma be late for work. Mommy kissed Yodi's two kids, Kamau and Chrissie, and grabbed her handbag. "Okay, now let's go."

I rolled my eyes and followed her down the hall to the elevator. Case and point, who was taking Mommy to get her hair hooked up now? Where's Toya's ass? I mean, I appreciated Mommy putting the rental car in her name, but she ain't have to always dismiss what I did do for her.

"You know Toya might be getting a promotion soon? Her supervisor resigning at the end of the month," Mommy said, smiling.

I rolled my eyes. Here we go again with this Super Toya shit. I blocked out the rest of Mommy's Toya brag-a-thon and focused on the thick traffic ahead of me. It took an hour to get to Lanham cuz of a car accident on 95, when it normally took thirty minutes. As soon as we pulled in the shopping center, I saw Peaches's blue Infiniti truck already there.

"Damn. She gon' be mad as hell as usual."

"Don't worry," Mommy signed.

Easy for her to say. Peaches was doing good on her

own. Thanks to the life insurance policy she cashed in on her husband, Nut, and the rental properties she sold, she was able to reopen her salon after he was killed and move on with her life. As much as she put on a front like she ain't miss him cuz he was an asshole who built his empire off of stolen drug money, flipping houses, and off of me, her, and my other girlfriends, she was ultra in love with that nigga. So in love that she worked the streets for years for him until he finally married her and put her up in a nice-ass house in bourgie Bowie, Maryland. The last time she saw him alive, her face was on his fist and he made her miscarry their second child. Their first son, Amir, was her new king.

What really bugged everybody out was the way Nut was killed. His body was found in a Dumpster around Savannah Terrace, but his head was taped up in a bag floating down the Anacostia River. All of us knew a Haitian dealer named Smurf was behind it, but Nut had did everybody so motherfucking dirty that we ain't have shit to say about it. Peaches was still depressed and spent most of her time in that big house with her son. Her ass needed to be in somebody's therapy sessions for real.

I pulled up to the salon Peaches named after herself and parked beside her truck.

"About time," Peaches said as soon as I walked in. She already had a client in her chair, even though the store had only been open for ten minutes. Knowing Peaches, she was probably there at the crack of dawn. She was a workaholic, looking like money first thing in the morning, with her fresh do, gloss, cute mint-green top, and charcoal stretch jeans.

"I know, I know. I'm sorry," I said, pointing at Mommy.

"Hi, Ms. Scott," Peaches said, smiling.

Mommy waved and said, "Sawry."

I looked at the book, checked the voice mail, and added new appointments to the schedule. Next, I went to make sure there was enough clean towels and that none needed folding.

"Anything you need me to do?" I asked Peaches.

"Yes, please, please, please go down to the beauty supply store and get me some color. I already called, and they holding three bottles for me."

"I got you." I signed to Mommy that I was going a couple doors down to pick something up for Peaches.

When I came back, I washed Mommy's hair and two other girls who had come in to get their hair done with Daneen and Kori. My phone vibrated in my pocket. Meeka had sent me a text:

YOU WANNA DO A PARTY WITH ME LATER?

I had to think about that one. Knowing Meeka, wasn't no money in it whatsoever. My wallet was empty as hell, though, and that rental wasn't free. I texted back:
FOR WHO, HOW MUCH, AND WHERE?

She sent me back: MY COUSIN HAVING A SMALL PARTY AT THE LA QUINTA IN WALDORF FOR HIS BOY THAT JUST GOT OUT.

Waldorf? That's too damn far, number one.

I texted: NAH, THAT'S OKAY.

Meeka sent: GIRL, HE GON' GIVE US $500 APIECE. YOU KNOW HE JUST GOT HIS TAX REFUND CHECK BACK. TRYING TO DO IT UP AND SHIT.

I laughed, then sent: DANCE OR PLUS MORE?

Meeka sent: DANCE, BUT MORE IF YOU WANT. TIPS ARE ALWAYS GOOD :-)

That wasn't bad. Maybe I can make next month's rent in just one night. After I finished washing another head and saw that Mommy was under the dryer, I asked Peaches what she thought about it on the low. Peaches was more than my boss, she was like my sister. Since we used to work the streets together for Nut, we was closer than me, Toya, and Yodi ever could be. I mean fighting bitches for each other, going to jail together, and everything. She knew what was up. My shampooing job was just a steady check and what I gave the IRS. I got as many hours as I wanted cuz I worked hard. I loved to see my girl doing good, plus she had been through so much. She deserved to have her dreams come true.

"I don't know, KiKi," she said. "That shit is far for you. Plus, you ain't got nobody watching your back. What if some hard-up nigga get outta hand?"

Peaches was right, I guess. "But it's her family, though," I tried again.

Peaches shook her head. "I know how it is, KiKi, but I just don't want nothing to happen to you. Those kinda parties can get crazy quick. You know how them niggas be drinking and shit."

Meeka sent another text. It said: SO WHAT'S UP? Even with all the hours I got from Peaches, it just wasn't as much as I really needed.

I sent Meeka one letter, K, then slid my phone back in my pocket. I ain't have no lump stash of money tucked nowhere like Peaches. It was just me. I had to do what I had to do. I smiled at Mommy, then walked over to the sink and washed another head.

Of course, I was the ride out to Waldorf since Meeka ain't never have shit. And 93.9 was doing their thing, too. I blasted Kelis's "Bossy" as loud as it could go. Meeka was in the mirror putting her makeup on, spraying way too much of her Juicy Couture Show Off that kept making me sneeze.

"Girl, my cousin ain't gonna be the only one with his refund check."

"Meeka, you don't mind stripping for your cousin?" I asked, still trying to wrap my mind around that part.

"He gotta be like my third or fourth cousin. Our blood more like Kool-Aid," she said, laughing.

"You stupid as hell. Your lying ass just wanted me to come."

"Money is money. Shit, you can give him a private dance. I'll get his money-making friends," she sang.

When we pulled up, Meeka called her cousin Harold

to come outside and get us. He was cute as hell with his caramel face, neatly shaved beard, and confident walk. Harold looked strong as shit, like a UFC fighter or something.

"How y'all doing," he said, smiling at me.

I winked at him.

"What's up, cuz?" he said, laughing and squeezing Meeka's round ass stuffed in those black liquid leggings.

That's when I knew for certain I had been lied to. I shook my head, then texted the address to Peaches, just in case. Back in the day, Nut took care of this part, but things had changed. Peaches sent me back: BE CAREFUL GIRL. LUV U. The music was low when we walked in the suite. Only four dudes was in there. Meeka gave me 250 dollars as soon as we got in the bathroom.

"He said we gon' get the rest when we finish dancing."

"Is this gon' be it?" Surprised at how few dudes was in there.

"Yeah, girl. It's private as hell, ain't it?"

I nodded. "But that's fine with me."

"Me, too. Shit. I hope they wanna fuck, too, cuz I ain't getting no damn tax refund check."

I laughed, then took a shot of Grand Marnier I had in my bag. Meeka fixed her breasts in her bustier. I fixed my fishnet bodysuit. It had been a long time since I danced. I ain't have no routine. All I needed was the music and somewhere to shake my ass.

"I brought this," she said, smiling sneakily, holding

up a three-foot-long, double-sided dildo. She raised her eyebrows, and I smiled. This girl was off the chain.

"Let's see what those tips looking like first."

"All right," she said, slapping my butt.

"You ready?" I said, stepping into my five-inch heels.

"Yeah, let's go!" Meeka squealed.

Jay-Z's "Big Pimpin'" played from the radio. Me and Meeka danced at the same time. First, we danced alone, and then we danced together. The guys seemed to be warming up, but none of them was raining dollars yet. I went over to Harold's sexy ass first, straddled his lap, and worked him so good, he nutted.

"Damn, girl," he groaned. He was loving it, too. His dick was still hard as hell. He yanked at my fishnets until a hole was big enough for him to pull my panties to the side. When he dipped his fingers inside, I stood up. Harold wanted to fuck. And now wasn't the time. I smiled and danced away to the next dude, a greedy-looking nigga with dollars in his hand. That's what I was talking about. T-Pain and Akon purred out the speaker as I got Big Homie up. Ain't take no time at all. As soon as my ass pressed against his jeans, he was rock. He must've been the one who was locked up. I took his money with the quickness.

"I'm saying, I want more than this," he whispered.

"I got you," I said. "Let's go."

Big Homie stood up and took me to a bedroom in the back. I could hear Gucci Mane singing, "She's a very freaky gurl/Don't bring her to mama," as he closed the door.

"You sexy as shit, but I just need some head."

"That's a hundred dollars."

He dug in his wallet and handed the bill to me. I put it in my bra with the other money I took from him, and then I sat Big Homie on the edge of the bed. As soon as I unzipped his jeans and pulled his dick out, nut drizzled all over my fingers.

"My bad," he laughed. "It's been awhile since a girl touched him."

"It's all good," I said, smiling to make him feel at ease. "You sure you can handle me?"

"That's all right. Let me just look at you or something."

"Okay." I stood up and danced to the faint music for him, then did a split and put my leg behind my head.

"Goddamn," Big Homie moaned as he played with hisself. "I'm cumming again."

"It's all good," I said, smiling. I got up and gave him a kiss on his cheek. "Do you mind if I go back out there with your friends?"

He shook his head, then left to go to the bathroom.

That shit was easy. I walked back to the living room. Meeka's ass already had a dick in her mouth and another one in her hand. Harold came up to me, rubbing his dick with one hand and holding a bottle of Cîroc in the other.

"I want your ass bad as shit," he said as he pushed me back in the room. Harold picked me up and carried me to the bed like a caveman. My pussy jumped. He bit my nipples through my bra and kissed down my stomach, and then he ripped my fishnet bodysuit apart like it was gift-wrapping paper.

"Wait," I said, pushing his chest up some. "You know you gotta pay for this, right?"

"Yeah," he said, burying his head in my neck. "I got you, I got you."

He was so fucking sexy. I swear I ain't wanna interrupt. I couldn't get enough of his Jean Paul Gaultier cologne. His beard tickled my neck as he kissed me.

"For real, Harold, you gotta pay me first."

"Man, fuck! I'm just trying to get this nut out real quick, then I'll get it." I saw a vein on his neck pulsate. Now, I wasn't no fool. I knew how this was gonna go. If he wasn't gonna pay me first, then he wasn't gonna pay it at all. But the tricky thing was, if I complained too much, he wasn't gonna give me the other half he owed me and Meeka for dancing and coming out here. This is what I hated about not having no pimp. A pimp would've made sure everything went the way it was supposed to go. Money first. See, for real, Harold ain't think he should have to pay extra since he's the one who orchestrated the whole little event. The best thing for me to do in this situation was to just take a loss and let him have a freebie. I'd be better off getting the other 250 than the *nothing* I'd get if I pissed him off.

When Harold was done, I got up and went to the bathroom. I wasn't even in the mood to finish dancing. I popped the X pill I had in my bag and swallowed another shot of Grand Marnier. Nah, fuck that. It was money in this suite. I wasn't leaving 'til I got what the fuck I deserved. I let the music and the pill work their magic, and then I went back out to the living room with Meeka's double-sided dildo in my hand. I joined her freak fest and gave them niggas the best show of their lives. By the end of the night, we walked out of there with all their money. I had eleven hundred dollars and Meeka one-upped me with twelve hundred. Even Harold paid his entire tab plus some and had the nerve to ask me for my number, talking about he wanted to take me to dinner. Nigga, please. Business is business.

3

ell, I know I flunked that one," I said, closing the
book. After comparing the answers I remembered
marking for the medical terminology test I just took to
the actual answers in the textbook, I knew I ain't pass. "I
should've fucking studied."

Meeka puffed her cigarette and leaned against the bus
stop. We both had to catch the train home, but we
wanted to smoke before we went inside the Silver Spring
station. I had to return the rental car cuz it was getting
way too expensive. Me and Mommy was gonna buy a car
together Saturday. Well, it was gonna be my car, but it
was gonna be in her name. If she ever needed it, I would
take her wherever she wanted to go. It was the best I
could do since I wasn't paying that fine on the Acura.

"What you doing this weekend?" I asked before I
took another puff.

"Girl, I promised Quentin I'd take him and his cousin to Chuck E. Cheese."

"Oh no. Not with all them wild, bad-ass kids running around," I said, laughing.

"Exactly," Meeka said, shaking her head. "But that's my baby."

I looked at my reflection in the glass on the bus shelter. "Ugh. I need to get my fade right." I had this bangin'-ass hairstyle Peaches hooked me up with, but she wasn't no barber. One side was tapered down low, like a boy, but the other side was long and multilayered, golden and feathered. I needed somebody who was nice with some clippers to edge up the other side. We both smashed out our cigarettes and headed to the train. Meeka transferred to the Green Line at Fort Totten, while I rode on until I got to Rhode Island Avenue–Brentwood. I walked down to Rhode Island Avenue and caught the bus, which was getting so old.

I stopped at the barbershop on North Capitol Street and told one of the barbers what I wanted him to do. He was cute and even asked me if I wanted a part or two etched above my ear. Not a bad idea.

"Can you make it go all the way down, though?" I asked, looking in the mirror.

"Like racing stripes?" he asked.

I nodded. It should be fly. He sat me in his chair and put the cape around my neck. As soon as he switched the clippers on and tilted my head to the side, I saw a

familiar face sitting in a chair across from me. He smiled
when he saw me. That same Cat in the Hat smile I remembered from years ago. *Dizzle*. Wow.

"How you doing?" he asked. He hadn't changed, just
looked a lot older.

"I'm all right."

"You look good."

I smiled. It was weird. Before Nut controlled my life,
there was Dizzle. He was the same person who took
my virginity, who took me off the street and turned me
out at the same time. The person who introduced me
to shrooms, Ecstasy, weed, and liquor. And there I was
smiling at him instead of spitting fire. His barber handed
Dizzle a mirror, then unbuttoned his cape and brushed
his shoulders off.

"You want to catch up later?" he asked.

I thought about it for a second. I mean, I really did
want to know what happened the day we was forced
to go our separate ways. Plus, I could use somebody
watching my back out here cuz I was still doing what
I needed to do to make money, but something wasn't
right about it. I told him I'd call him, but I knew
I wouldn't. His trifling ass preyed on runaways. He
couldn't be trusted.

"You know you still my favorite," he said, winking.
Dizzle was a genius at mind games, at least with girls
who was eleven and twelve. He ain't deserve to know
how I turned out or that I was still doing what he taught

me to do. Surviving. I sat there thinking about those days. A lot had happened, and he still seemed like the same person, only much older. I watched him walk out the door with the same bouncy stride I remembered. Two girls came in the shop not long after Dizzle left. One was a bombshell with a boy haircut but was in bad need of a shape up. The other was an albino. She was tall and had a body like she played basketball for the Mystics. She had such an eye-catching face, tiny blonde cornrows hidden underneath her fitted cap, and a pair of cute shades covering her eyes. I watched her take a seat and wait for her friend to get in the chair she wanted. Every time my barber spun my chair around, I could feel the albino staring at me, even though she had a magazine in her hand. I looked down at my phone and sent Peaches a text to see if she needed me to work later.

"What kind of phone is that?" the girl in the shades asked.

"Oh, it's a Palm Pre."

"You like it?"

"It's all right, except the keyboard is jive cramped."

"You mind if I see it? I'm thinking about upgrading my phone," she said.

"No. Here you go."

The girl walked over and took my phone. I could see her playing with the keyboard and scrolling through the menu screen.

"It's nice, but I think I'ma go ahead and get another iPhone." She handed it back to me.

I smiled.

"I think you gotta new text. I felt it vibrate," she said.

"Oh, okay," I said, looking at my phone. I laughed when I saw that she was the one who actually typed a message that was still on the screen. It said: YOUR SEXY ASS NEED TO MAKE IT YOUR BUSINESS TO CALL ME. I'M AUDRI. 202-555-2131. She was bold as hell. Her girl was sitting right next to her. That shit turned me on for some reason. I saved her number in my phone, then sent her a text: I'M KIKI, AND I MIGHT OR I MIGHT NOT.

"You're all done, beautiful." The barber handed me a mirror. "You like it?"

"Yeah, it's real cute."

He took off my cape and wiped off my shoulders. I paid him and walked out without even looking at Audri. I mean, that was just too much for one day. First Dizzle, then her going hard in front of her boo. Shit was crazy. I waited for the next bus to take me back up the street. I thought of just going over to Mommy's later so I wouldn't have to wake up early in the morning. When I hopped on the bus and got settled in a seat, I saw Audri come out the barbershop. She was grabbing something out of her burnt-orange Challenger. That shit was hot. A black racing stripe went down the front, and it sat on twenty-two-inch rims. I might have to call Audri after all.

* * *

The next day me and Mommy met this girl on Orleans Place to look at her white 1996 convertible BMW. She was a student at Gallaudet University, the top college for deaf kids. She was trying to get rid of it for some quick cash. I mean, it looked all right for it to be so old, except for the duct tape on the convertible part. The best part was she only wanted two thousand for it. We did a test-drive up Florida Avenue, down West Virginia, and back. I couldn't believe how clear she was able to talk to be deaf. She said it was cuz she had cochlear implants since she was little. I had never heard of that, but Mommy said the surgery was too expensive for her and that a lot of the kids at Gallaudet had it. It made me feel bad for Mommy cuz this girl sitting behind us could hear so well. She ain't need to read my lips or see me sign for her to understand me. I mean, for real, I couldn't hardly tell that she was deaf, except some of the words she said wasn't pronounced real clearly.

When we got back to Orleans Place, I talked the girl into going down to seventeen hundred dollars since the side mirror was cracked and cuz of the torn convertible cover. Mommy's name went on the title.

"Do you get jealous of those kids, Mommy?" I asked when we left.

"Dat's a hod queshun to ansur. God gave me dis life," she said smiling, but her eyes looked sad.

I wished he hadn't.

"Things aren't so bad," she signed.

I shook my head cuz it wasn't fair. We had to leave the car with the girl until we could register it and get paper tags. I caught the bus with Mommy to her house since I ain't have no plans for the day yet. When I walked in, Yodi was lying on the couch watching TV. My niece and nephew played with toys on the living room floor. I went straight to the kitchen to get something to drink. All of a sudden, Ryan came out of the back room mumbling something under his breath, and then he stormed out of the apartment.

"What's his deal?" I asked.

"Who knows with his weird self. Ain't like he ever talk to nobody."

She right about that. Ever since we had been back together as a family, something about Ryan had changed. He stayed quiet and to hisself mostly. None of us could read him. Besides a sideways look every now and then, nobody knew what was really on Ryan's mind. Guess I couldn't blame him about being overprotective about us. He was the man of our house. I always felt like he was just a little extra protective over me. The few friends Ryan had always said I was the prettiest of all his sisters. His boys stayed, calling me the one with the cat eyes. Some said I looked like I could be a model. Whether I believed it or not was a different story, but Ryan never played that shit with his friends who tried to holla at me every chance they got. I knew Ryan hated that shit, and one thing he made sure me, Yodi, and Toya knew was that we better never mess with any of his friends.

My phone started ringing Wale's "Chillin," which meant whoever was calling wasn't saved in my phone or maybe it was Kareem calling me from jail. I started not to answer it, but since I was bored, I did. "Hello?"

"This KiKi?" the person said.

"Who this?" I asked, not recognizing the voice.

"Audri."

Oh, the girl from the barbershop. "Oh, hey. This ain't the number you gave me yesterday."

"I know. That was my friend's phone number."

What? Not the girl who was in the shop with her? "Oh, so that wasn't your girlfriend?"

"Nah, but I see if it was, you ain't give a fuck."

She caught me there. I sat down at the kitchen table. "I mean, I figured she must not be doing her job if you giving me your number."

Audri laughed. "You something, I see. What you doing later? I'm tryna see you."

"Hmmm . . . Depends."

"What it depend on?"

"It depends on what you wanna do."

"I'm saying, we can go get something to eat or we can go shoot some pool. I don't know. I just wanna see you."

That made me feel good. I smiled and said, "Okay." I told her to meet me at my apartment at six. I never really dated girls. I mean, I did whatever when I was working. That was different. But a relationship? Never. Unless you count Nausy back when I was little. Audri seemed like a challenge. Maybe it was cuz she was an albino. I don't know. I was just curious. Toya always said that was my problem. That I'd try anything once. But that bitch could suck a dick for all I care.

I told everybody bye and dipped cuz I had to catch the bus home to get dressed. I thought about what I was gonna wear. It was between the royal-blue Dolce & Gabbana silk shorts and matching top with the YSL heels Trina Boo sent me for my birthday or the sleeveless super-short nude Marc Jacobs dress I got from Lord & Taylor with my Gucci pumps. I mean, every girl gotta have some elegant fly shit for their first date. Not the cheap stuff you mix and match later. Audri needed to know what I expected her to help me maintain if we was goin' be goin' on more dates in the future.

Later, when Audri showed up in front of my R Street apartment building, I stepped out the door in my royal-blue outfit. I ain't wanna hurt her too much with the nude dress. My hair and makeup was flawless, too. Audri looked cute in her black Lacoste polo, some jeans, and some fly Jordans. Her Nationals cap was cocked. She raised her shades for a second, like she was getting a better look, and then she smiled. She closed her phone, then said, "Hey, you."

"Hey," I said, getting inside.

"You look good."

"Thanks. You do, too."

"So you wanna get something to eat first?"

"Yeah."

I listened to music as she drove, not knowing where she was taking me, but we ended up on H Street in Chinatown. Audri parked, and then we squeezed inside Matchbox, which always stayed crowded. It was a long wait to get a table, and it was too many people there to really talk, so we ate without saying much. I couldn't believe she still had her shades on inside the restaurant, but I ain't mention it. When we was done eating, she asked me if I knew how to shoot pool.

"No, but I can learn."

Audri smiled and led me to the parking garage. In the car, she asked me how old I was, where I worked, and how long I been single. She told me she lived uptown on Kenyon Street, that she was twenty-two, and that she worked in a mailroom downtown.

We ended up at a pool hall on Benning Road. I had seen it before when I used to live on Nineteenth Street, but I ain't never go inside. Audri seemed like she been playing for a while, the way she lined the balls up and sharpened her stick. When she cracked the balls apart with her first hit, two balls went flying down holes. I was impressed, especially after she got the next three balls, too. The fourth ball went in and out.

"About time I can get a chance to play."

She laughed, then tried to show me how to do it.

"When you gon' take your shades off? I wanna see your eyes."

She smiled and backed away. "Nah."

"Why not?"

"They're medicated."

"No, they not."

"Yeah, they are. All my shades are."

"Why?"

"I got bad eyes."

I mean, I guess I had to believe her, but until I saw her eyes for myself, I ain't know if she was gonna look crazy or what. We played a couple rounds of pool. Of course, Audri beat me each round, and then she asked if I wanted to hit a lounge on U Street. I said okay. She bought me a Grand Marnier mixed with pineapple juice, and then we sat on a plush sofa in a corner. Some people danced around us, but it was more people chilling, drinking, and talking, listening to Maxwell-and Chrisette Michele–type music. I hadn't been to a place like this in a long time.

"So what's up with you?" Audri asked.

"Nothing."

A dude I recognized from a party waved at me. I waved back. I felt my phone vibrate and decided to sneak a peek to check who it was. I smiled when I saw Camille's picture pop up. I hadn't talked to her in a minute, but I couldn't answer it now.

"You wanna get that?" Audri asked with a little attitude.

I slipped my phone back in my clutch, then took another sip of my drink. I guess I was being rude. Audri looked disappointed for a while, and then she said she was going to the bathroom. I sent Camille a text that I was on a date and that I'd call her back. When Audri returned from the bathroom, she said she was ready to go. I followed her out of the lounge, then down the street to her car. Inside, she said, "What made you give me your number?"

"I don't know. You seemed interesting, I guess."

"Am I?"

Was this a trick question? I nodded.

"Tell me more about you then," she said.

"Umm...ain't much to tell. I got two sisters and a brother. A niece and nephew. I'm taking classes at Everest to be a medical assistant. I don't know. What else you wanna know?"

Audri shook her head, then started the car. She drove down Florida Avenue, then headed toward my apartment. I guess the date was over. When we got to my street, she double-parked.

"I don't mess with broads who only curious about what it's like to fuck albinos."

My mouth fell open. No, this bitch ain't trying to carry me. I climbed out of her car and headed up the stairs to my apartment. I ain't even look back, even though she made her engine roar like it was saying, "Fuck you, too."

4

A month later Meeka called about doing another party. This time it was at a house in Takoma Park and all we had to do was dance. Again, I wasn't feeling this house party shit without some type of protection, but the money was gonna be too easy. Meeka wanted me to bring my cousin Marcha since she was gonna bring her friend Quita. At least it wouldn't just be us two, and if it was packed, then I wasn't doing no extras. Just dance and keep it moving. If it got too out of hand, I knew how to get home, and I was driving my BMW that I finally picked up two weeks ago.

When I pulled up to the house, I saw a handful of dudes standing on the porch smoking and talking. Me and Marcha waited in the car until Meeka showed up. A couple minutes later, her and Quita walked over to my car. Music vibrated the house, but it wasn't loud enough that the neighbors would call the police. Niggas was packed all over the place, looking hungry for some ass. They was crowded on the steps, all over the living room, in the kitchen, in the bathroom. The dude Kenny who was throwing the party was having it for his best friend's birthday. Backyard Band thumped from the speakers as he pointed us to the room where we could change and get ready.

"Girl, it's a lot of money in that room!" Marcha shouted and clapped her hands together. Her and Quita was the pros, since Marcha worked at the Skylark on New York Avenue and Quita at the Penthouse on Georgia Avenue.

"I just hope they not broke," Quita said, rubbing glitter body butter over her skin.

Me, either. Hell, I was only getting five hundred for this party. My plan was not to dance longer than twenty minutes. But when I looked at Quita, seeing how pretty she was, her perfect brown skin and her banging shape, I knew I wasn't gonna make a lot of tips, just grinding. There wasn't a scar, pimple, or stretch mark on her entire body. She looked like a trophy with her small waist, big ass, and titties. Quita put on a cute, short bob wig and lined her eyebrows. I watched Marcha light up a blunt and finish her makeup. She let me take a few puffs. Meeka poured herself a cup of Patrón. I already knew that I was gonna have to work extra hard if I wanted to make more than five hundred tonight with these thirsty bitches.

A few minutes later, I heard Meeka's CD playing Lil Wayne's "Lollipop" and knew that was our cue to get our asses out there. I let Quita and Marcha go out first since those hoes had a real routine. I popped an X pill and chased it with Meeka's Patrón before I marched out behind them.

"You good?" Meeka asked, grinning.

I nodded.

"All right now. Let's get it in," she said, smiling.

Dancing was easy. Same old shit. Shake like a tambourine. Add squats and shake. Pop and split. Next, grind my hips, move my body like a snake, and do it all over again. Niggas smiled, damn near slobbed on themselves. Touching and squeezing. Rubbing shit they ain't wanna pay extra for. Cheap niggas after all. I was sitting on a dude's lap, grinding with my back to his chest, when I saw my brother Ryan walk in the room with his friend Marlon. "Oh, shit," I whispered. My body froze for a second, and then I snapped out of it and tried to run out.

"What the fuck?!" Ryan yelled as he snatched my wrist. He looked at me like my face was covered in shit. I pulled away until he let me go. I ran back to the bedroom where I had my stuff, threw on some clothes, then stormed out. Ryan's fist slammed into my face as soon as I hit the porch.

"Damn," I heard people say.

My nose felt cold, then hot, as tears mixed with the blood. I had a flashback of Nut.

"What the fuck you think you doing?" Ryan yelled as he snatched me off the porch and shoved me down the street. I tripped over my feet and caught myself from falling.

"Stop, Ryan," I cried, trying to get away from him.

"Fuck no! Where your car?"

I pointed.

"Get your ass in the muthafucking car! Embarrassing me and shit!" he said, dragging me down the street.

"KiKi!" I heard Meeka's voice screaming. Even though she grabbed a T-shirt before she left the house, she was still in her panties and barefoot.

"Leave her alone, Ryan!" Marcha shouted behind him.

"Ryan, stop!" Meeka screamed and threw her body in between the two of us.

"Get the fuck off of me, fat bitch!" Ryan yelled, pushing her hard, making her fall to the ground.

"Go, Meeka," I begged. "Please."

"Ryan, leave her the hell alone. She grown!" Marcha chirped behind me.

"What? Don't be telling me what my sister can do!" Ryan barked. "I expect your ho ass to be doing this shit, but not her!"

Ryan snatched my car keys from my hand and opened the door. He threw me in the backseat. I couldn't believe this was happening. He jumped in the driver's seat and started the car up, pulling off before I could see what had happened to Meeka. I was bawling my eyes out and trying to stop my nose from bleeding with a shirt I had in the backseat. Seemed like every traffic light we hit, Ryan called me a new type of ho or bitch. Nasty ho. Trifling bitch. Dick-sucking roller. Money-hungry bitch. I could see his wide eyes jumping around like a rabid animal in the rearview mirror. He was scaring me. The more he cursed me out, the more the car began to smell like liquor. It wasn't the Ryan I knew. I had never seen him so heated before in my life. He drifted across the double lines into oncoming traffic. Horns blared.

"Ryan, watch out!" I screamed as he drove down Blair Road, swerving across the line again. "Stop!"

"Why? Your nasty ass living reckless anyway!" he yelled and veered back over. "Trick-ass bitch! I knew about Marcha, but your ass, too?"

The only person in my family who knew about me besides my cousin Marcha was Yodi—except she only knew about me stripping every now and then. I told her only cuz she ain't judge and she knew how hard it was to put money in your pockets when you dropped out of school. Yodi ain't know about me working the streets. I mean, I moved out on my own when I was fourteen to work for Nut. How the hell did my family think I was eating? If it wasn't selling my body as a prostitute or stripping, then I was definitely fucking somebody who was taking care of me. Same difference. All I could think of as Ryan burned down the street was if I had a pimp, they would've whipped his ass for punching me. Brother or not.

When Ryan pulled up to my apartment, he ain't even put the car in park. He just told me to go in the house, talking about he was keeping my car.

"What?" I asked, confused. What he mean he was taking my car?

He ran the car up on the curb, like I had pissed him off, fucking my tires up. Then he put the car in park, snatched me out of the backseat, and dragged me up the stairs. Tears burned my eyes. He gave me the keys to unlock my door, and my hands shook the whole time. Then he said, "Don't even think about leaving tonight. You hear me?"

"How you gonna just take my car?" I cried.

"I should fuck you up right now. Got my friends watching your ho ass and shit! Grrrargh," he groaned, making another fist like he was gonna hit me again. I walked backward into my apartment. He walked toward me and glared at me hard with his fists balled up. My mouth flew open, but instead of hitting me, Ryan punched a hole in my closet door. I screamed and ran to my bedroom. Instead of Ryan following me, I heard the front door slam shut. I peeked out the window and saw him pull off the curb and peel off down the street.

I took a deep breath. I looked at the splintered wood on my closet door, surprised that he was strong enough to do that kind of damage. My nose started to throb, so I went to the freezer to get some ice. Since there wasn't a lot, I grabbed the bag of peas, and then I laid on my bed. I wanted to call Meeka to tell her I made it home okay, but I left my phone in the car. My makeshift ice pack took the pain away a little, but I popped some Tylenol and took some Ambien so I could go to sleep. I laid there replaying the night in my head, wondering how long Ryan had been at the party. *How much did he see?* I drifted asleep.

It wasn't long before I was yanked out of my sleep by the weight of someone lying their heavy body on top of me. Strong, rough hands groped my breasts and my thighs. I struggled to fight through my grogginess, trying to push the person away. Nothing but darkness and the smell of liquor and cigarettes flooded the room. Sloppy kisses covered my face and my neck, then my breasts.

"No," I cried out.

It was way too dark to see, but I felt the face—their eyes and nose was covered by what felt like stockings. I could feel my panties ripping off of my hips, then the violent thrust of two fingers being shoved inside of me.

"Aiiiiiiiiiii," I screamed. But I felt strapped to the bed, even though it was the force of the person holding me down with one arm. He pressed his dick against my thigh. I tried to scratch his face as he rammed harder against me. "No! Get off me, please! Get off me!" I

begged so loud, I knew my neighbor had to hear me.
But he ain't stop. I scratched the stockings until I felt
them shredding, then suddenly he punched me in my
jaw like a man. The pain was too much, but I caught a
glimpse of Ryan's face before I passed out.

When I finally woke up, the sun was shining directly
on me through slightly cracked blinds. I touched my
throbbing lips, feeling the split center before I sat up. I
was naked, the sheets splattered and smudged with dried
blood. My nose was caked with more blood. My ripped
clothes huddled like my fear in a pile on the floor. My
arms felt swollen, and light-green bruises covered them.
My inner thighs were sticky and tender. I softly pat-
ted them with my fingertips, screaming instantly at the
horror of what he'd done. I screamed and cried until I
couldn't cry no more. Memories of us playing as kids
flashed over and over in my head: Him shooting a water
gun at me, us playing Red Light, Green Light. Birth-
days, cookouts. Him on top of me. Him beating me
until I was unconscious. The moans of pleasure that
poured out his throat with every thrust. I wailed into
my pillow.

After laying there for what felt like hours, I found
the strength to stand up. My thighs felt bloated, and
I couldn't stand to have them brushing against one
another. I took baby steps to get to the bathroom, grip-
ping walls for support. My body too weak and sore to
move faster, but I had to get it off. I had to get it off

now. I ran the bathwater and cried on the toilet until the tub was full of water. I looked in the medicine cabinet and under the sink for something strong enough to erase his touch. I cried when I couldn't find what I needed, and then finally, I half crawled to the kitchen.

Tears streamed down my cheeks as I pulled everything from the shelves and the cabinets, letting them fall wherever. I needed to get it off. I had to wipe off all the sickening stickiness he left behind. His touch. His smell. His taste. The memory of everything. I wanted it gone! I grabbed the vinegar and limped back to the bathroom. I emptied the whole bottle in the tub, the pungent odor much sweeter than Ryan's vile stench. My body shivered thinking about what had happened. I scratched at my arms and my legs until every inch was covered with the mixed water. The stings of the vinegar seeping into my scratches hurt like hell, but I had to scrub it everywhere. If only it was a magic potion that could erase every bad thing that ever happened to me. I stared at the murky bathwater until tears clouded my vision. I wiped my face with the back of my hand just as the sudden rush and heat of something rising up from my stomach landed on the bathroom floor. I cried as I watched the yellow fluid splash everywhere, hating myself for not being stronger. Hating myself for making my brother want me. Hating myself for being alive. I hated Ryan. I hated the world. How could this happen to me?

NINE YEARS EARLIER...

2000

5

Me and Nausynika shared a room with two twin-sized beds at Ms. Val's foster house on South Dakota Avenue. We was in the same sixth-grade class at school, too. Nausy was real nice to me from the start, and she bullied Taysia until she moved her seat, just so I could sit at the long rectangle table with her in the back of the classroom. Our teacher didn't care as long as we ain't talk. One day I noticed Nausynika rubbing her eraser back and forth in between her legs. She moaned softly for a few minutes before she stopped, looking both tired and sleepy. I thought it was weird, but I ain't say nothing.

When Nausynika did it the next day, I wrote her a note asking her what she was doing. She didn't write back. She just smiled. Then she put her hand in between my legs underneath my skirt. She used her fat fingers to rub circles on my coochie. My eyes grew big and slowly rolled to the ceiling. It felt soooo good, like a tickle, but warm and smushy and so much better. I ain't want that feeling to stop. Then Nausynika slipped her finger inside my panties and pushed it in and out. A moan slipped out, and I looked around to see if anybody heard me. Nausynika warned me to be quiet with a soft *shhhh*, and then she stopped. I felt tingly. I wanted her to do it some more, but she just smiled at me. I couldn't believe this big, fat, ugly girl could make me feel so good. I didn't even know I could ever feel that way. I wondered if the other kids knew about that same feeling. I could tell by the silly games they kept playing on each other that they had never felt that feeling before. Now I knew why Nausy seemed so much different than the other foster kids I had met before. She knew a secret.

When we got home, Nausynika made me lay down. She climbed on top of me and used her knee to rub in between my legs. I ain't stop her when she rubbed my chest or when she planted kisses on my neck. It felt so good. My body shivered. Me and Nausynika kept touching each other until Ms. Val came home from work. We touched each other every day. I couldn't wait to feel that warm, tingly feeling. I ain't even see Nausynika as ugly no more. Whenever she looked at me like she knew my secret at dinner, it made me feel silly and guilty at the same time. I giggled a lot around her. Ms. Val just called us childish and left us alone.

Before I came to Ms. Val's, I was at the Moodys'. They was real stingy with their food. Thank God I got breakfast and lunch at school cuz I wasn't allowed in their refrigerator. And before the Moodys, I was at the Garys' house. Ms. Gary threw shit at me from across the room for petty mistakes I made like leaving the light on in an empty room or for accidentally leaving the door unlocked. She threw a bottle of bleach at me while I was washing dishes cuz she said I was giving her lip. It splattered all over my clothes. She made me finish washing and drying dishes even though my butt burned until I was finished. I hated Ms. Gary with a passion.

A year later, I finally went to Ms. Val's. I liked her a lot cuz she ain't do nothing to hurt me like the other people did. Ms. Val really understood what I was going through. She told me it was okay if I missed Mommy. "It's absolutely normal to miss the people you love," she said. Her and Nausynika made me feel like I was at home and not just like I was passing through or taking up unused space.

But everything changed the day we got caught fingering each other in Mr. Breyer's classroom. There was a big meeting with the principal, the vice principal, and the counselor. Everybody was looking at us with disappointed eyes, and when Ms. Val took us home, she called us every name in the book and promised to have us separated and sent to different homes in the morning after she met with our caseworkers. Me and Nausynika stuffed our book bags with clothes and snuck out of the house as soon as we had a chance to that night. We made the long, scary walk from South Dakota Avenue all the way down to Union Station, just so we could sleep in front of the Amtrak train station.

The next day, even though we was supposed to be in school, we spent the whole day downtown, going to all the Smithsonian museums. Nobody messed with us cuz we blended in with all the tourists' kids on their field trips. When it got late, we walked back to Union Station. My feet hurt so bad. They felt swollen and on fire, but we ain't have no choice. I followed Nausynika. She said it wasn't the first time she had to sleep out in the street like this. She showed me how to get free food from McDonald's when they was about to close and throw all the leftovers away. She taught me how to wash up with nothing but paper towels and hand soap and how to beg for money with nothing but a plastic cup. All I had to do was shake it at the people getting off the Metro trains and some of them dropped money inside, just like that. We did that for three days before security started noticing our routine and followed us around Union Station, forcing us to leave.

We walked down a few blocks to the bus station on First and L Streets. The station seemed crowded with people that looked lost and alone like us. Some people tried selling CDs, socks, and umbrellas even though it ain't rain in I don't know how long. It was hard to sleep there cuz it was so noisy and bright. Then out of the blue, a tall dude with a thin mustache walked up to us, wearing a green Celtics hat with some long plaits peeking out. His hat matched his green-and-white striped polo shirt.

"Hey, y'all need a ride?" he asked.

"We ain't got no money," Nausynika said, holding her book bag tight. It was after eight o'clock. The later we stayed in the bus station, the more it seemed like nothing but suspect-looking people was coming around us. An old white man whose skin was so dingy you couldn't even tell he was white for real sat on a chair across from us. He had like twenty raggedy plastic bags piled around him, and he kept staring at us with his see-through green eyes, looking all creepy.

"Man, you don't need no money," he said, smiling. "I'll take y'all wherever you need to go. On the real, y'all look like you need to be somewhere and not hanging out here. I don't mind helping y'all out."

Only problem was we ain't have nowhere to go, and I guess we looked like it cuz he said, "I know somebody worried about y'all right now. Where you supposed to be?"

Neither one of us said nothing. Nausynika shook her leg nervously like she always did and looked away.

"Listen, don't look so sad. Why you two pretty girls looking all sad for and shit?" he said, stuffing his hands inside his pockets.

We still ain't say nothing. I just looked down at my feet and the book bag that sat there so full that the zipper ain't wanna stay closed.

"Listen, I'm the type of person who like to help people, and y'all just look like you need some help, for real. You ain't gotta say nothing. I'm a good dude. Here's my ID," the man said, taking his wallet out.

Me and Nausynika leaned over to see Daniel Wise's face. He ain't have no plaits in the picture, though. I saw that he was born ten years before me and that he lived on Q Street.

"My name Daniel, but my friends call me Dizzle," he said, smiling again, reminding me of the Cat in the Hat with his high cheeks and big grin. "I can help y'all if you want. Take you somewhere that you can get cleaned up. Maybe get y'all something to eat. What you think? Seem like y'all ain't sleep in a nice bed in some days."

He was right about that part. Nausynika said, "You said you gon' feed us, too?"

He nodded. "What y'all want? It's a Wendy's and McDonald's right up the street."

"Wendy's," I said. I was so sick of eating McDonald's.

"Then Wendy's it is," he said. "Follow me."

Nausynika looked at me with a face that said she wasn't sure if it was the right decision, but neither one of us wanted to get sent to yet another foster home, especially without each other. Dizzle seemed nice and didn't look like he could hurt us. I checked his hands.

Yep, his nails was clipped and clean. Mommy used to always say cleanliness is next to godliness, so I nodded at Nausynika, and then she tucked her lips back to signal that she was cool with it, too. We both stood up to follow Dizzle to his car. He walked with long, smooth strides but added a little bounce with each step.

"Hey, so what's y'all's name, then?" Dizzle asked us.

"I'm Nausynika, and this is Shakira."

"Oh, okay. That might be kinda hard to remember. Is it all right if I call you Nausy and KiKi?"

We nodded and waited for this stranger to open the door to an old white Lincoln with tinted windows. His car was clean on the inside, too, so I took that as another sign that Dizzle was okay. "Hot Boyz" was playing on the radio with Missy Elliott and Eve rapping. I nodded my head to the beat and tried not to think about the risky ride me and Nausynika was taking. I wondered what she was thinking. Dizzle was true to his word when we pulled up at the Wendy's. After me and Nausynika ordered our food, Dizzle drove down New York Avenue and turned into the parking lot of a motel. We stayed in the car while Dizzle went inside to get us a room.

"You scared?" Nausynika asked me.

"A little," I said as I bit my lip. "You?"

She raised her shoulders quickly and let them drop just as fast. "I mean, he seems okay, I guess."

I ain't never in my life stayed in a motel before, but then I ain't never sleep at a train station before, either. If

she wasn't scared, I wasn't gon' be scared. We stared out
the window without saying another word, waiting for
Dizzle to come back. I wondered what Nausynika was
really thinking.

"I got y'all's room," he said, showing the room key.
He parked near the back of the parking lot, and then
we climbed out of Dizzle's car, following him to our
room that was on the second floor. He unlocked the
door and stepped back so we could go in first. There
was only one big bed with a burgundy blanket drenched
in flowers.

"I could only get y'all a queen-size bed. Is that
okay?"

Nausynika shrugged.

"Okay, good. Here's a nice-size TV, and there's the
bathroom over there. You might as well put your stuff
in the drawers. I know you tired of carrying them bags
around."

Nausynika sat on the edge of the bed and looked
around.

"Well, I'm not gon' stay long. Y'all go 'head and get
comfortable. I'ma write my number on this pad," Dizzle
said, scribbling, "then I'ma get outta here. If y'all need
something, let me know. Here's twenty dollars so you
can order something to eat later, too."

He laid the money by the pad.

"Thank you for helping us," I said.

"Not a problem. But really ... don't feel like you have

to leave. I know how it is when you ain't got no place to go." He locked his eyes with mine. "I ran away before, too, and know for a fact how dangerous it is out there. People don't care about you and want whatever you got. Even if they have to take it from you."

My heart skipped.

"Anyway, y'all take care, okay?"

Dizzle closed the door with that same smile he introduced hisself with. We both let out a deep breath. Seemed like we had been holding it ever since we left Ms. Val's.

"Can you believe this?" I said, my eyes bigger than usual. I felt like it was our lucky day.

"Girl, I don't know about you, but I'm taking a bath!" Nausynika shouted and ran to the bathroom.

"Hurry up because I'm right behind you."

I laid back on the bed and stretched my arms and feet out as far as I could, and then I reached over and cut the TV on. Before I knew it, I had fallen asleep. When I woke up, I saw the sun shining through a crack in the curtains. I looked at the clock and then at Nausynika laying under the blanket beside me. She could've woke me up so I could take my bath last night. I rolled out the bed and went to the bathroom. After I ran the bathwater, I emptied the free shampoo bottle in the tub for some bubbles. I felt so grimy. I couldn't have been there long before Nausynika woke up and stood in the doorway.

"What we gon' do today?" she asked.

I shrugged my shoulders.

"We got twenty more dollars than we did yesterday," she said, snapping the bill Dizzle left us.

"Yeah, but don't we gotta make it last?"

She rolled her eyes and left the bathroom. "But I'm hungry!" she yelled.

"Your ass always hungry," I mumbled into the bubbles.

Just as I finished washing up and wrapping the towel around myself, we heard a knock at the door. Nausynika looked out the window.

"Oh! It's Dizzle with Burger King, girl!"

She unlocked and opened the door. I stepped back in the bathroom and looked through the half-cracked door.

"I thought y'all might be hungry. Hope you like French toast sticks and orange juice," Dizzle said.

"Sure do!" Nausynika said, taking the bag.

"Cool. I'm not gon' stay long, but I just thought y'all might want to go see that new Martin Lawrence movie later. What's it called again? Damn, I can't remember," he said, looking stuck.

"*Big Momma's House?*" I asked, smiling.

"Yeah, that's it. Y'all down?"

Nausynika smiled, too. Ms. Val said she wasn't gonna take us to see it cuz it was PG-13 and I was just eleven and Nausynika was twelve. But I was about to be twelve, and everybody said we looked at least fifteen, especially since I already had breasts as big as girls in high school.

Ms. Val said my shape was too much for my age, so she made sure if I wasn't in my school uniform that I was in clothes she said I could grow into. It ain't make me no difference as long as I had clothes that was mine and not another foster kid who I had to share with like at the other places.

Dizzle took us to the movies all the way out Marlow Heights later that day, and the next day he took us to the skating rink off of Branch Avenue. When he showed up the day after that, saying we was gonna go to the ESPN Zone for lunch downtown, we couldn't believe our luck. It was like this for the rest of the week. The way he looked out for me reminded me of Ryan. Everywhere we went he made sure I had what I needed and what I wanted. He even took us to Rainbow on H Street to get three outfits apiece. But it was a couple days later, after we went to Dave and Buster's, that changed our lives forever.

Dizzle said he was too tired to drive home. We had been out all day, chilling at Anacostia Park. He had a little grill that he used to cook us hot dogs and burgers while we laid on a blanket from his trunk and listened to the radio coming from his car. It was a hot day, the kind where the air was too muggy and thick to breathe. Seemed like all our energy was drained when we finally left the park. By the time we got back to the motel, I couldn't wait to climb in the bed and go to sleep.

"Y'all mind if I crash here tonight?" Dizzle asked when we pulled up.

"Not really," Nausynika said.

Dizzle seemed like our older cousin, so I ain't care, either. He could sleep on the floor or in the chair. As soon as we got inside the room, I kicked my shoes off and went to the bathroom. When I came out, Nausynika and Dizzle was watching TV sitting on the bed. I ain't know about them, but I was sleepy. I crawled in the bed under the covers and closed my eyes. I woke up when I heard Nausynika and Dizzle giggling non-stop. I rolled over and saw that she was staring at the ceiling and Dizzle was watching her with a sandwich bag in his hand.

"KiKi, you want some?" Dizzle asked.

"Want what?" I asked, sitting up with one arm.

"Girl, everything look funny," Nausynika said, reaching out toward the ceiling. "You gotta try it."

Dizzle handed me the bag. Inside looked like mushrooms. "What is it?" I asked.

"Shrooms. It ain't gonna hurt you. Just eat a couple of them, and tell me what you think."

"Raw like this?"

He nodded.

I looked at Nausynika again, and she was all smiles, still staring at the ceiling, giggling. The mushrooms looked like dried tiny bits of the kind that grow around trees whenever it rains a lot. I took a couple and put them in my mouth. It felt like Styrofoam, but the shrooms didn't have a flavor, so I chewed faster and swallowed. Ain't nothing happen at first, so I lied back and watched Dizzle and Nausynika, who both was smiling and laughing. *CSI* was on TV, and the colors on the screen looked extra colorful. Suddenly, blues, greens, yellows, and oranges seemed like they was pouring out of the screen. I leaned closer.

"You all right, young?" Dizzle asked.

Each of his words suddenly had a taste. The *you* tasted like a Twizzler. *All right* tasted like a slice of toast, and *young* tasted like a Sprite. I laughed just thinking about it. The motel room was a rainbow of colors, from the bright sunshine-yellow curtains and chocolate-brown carpet to the velvet cupcake burgundy blanket. The flowers on the bedspread seemed like they was in 3-D. I reached out at the dreamy petals that danced around the room. Nausynika and Dizzle smiled at me. I felt like the bed was moving in circles. Dizzle kissed me hard on my lips next, pushing his swirling tongue in my mouth. I saw him taking his shirt off, then his jeans next. Dizzle gently pushed Nausynika's head toward his shorts and used his other hand to rub my breasts. This had to be a dream. I closed my eyes so that the next time I opened them I'd be fully awake. But even with my eyes closed, I could feel his fingertips rubbing my nipples. "Stop," I barely breathed out. Was he supposed to be doing this?

Dizzle's laughing and moaning bounced off the walls

quick and innocent, like pebbles skipping across a creek. His soft, wet kisses made me feel like I was swimming. I shook my head from side to side. This couldn't be right cuz he was a full-grown man. It was like I was inside of a bubble floating above, watching this man twice my size kissing and rubbing his large, warm hands all over me. I wanted him to stop. Even though he was older and stronger, this wasn't something that was supposed to be happening to me. Not me. Unless I was being punished for running away from Ms. Val or for not being more careful helping Mommy pack Yodi's diaper bag. Maybe if I would've double-checked that day them drugs fell out, none of this would've ever happened. My family being split up, me being sent from one foster care house after the other, me laying here with a grown man who was peeling my panties off.

"You're so pretty," Dizzle whispered between kisses. I took a deep breath as if I had been holding air in my lungs. That's when I tried to scream, but the only thing that came out was a dry gasp. I shut my eyes tight, try-ing hard to block out what I was feeling Dizzle do to me, how his soft touch made me feel warm all over. Mommy's face appeared in my head. She was standing in the kitchen washing dishes. Every now and then, she looked down at Yodi playing with a puzzle on the floor by her feet. I wanted to be home with her and Yodi. I wanted to be far away from this room, from this mo-tel in a part of the city I ain't even know nothing about

until this week. I looked at Nausy. She had a strange expression on her face. I couldn't tell if she liked what was
happening to her or not, but she definitely wasn't fighting Dizzle off, either. All of a sudden, a thought popped
in my head that made me panic. If I made Dizzle stop,
would he treat me and Nausy differently? Would we be
put back out on the street? What would happen to us
next? Where would we go?

Suddenly his touching me didn't seem so bad.

6

I felt strange cuz in a weird way I liked Dizzle. He was good to me and Nausynika, especially cuz we ain't have nobody in our corner. Both of us ain't have no family. Me, well, I ain't know where mine was, and Nausy, well, her mother was in jail in North Carolina for lying to the welfare people about something and wasn't getting out for three more years. Dizzle was the only person who been nice to me and who been taking care of me since Ms. Val looked so outraged a month ago at the school. I guess it was weird cuz deep down I knew what me and Nausynika was doing with him couldn't be right, even though the way he made my body feel so good with his soft kisses and gentle touch. I was so confused. He made sure we had whatever we wanted. We ate whatever we wanted, and he still took us different places and bought us stuff.

Lately, I had noticed that Nausy was acting different around me. She said she ain't like that Dizzle always wanted her to put his thing in her mouth and he ain't never ask me to do it. I ain't know why Dizzle never asked me to do it, but I really ain't want to. I did notice that he never really touched Nausy the same soft way he ran his hands over me. He kissed me long with his tongue and only gave her kisses on the cheek or on her neck and forehead. But I mean, he took care of both of us the same. Buying us whatever food we wanted, letting us pick clothes out that I knew fit and that girls at our school would be jealous about when I got back, and even getting us makeup and cute earrings. Dizzle took care of everything—soap, deodorant, toothpaste, and all. I ain't know why she had to be complaining. Shoot, as long as we ain't have to live on the street, she needed to suck it up.

After spending twelve days with him, Dizzle said we had to leave the motel. Said he found a cheaper spot in Capitol Heights that had a kitchen and two queen-size beds. "Y'all gon' like it," he said. "It got closet space for both of y'all, too."

I was happy. I mean, I wished we could've lived in our own *house*, but this was better than living by somebody else's rules. After we grabbed all of our stuff and filled Dizzle's car, we left and headed to Maryland. When we got to Central Avenue, he pulled up to a motel across the street from a 7-Eleven. Inside Dizzle was right. There was a little more space than the other motel. We ordered a pizza and watched TV. Dizzle poured us both a small cup of a strong coconut-tasting drink, before he gave us more shrooms that made us feel giddy. Next, Dizzle made us undress. After that he told Nausynika to suck on his thing. She sucked her teeth loud enough for Dizzle to hear her, and then she rolled her eyes as she picked it up slowly.

"What's wrong, Nausy, baby?" Dizzle said, rubbing her cheek.

"Nothing," she said, even though it was clear she was mad and that she wanted everybody to know she was.

"You don't wanna do it?" Dizzle asked.

She shook her head.

"Why not?" he asked.

"How come you never ask her to do it?"

"Cuz you can do it better than KiKi," he said. "I love the way *you* do it. I ain't never had it done so good before I met you. Don't you want me to feel good?"

She rolled her eyes. I knew she was still upset. "How you know she can't do it better if you ain't never ask her to do it?"

"Come on, Nausy. She tried before...once in the bathroom." Dizzle was lying. I ain't know why, and I ain't speak up, either. If he wanted her to do it, I ain't see what the big deal was. It just looked like she was kissing and sucking it like a Popsicle. How hard could it be?

"Her lips ain't like yours, girl," he said. "Look how thin they are. Look at yours. They all juicy."

Nausynika looked up at me, then smiled. "But if you like my lips, why you never kiss me like how you kiss KiKi?"

This time it was Dizzle's turn to roll his eyes. "Come here, girl. If that's what you want, here."

Nausy leaned closer, and Dizzle kissed her long and hard. Nausy melted, and then she bent down to put his big thing in her mouth.

"Don't y'all know, I love y'all," he whispered before he leaned back and let Nausy do what she always did. "I'd do anything for both of y'all. We like family."

This was the first time in a long time that me and Nausy ain't sleep in the same bed. For some reason, Dizzle decided he wanted to sleep in my bed. I ain't mind cuz it was better than all three of us squished up in one bed like we had been before. Just when I was about to sleep, I felt Dizzle trying to take my panties off. He rubbed his thing against me from behind. It felt warm and thick. He pulled me closer to him, hugging me real tight. Soon he was pressing his thing harder until he pushed all the way inside me, scraping and stretching my private part. A loud sound jumped out of my throat. He slipped his hand over my mouth. "You know I like you the best, right?" Dizzle whispered as he moved real slowly. It was the first time he ever did that to me. "You the best, right?" he whispered again. "Right?"

"Unhunh," I tried to say, but he was hurting me.

"Your body feel so soft. You fit me like a glove. Just right," Dizzle kept whispering with every stroke. "KiKi, you *are* my favorite."

Somehow his words made me feel good at the same time, like something about me was special. I knew he was telling the truth cuz in a way he was treating me better than Nausy. I wondered if it was cuz he thought she was ugly. I wanted Dizzle to like both of us the same. Nausy was my best friend, and I ain't want her to feel bad. He groaned real loud and held me tighter. Dizzle's body shook, and then he loosened his grip, but he ain't let me go. He held me even when I finally fell asleep.

The next couple of days was a blur. Nausy wasn't talking to me no matter how much I tried to talk to her. When I asked her for the remote control once, she said, "Fuck you," for no reason whatsoever. I ain't say nothing cuz why was I gon' pick a fight over something stupid like that? Then when I asked her to go with me across the street to the Laundromat to wash some clothes, she said, "I ain't going with your ass nowhere!"

"What's wrong with you?" I asked her. "Why you got a attitude for?"

She looked at me like she could kill me. "Your ass think you better than somebody, that's why!"

I was so confused. "What?"

"Bitch, you heard me."

"Nausynika, what you talking about? Don't nobody think they better than you."

"Yes, you do. You think I'm blind or something?"

I crossed my arms over my chest. She was speaking in codes, and I couldn't figure out what was plucking her nerves so bad. When she ain't say nothing else, I walked out with a bag of my dirty clothes and headed to the Laundromat across the street. Me and Nausy was definitely growing apart. We ain't even mess around with each other no more unless Dizzle asked us to cuz he wanted to watch. She slept in her bed by herself, and Dizzle slept with me. I did wake up once to see her bent over the bed with Dizzle standing naked behind her. I was happy cuz maybe she wouldn't be mad at me no more since he was pushing inside of her the same way he be pushing inside me. Nausy moaned just like I did when he was inside of me, and he groaned and shook the same way he did with me. Only difference was when he was done, he ain't sleep next to her. He always went to the bathroom and took a shower. *Did she know he called me his favorite?*

I took my time loading the washing machines cuz I ain't want to be in the room alone with her attitude all day. Dizzle hardly came to the motel until it had started getting late, so I was gonna have to be with her at some point. There wasn't no rush, though. A lady in a purple leotard, a see-through white skirt, and some leggings washed a load of clothes, too. She had on flat black shoes that looked like footies. I couldn't stop watching the way she walked from the machine to the sink while she sprayed some stuff on a few stains. I ain't never seen nobody walk like that in real life. It was like one of those birds I seen at the zoo. The pink kind with long, skinny legs that walked real slow and stopped real sharp before turning and walking the other way. She was so pretty. Her hair in a pony-tail bounced just like a horse's tail. Maybe she was a real dancer. She floated across the room with her skirt moving like a cloud around her. I bet if I could walk like her, I wouldn't have to be living in a motel in a place I ain't know nothing about.

The lady saw me looking at her and smiled. I smiled back, then looked away. There was some kids play-ing with the laundry carts while their mothers folded clothes. *Judge Judy* was on the TV hanging over the soda and snack machines. I bought an orange soda and sat down to watch TV until my clothes finished washing, and then I put them in the dryer. I dug in my pocket for the two quarters I had left and put them in the machine. I went back to watch TV until my clothes dried. The lady in the leotard floated over with her basket to grab the clothes out of the dryer. I watched her glide back. I waited for her to fold her clothes on the table before I checked to see if mine was dry. Dag, half of them was still wet. I checked my pockets to see if I had at least one more quarter but wasn't nothing in there. Only if I ain't buy that soda, I'd have enough. I guess I could hang them up in the bathroom to dry.

"You need some more change, sweetie?"

I turned around to see who was talking to me. It was the lady with the bird walk. I felt so embarrassed and looked down.

"Here. I still have some quarters left," she said, floating over and handing me three quarters.

"Thank you," I said. The pretty lady smiled. I put the quarters in the slot and walked back to my seat. Since she was being nice to me, I had to ask her. "Are you a dancer or something?"

Another smile lit up her face. "I sure am. Do you dance, too?"

I shook my head.

"Would you like to learn how?"

I nodded.

"Well, my name is Brianna, and I give lessons at a rec center in Landover. Here," she said, digging inside her bag. "Here's my card. Give this to your mother. Maybe she can bring you."

"Okay," I said, but I knew I'd never be able to go. I smiled and put the card with the ballerina picture in my pocket. Brianna finished folding her clothes, packed them up, waved good-bye, and glided out of the Laundromat. I watched her get in her green convertible Volkswagen and pull out of the parking lot. One day that was gonna be me.

Nausynika was sleeping when I got back to the motel room. I was putting my clothes in the dresser when Dizzle came through the door practically singing.

"Hey, I got news for y'all," he said, throwing his keys on the table near the window and sitting down. He rubbed his hand over his plaits. "Hey, Nausy! Wake up, girl."

She rolled over and wiped her eyes. I sat down on the edge of my bed.

"So I got us our own house!" he said, smiling that huge Cat in the Hat smile he always had. "So pack your stuff up. We leaving."

"House?" Nausynika said. "Where?"

"It's not too far from here. Y'all excited?"

Nausynika rolled her eyes. I guess she ain't care, but I was happy. We could finally be somewhere for good. I grabbed my bags and stuffed all my clothes inside them. Nausy took her sweet, precious time about getting her stuff together.

"What's wrong, girl?" Dizzle asked.

She shrugged her shoulders. Dizzle must ain't notice how mad she been acting lately.

"Come here, Nausy."

She ain't move.

"Didn't I say come here?"

She stood up and pulled her tight shirt away from her stomach before she walked over to him with an attitude.

"Tell me what's wrong? I don't like seeing you all mad and shit."

"Ain't nothing wrong," she mumbled, but she cut her eyes away from him at the same time.

"Yes, it is. I know how you get when you pissed."

"Nothing," she said again.

He pulled her to him and sat her on his lap. She smiled, then said, "I know I'm too heavy for you."

"Girl, please. I love all this chocolate," Dizzle said, hugging her tight and squeezing her butt. She giggled and ran her hand over her two French cornrows. "You gonna tell Dirt Dizzle what's wrong with you now?"

"Why don't you *like* me like you *like* her? Huh?" she said real low.

"Nausy...come on now...I love you, girl," he said, kissing her cheek. "I'm the luckiest nigga on the planet. Don't you understand? I got the two most beautiful girls on the East Coast with me, and I'd do anything for y'all. Let me tell you something...you, too, KiKi. Come over here."

I sat in the chair across from him. He picked my hand up and squeezed it.

"Listen, y'all treat me good. I ain't never feel this big. I mean my head swole like a muthafucka. Y'all kick it with me. Make sure I laugh. Keep me company and make me feel good. I don't wanna lose that. Both of y'all special to me. You understand? If you ain't got no-body in your corner, you always got me. You hear me? I'ma make sure y'all have, even when I don't have. I don't want y'all to ever doubt how I feel about y'all."

I believed him.

"Understand, Nausy?"

She nodded, then reached over and held my other hand. I guess she wasn't mad with me no more. He kissed her forehead.

Later, we all headed down Central Avenue to get on the highway. Dizzle drove a long way until he turned off an exit onto Route 301, then down 97 to Severn and into a neighborhood called Crestwood Mobile Park Community. Some little white kids was playing in the street with a dog tied to their bike. Dizzle waited for them to move, and then he drove slowly down the grav-elly road.

"There it go, right there. The yellow one," he said, pointing. "Y'all like it?"

My forehead crinkled immediately. I bit my lip and looked over at Nausy. I could tell she ain't like it either by the way her top lip curled up.

"Wait 'til you get inside. It's much better. I promise," he said, unlocking the car doors.

We got out and looked around the neighborhood. All the houses looked like they was made out of plastic or tin and like the long trucks that I saw on the highway, except without the front part. Not brick or stone like all the houses I ever seen. There was a couple of flimsy bushes in front of ours and a funny-looking mailbox that leaned so far forward I thought it was gonna fall. The windows was tiny, like the kind in Ms. Val's bathroom. I counted two.

"Come on. Let's go inside. You can get your bags in a minute."

Dizzle walked up the two stairs, opened the screen door, and then he unlocked the other door that wasn't that thick and seemed like somebody could kick it in if they really wanted to.

"Are we gonna be safe?" I asked.

"What you mean, girl?" Dizzle said with an attitude. His jaw locked tight. He ain't never have no attitude with me before. I ain't know what to say next. I looked down and waited for Nausy to go up the steps. The inside was smaller than I thought it was. The kitchen sink was the first thing you saw, then the long counter that had two wooden chairs underneath it. There was some little cabinets on top of the stove and a microwave. A beat-up gray couch was on one end of the trailer facing a little TV. Behind me was the bathroom and a short hallway that led to a room with one bed the size of the one me and Dizzle slept on back at the motel. We already tried sleeping three in a bed that big, and it was too tight.

"Where we all gonna sleep?" I asked. And just like that Dizzle slapped me across my mouth. He did it so fast that I had to blink away the hurt. I heard Nausy suck in air cuz she was shocked, too.

"Shut the fuck up! I ain't bring you all the way out here for you to think you can start disrespecting me. I don't see you paying for shit."

I sucked my lips, hoping the sting of his words and my mouth would stop hurting. A tear rolled down my cheek.

"Get in there and lay the fuck down until I tell you to come out," he said, like he was trying to calm his-self down. "I'm so fucking pissed off at you right now. Questioning me and shit."

More tears fell from my eyes. I couldn't believe he hit me. Him and Nausy both walked out of the trailer, the weak door snatching shut behind them. I heard the car start up outside, so I jumped up to peek out the window where I saw Dizzle backing out of the parking space. *Where was they going?* Tears kept coming, so many I couldn't even see his car when it turned off the road.

7

Where was I? I waited in the quiet tin house by myself wondering if Dizzle left me out here for
making a stupid mistake. In next to no time, the trailer
got dark as the sun went down. I was scared. Way too
scared to leave the room. Even when I had to use the
bathroom, I stayed on the bed. I could hear the crunchy
sound of cars driving over rocks on the road, but none
of them stopped at the house. *What was I gonna do if he
left me out here for good?* I ain't even know where I was. I
could still hear Dizzle telling me to "shut the fuck up"
in my head. Soon I fell asleep waiting for him and
Nausy to come back.

The next morning when I woke up, nobody was in
here with me. I ain't even have my bag cuz it was still
in Dizzle's car. I felt the tears coming again. What was
I gonna do? Why did I get smart with him? Nausy ain't

even stand up for me. I shouldn't have never run away in the first place. I cried and cried until my throat felt raw. I ain't care if somebody heard me. I laid on the bed and thought about all the stuff that happened over the past two months. I started thinking about all my old foster homes, the Moodys and the Garys and all the bad stuff that happened to me there. I thought about my mother and how she used to make my brother Ryan or my sister Toya read to me and Yodi. How Mommy taught us some sign language with books she got from the library. I missed her. I missed the funny way she used to sing "Twinkle, Twinkle, Little Star" to Yodi. It was the same way she used to sing it to me. I was six when I found out the real way she was supposed to sing it, but cuz she was deaf she had been mispronouncing most of the words.

The fourth birthday without my family was coming up, and I was gonna be twelve. Yodi had to be the same age I was when we split up, eight. I wondered what she looked like now. Ryan was fourteen, and Toya was about to be sixteen soon. I thought about them all the time. I wondered where they could be and if they had been going from one foster care house to another like I had. Did Toya ever do what I did with Dizzle or Nausy with somebody? Did she know about that feeling?

I stared at the ceiling for a while, and then I practiced signing the lyrics to "Twinkle Twinkle, Little Star," and then I signed all the letters of the alphabet and all the words I could remember. I signed what I would say to

Mommy if I ever saw her again—that I loved her and I missed her and that I wanted to come home.

I was wiping away tears when I finally heard the door unlock. I sat up. Nausynika walked in with a white carton of food and both of our stuff from Dizzle's car. I could smell pancakes. She threw the food on the long counter with the two chairs, dropped the bags by the door, then went to the couch to take off her shoes. I ran to the window and saw Dizzle driving down the road. She stretched out and fell asleep, though it was morning. Where was she last night, and where was Dizzle going now? Was he still mad at me?

I opened up the carton and cut off a piece of her pancakes and some of her sausage. I chewed two more bites and then closed it. I hoped she wasn't gonna be mad, but I ain't eat since lunch yesterday. *Why Dizzle ain't buy me no food?* I sat in the chair and waited for her to wake up, my stomach growling loud. Nausynika needed to wake up and tell me if he was still mad at me. I leaned over and tapped her shoulder. "Nausynika?" I said, but when she ain't move, I pushed her shoulder again. "Nausy!"

"What . . . ?" she groaned.

"Wake up. Tell me what happened when y'all left."

She looked up at me and rolled her eyes. "Just leave me alone."

I turned my lips to the side. Dag, what was I supposed to do while she was sleeping. "Can I have your food?"

"No," she mumbled.

"But I'm hungry."

"Good."

"Why you so mad at me?"

"Cuz of you, I ain't get no sleep last night!" she screamed angrily.

I winced at her loud voice. "Where was y'all?"

She sat up and stared at me so hard I thought my head might explode or something. "Don't even worry about it. Your turn coming," she said, lying back down.

What was she talking about? I chewed the inside of my cheek for a moment, then went to get my bag from the door. I washed up in the bathroom and put some clean clothes on. I was starving like Marvin when I came out. I still ain't believe Dizzle ain't get me nothing to eat. Her food was smelling so good, but the last thing I needed was for Nausy to go off on me next. I pulled a chair up in front of the TV and cut it on. Wasn't no remote control nowhere. I had to push the buttons on the TV. I flipped through until I stopped on *Good Morning America*. Nothing else was on. I watched *Live with Regis and Kathie Lee* next. Kathie Lee was talking about how even though she was gonna miss being on the show, she couldn't wait to spend more time with her family in a few weeks. I bet Mommy wanted us to be together, too, wherever she was. When Nausynika finally woke up, she went straight to the bathroom without saying a word. After she got dressed, she put her carton in the microwave.

"You ate some?" she asked with an attitude.

"Nausy, I was starving, okay?"

"See, that's what I'm talking about."

I sucked my teeth and turned back toward the TV. When the news came on at twelve, Dizzle came in the door with some older dude behind him. Maybe it was his father or something.

"Hey, y'all. This Clayton. He's my friend. Say what's up."

I said hi to the man with a stomach shaped like a basketball and a head that was balding, but I couldn't get over the fact that Dizzle ain't bring me nothing to eat. Clayton nodded and sat on the couch.

Nausy said hi, too.

"Dizzle, I'm starving," I said.

"You are? Okay, I'll go out and get you something to eat. But first I want you to do something for me."

My forehead got tight. "What?"

"Come here real quick. Clayton, give me a second." Dizzle pulled me down the hall to the room. He shut the door, then sat me on the bed. "I need you to do me a huge favor. You trust me?"

I nodded.

"My friend's wife is in the hospital. She dying. Ovarian cancer and shit."

I covered my mouth. I ain't know what *ovarian* meant, but I knew the word *cancer*.

"He's good folks. You understand?"

I nodded.

"He looked out for me when I was young. Made sure I had food when my father wasn't around. It hurt me to see him hurting, you dig?"

I nodded again.

"KiKi, all I want you to do for me is let him lay with you."

I looked at him, confused. "Lay with me?"

Dizzle nodded. "Clayton said he miss sleeping beside his wife. See, I figured since you kinda look like her a little bit—red bone and cat eyes—that maybe he could imagine he was with her."

I shook my head. Heck no. I couldn't believe Dizzle would even ask me to do that.

"Look, KiKi, damn it. I need you to do this favor for me," Dizzle said with a harsh voice. "He gon' pay us. You can't do that for me? For *me*?"

I bit my lip and crossed my arms over my chest. "He just gon' hold me and sleep beside me?" I asked, scared to say no.

"Yeah. That's it. I'ma run out and get you something to eat, and by the time I get back, Clayton should be ready to go. Okay?"

I took in a deep breath. "Okay."

"Here, take this. It'll help you block everything out."

I looked down at the yellow pill stamped with a star. I ain't never seen it before, but as much as I wanted to know what it was, I ain't dare question Dizzle again. I popped the pill in my mouth and tried to swallow it dry.

"Good girl," Dizzle said, smiling, and then he kissed me on my forehead. "I'ma send Clayton in here, then run out to get you something to eat. You want some McDonald's or Burger King?"

"It don't matter," I said.

"Okay, I got you. You gon' let him lay with you?"

I nodded, even though I ain't wanna do it, especially if Dizzle wasn't gonna be here, too. A few seconds after Dizzle closed the door, the bedroom door opened again. Dizzle's older friend was standing there smiling, smelling like he had on too much deodorant. I heard Dizzle leave the house cuz the flimsy door snatched shut, and then I heard his car start up as soon as Clayton said, "You are so goddamn fine." The crunchy sound of Dizzle's tires riding over the gravel outside ain't mask the sound of Clayton's voice when he said, "Take your shirt off, baby girl, and let me look at you."

8

Ever since that first week in the trailer park, Nasty Nausy was what all the men kept calling her when they showed up at our door. I was still just KiKi. Dizzle ain't never sleep by our house no more, he just came and went. Each time with a new face behind him. Fat men, skinny men. White men, Spanish men, black men. Clean men, smelly men. Happy men, angry men. Dizzle kept our refrigerator stocked with food and beer and made sure the cable was on. He also gave us plenty of condoms, soap, and toilet paper. We wasn't supposed to ever leave the trailer in the daytime, not before three anyway. He said if he found out we was outside that he'd hurt us so bad that nobody would ever recognize us again. After how he had tricked us into moving all the way out to no-man's-land and into doing trifling stuff with all kinds of men, I was scared of what else he might do to us.

Dizzle wasn't the same person we met in the beginning of the summer. He kept his distance it seemed like as much as possible. Nausynika and me had picked up a gross habit of smoking cigarettes, which Dizzle also made sure we had enough of. As disgusting as they tasted, I liked how the cotton feeling in my mouth after I smoked blocked out all the different tastes of the men. Sometimes we opened the door in the morning and opened all the windows just to get some fresh air. The trailer was so small and cramped, the odor of the men that came in and out seemed like it was soaking into the wallpaper. Dizzle took us to the Laundromat to wash sheets and clothes every Thursday night. He hardly even touched me or Nausy anymore, either. Sometimes she went down on him, and a couple times he made me open my legs for him, but he never stayed long and never kissed me no more. I felt hurt. He was the one who made all those men do horrible things to me, touch me and drip inside me, and now he seemed like he ain't really like me no more. When Nausy had her period that's when he told those men they couldn't drip in her no more. She felt lucky, but me...he ain't say nothing about me. I couldn't wait for my period to come, too.

A couple months after we had been living there, me and Nausy sat in the plastic chairs in front of our house to stretch our legs and get some air. Dizzle had just left from dropping off some groceries. Indian summer made the trailer muskier than usual, and all we had was fans inside. Nausy had lost a lot of weight since we first moved in. She wasn't my size, but she was getting close quick. I handed her my bag of sunflower seeds so she could share some with me. She poured herself a handful, then passed it back over.

"You ever think about school?" she asked while she cracked open some shells.

"Sometimes."

"You know, we'd be going to Mrs. Tobias class this year?"

I cracked open some more shells and spit them out. "Yeah, I know."

We sat spitting shells for a while, watching cars drive up and down the gravel road. Some of the little kids in the neighborhood screamed and laughed as they played in the street with their bikes and wagons. A dingy, straggly dog ran behind them with its leash dragging through the gravel.

"I get jealous when I see them catching the school bus in the morning."

I looked at Nausynika and wondered what she was really thinking but not saying. I missed school but not as much as I missed my family. I couldn't believe all that we had been doing. Was this how life was for everybody? Now I know why Mommy always complained about bills. The way Dizzle complained about how expensive it was to take care of us, I felt guilty. I did what he said so he wouldn't be disappointed. If all I had to do was let those men touch me so we could have food and clothes, then I guess it was worth it. I just closed my eyes and counted the whole time in my head. Sometimes I practiced all the short and long vowel sounds like I heard Nausy doing when it was her turn. "Auu, auu, auu, ehh, ehh, ehh," I'd go until I got bored. Other times I hummed. If they ain't want me to hum, then I thought about Brianna dancing in her white skirt. Or I thought about the sign language alphabets. Anything to forget what was happening and to erase the sweaty, funky stench that was in the room. I knew this wasn't supposed to be my life, but I felt like I had done too much to ever erase it totally from my head.

Every now and then, Dizzle wanted me and Nausy to do it with the same man at the same time. Those was times I hated the most, but I tried not to complain, especially not after the time he beat Nausy up for saying she ain't wanna do two men at the same time. I was so afraid that he was gonna have to take her to the hospital when he was done whipping her. Nausy screamed and hollered so bad, I cried in a ball by the bedroom door. Dizzle stormed out the trailer, and I ran to the window to see him drive the two men away.

"Let me get some more," Nausy said, reaching for the bag.

I gave it to her.

"I think I'ma run away again."

I looked at her, my eyes bigger than before. "And go where?"

She shrugged her shoulders. "I can't keep doing this." Nausy spit out more seeds. I knew how she felt, but what else was she gon' do for money? Live out of her book bag and eat out of trash cans? I'm sorry, I ain't wanna do that, either. I thought about all the things she had taught me over the past few months, like how to talk pig latin, how to make grits just right, and how to stitch on a button. I had taught her a little bit of sign language and how to neatly paint her nails using her left hand. Even though we learned a lot from each other, as much as I hated to admit it, I knew we both needed to be in school somewhere learning real stuff like dividing fractions or something. We sat outside for another hour finishing the bag of seeds, hoping and praying Dizzle ain't come back that night with more strange men.

About a week later in the middle of the day, there was a knock at the door. Me and Nausy froze and looked at each other. I got up and turned the TV down. We wasn't supposed to have nobody by the house unless Dizzle brought them by, and it was too early for company. Whoever it was knocked again. Loud and hard, and then a woman's feeble voice said, "I know you in there. Open the door. I live across the street."

Nausy looked at me, and I looked back just as worried.

"What should we do?" I whispered.

"Nothing. Just be quiet."

"It's two of y'all in there. One light one and one dark one. If you don't open up, I'm calling truancy. You supposed to be in school!"

"Oh my God," Nausy said, standing up. She tried to peep through the curtain covering the front window. "Shit, what we gon' do?"

I stood up and started walking around, rubbing my hands together. Then I said, "Open the door. We can just tell her we sick and we got the chicken pox or something."

Nausy thought for a second, and then she nodded and cracked open the door. "Hi," she said to the old white lady.

"You and the other one home alone, ain't you?" she asked.

"We both sick."

"You don't look sick to me. Where the other one?"

"In the bathroom."

"I've been watching you. Where are your parents? The two of you don't never leave this house like the other kids do in the morning. I've been watching you for a while now. So sick or not, you ain't supposed to be here by yourself all day."

"Well, I ain't supposed to be talking to no strangers

now, either, but I am. Plus, it ain't none of your business anyhow," Nausy said before she slammed the door shut.

My hand flew up to my mouth. I couldn't believe she slammed the door in that old lady's face like that. "Oh my God. What we gonna do now?" I asked, a little scared.

Everything was about to unravel. Nausy took a deep breath, and then she said, "We gotta call Dizzle to come get us, that's what!"

We waited for the old lady to go back inside her house before the two of us snuck outside. We had to use a pay phone cuz we ain't have no phone in the trailer house. Dizzle said he ain't think we needed one since he was the only one who we needed to be talking to on the phone anyway. Me and Nausy walked as fast as we could to the gas station at the end of the road before we bummed change from a man pumping gas. He gave us just enough to use the pay phone. A second later I listened as Nausy told Dizzle what had happened, and then she told me Dizzle said he was on his way, that we was supposed to pack up all our things and be ready to leave when he got here.

"He said we going to a motel until he can figure it out," Nausy said as we walked fast back to the house.

"Dag. All because of her?"

"Dizzle said if she been watching us, no telling what else she done seen."

"True."

Me and Nausy threw clothes in plastic bags and emptied out the refrigerator. When I took the sheets off the bed, I heard a lot of commotion outside and cars driving over the gravel up to the house.

"Dang," Nausy said, looking up.

"Oh no." I froze, then rushed to look out the window. There was two police cars and the old white lady who had knocked on the door. They was all marching straight across the street toward our trailer like a mini-army. Before I could even tell Nausy, somebody knocked on the door. One lie led to another, and then next thing I know, me and Nausy was sitting in the police car waiting to pull out of Crestwood. I saw Dizzle's white Lincoln slowly driving down the road. I couldn't see his face cuz of the tinted windows, but I knew it was him, and of course he ain't stop.

After a long night at the hospital where the nurses and doctors took my blood, made me pee in a clear cup, checked inside my coochie with odd-shaped plastic things, and gave me a shot in my butt, I finally saw Nausy again. We walked past each other in the hall as some counselors led her one way and me another. "Ont daga ell taga em thaga othing naga," she said in pig latin. I knew I wasn't gonna tell them nothing even before she said that. Who knew if they was gonna try and split us up again?

As soon as the short counselor with microbraids and the white one with long brown hair got me alone in a tiny room with three cushy chairs, they asked me if I was okay and if I wanted something to eat or drink. I nodded. The white one left the room. As soon as the door closed, the short one started asking all the questions. "So how long was you in that trailer anyway?"

I shrugged my shoulders. "I don't remember."

"Well, how did you get there in the first place, then?"

"I swear I don't remember," I said.

"Well, who brought you out there?" she asked.

"I really can't remember nothing."

Just when the short counselor tucked her lips back, like I was getting on her nerves, the white one came in with a cheeseburger and a Sprite.

"Eat up," she said.

I took a bite and thought about why I didn't wanna tell on Dizzle. For a strange reason, I ain't want nothing bad to happen to him. The counselors watched me chew for a couple minutes before they started asking me more questions. They was being so strict and nothing like no counselors I had ever seen before at school. Seemed like they ain't believe me when I said I couldn't remember nothing about who we had been staying with. When the short counselor described Dizzle to a tee, I told her they was totally wrong. I don't know why I was protecting him.

"Well, at least tell us where you met him at, Shakira?

Was it in D.C.? Your neighbor gave us the tag number to his white Lincoln. I know you remember that much," said the short lady with microbraids.

I bit my lip and looked away. If they had all that info, then they definitely ain't need me. I ain't have nothing to lose if I told them how we was stranded out there and how he made us do things I wished I could forget, but I just couldn't do it. Why hand Dizzle over to them when he was the only one who had took care of us? He ain't never try to split me and Nausy up like Ms. Val. Dizzle said we was family, and as far as I was concerned, family ain't turn their backs on each other.

Once the short counselor and the white one finally realized I wasn't gonna say nothing else, they left me alone for a while. Soon the short lady introduced me to a nun named Sister Melanie.

"I'm gonna take you and your friend home with me if that's okay?" She smiled a weird way, not showing her teeth.

"Nausy's coming with me?" I asked.

She smiled again and nodded, and then I smiled, feeling relieved for the first time since we got to the hospital.

Life with Sister Melanie was simple. She prayed for us, clothed and fed us. All we had to do was small chores like wash the dishes and keep our rooms clean. Sister Melanie asked lots of questions about our families. I guess she seemed nice, but whenever she looked at me, it was like she felt sorry for me. I already felt ashamed of what I had been doing, and the look she gave me ain't help the situation. Even though deep down, I knew she really wanted to help, I hated her sad eyes. Then one day Nausy told her that she'd rather go back to school instead of seeing the tutor.

"Oh. I just didn't think you girls were ready," she said. "But I guess I can enroll you in St. Francis Middle School tomorrow morning."

I was nervous about going back. Everything had changed so quickly. One minute we was doing whatever disgusting thing the men wanted. Now, all we did was whatever our teacher wanted us to do. It was hard keeping up with homework and paying attention in class. The other kids ain't seem to have none of the same problems I was having staying focused. They was moving past me so fast. Nobody wanted me to be in their group whenever it was group time cuz they said they would end up doing all the work. It's not that I ain't understand what I was doing, it was just hard to finish it when the teacher said we was supposed to be done. I couldn't concentrate with all them in my face, rushing me.

Kids from Severn, Maryland, was so different from my old classmates in D.C. All kinda color kids went to St. Francis. White, black, Chinese, Spanish, and even some Indian. They talked about stupid stuff like *Jackass* on MTV or *Malcolm in the Middle* during lunchtime. Me and Nausy just couldn't relate to them, so we stayed to ourselves mostly. Me and her ain't talk about the trailer or the motel, either. Sometimes we wondered where Dizzle was, but we never talked about him at Sister Melanie's house. It was January, three and a half months after we last saw Dizzle, when Sister Melanie told me Mommy was looking for me.

"Looking for me?" I couldn't believe it.

"You're going home tomorrow," she said, smiling.

I ain't know what to say or how to feel. Instead of feeling happy like I thought I would, I felt sick to my stomach. *What was Mommy gonna think of me after all this time? After all the gross things I had been doing?* I looked at Nausy and she looked away. How come now they gonna let me live with Mommy when they said she couldn't keep us at first?

"Maybe Nausynika can help you pack your things tonight," Sister Melanie said with a warm smile on her face, but after dinner I found Nausy crying in her room. She was lying on her bed, her face buried in her pillow.

"What's wrong?" I asked.

"You leaving," she said through snotty breaths, "and I'm gon' be here all by myself."

I rubbed her back, not sure what to say to her. "Wherever I go, I'ma leave you the phone number so you can call me. I know Sister Melanie won't mind."

She sniffed. "I'ma be in that dumb school all by my-self."

I bit my lip as I tried to think of something to say. "Well, can you do me one favor?" I asked.

She rolled over and looked at me. "What?" she asked, wiping her face with the back of her hand.

"Can you at least make sure you don't run away so I can come visit you?"

She gave me a half smile. I reached out and hugged her as tightly as I could. Nausy hugged me back tighter.

"Come on," I said, smiling.

The next morning while Nausynika was getting on the school bus, me and Sister Melanie was pulling out the driveway, headed for D.C. I waved bye to Nausynika, and she waved back. I was gonna miss her a lot.

Sister Melanie got on the highway and drove for a long while until we hit Rhode Island Avenue. Every-thing looked the same in the city, just like it had looked at the beginning of the summer. Sister made a right on Fourth Street, then a left on W Street.

"Well, Shakira...this is it. You're home. It's right there," she said, pointing to the brown brick building with four levels. "Let's grab your stuff and head up-stairs."

It wasn't the same place where we lived before we got split up, but if Sister Melanie said this was home, then it was home. I felt so nervous. Would Mommy tell I was different? That I had been doing strange things with my body? Would she still love me?

"Let's go, Shakira," Sister Melanie said.

I bit my lip and squeezed the latch to open the car door.

9

Once inside the building, it wasn't just Mommy who opened the apartment door. It was Toya and Yodi standing there, too. Mommy screamed and hugged all over me. Yodi was so much bigger and looked more like Daddy than I remembered. Toya waved and stepped back so me and Sister Melanie could come inside. Sister Melanie waited for everyone to calm down, and then she came in with my bags. Mommy tried to tell her how the system had lost track of me, but Sister Melanie was having a hard time understanding everything she said. Toya explained what Mommy was saying and signed for Sister Melanie that Mommy was finally able to prove to the courts that she was a good enough parent to get all her kids back.

Mommy said, "Seemed like they ain't wanna believe me cuz I'm deaf, but once they sarr I had a job at

Gallaudet, working in the cafaturia, they funally let me have another chance to have my kids."

Toya and Yodi took me around the apartment while Sister Melanie and Mommy wrote on a notepad to each other. Yodi tugged me down the hallway to show me the room I was gonna share with her, then Ryan's dark room.

"Where Ryan at?" I asked.

"Outside, I guess," she said, looking so much older and different than I remembered. She seemed quieter, too. Yodi was the opposite and full of energy, holding my hand and tugging me around the apartment.

Toya showed me Mommy's room and then her room with all her posters on the wall. We was in there for a while looking at CDs before Sister Melanie came in to tell me good-bye. She gave me a hug, and then I re-membered to get Mommy's phone number for Nausy.

"Please, don't forget to give this to her. Please," I begged. "She's my best friend."

"I won't, sweetie." Sister Melanie hugged me again and walked out the door.

I looked at Mommy and signed, "I missed you, Mommy."

She signed, "I love you."

It ain't take me long to figure out how different we all had become. True strangers for real. It seemed like we only remembered bits and pieces of what life used to be

like before we got separated. It had been four years since
we all was together last. A lot seemed to change, too.
Mommy had a weird new habit. She colored in coloring
books and cut out coupons whenever she got stressed
out. Toya and me ain't never seem to get along. She was
always extra mad now and treated me like I wasn't even
her sister, especially whenever we was in front of her
friends. I knew she was sixteen and I was just twelve,
but she acted like she ain't want me around her. Whenever Ryan was around, he was in his room with the
door closed shut, blasting music, playing video games,
or watching movies. He was so strange to me and not
the same brother I remembered.

Ryan used to talk a lot more. I asked him once
why he was so different. He shrugged his shoulders
and kept playing his video game. I wondered if it
had something to do with where he was sent when
we was all split up. Toya told me he was put in a
group home for young boys uptown, a place where
she heard all kinds of strange stuff happened. Sometimes his friends Marlon and Kris came over to play
video games. The only time I seen Ryan kirk out was
when Kris grabbed my butt when he thought nobody
was looking. Before I knew it, Ryan punched Kris in
his throat and kicked him out. I couldn't believe how
pissed Ryan was.

After I finally got settled back home, I called Nausy a
couple times. She said she was actually starting to like St.

Francis since I left. She was in the drama club, and she had a huge part in a play that her and her new friends made up. Whenever we did talk, the less we had to talk about cuz our lives was so different now. She talked about people and places I ain't know nothing about. Nausy was so excited about a school trip she was gonna go on at the end of the year to Philadelphia. I felt a little jealous and sad about it.

My school was okay. No amazing school trips to talk about, though, and I still couldn't focus in class. When I found out my new school had a step team, I tried out for it, thinking that was probably my best chance of learning anything about dancing since Mommy still wasn't making a whole lot of money.

The day after I tried out, Toya came home and found me crying in my room.

"Come in my room and show me your moves," she said after I told her what had happened. I wiped my face and followed her down the hall. She turned on her radio, and 702 was singing "Where My Girls At?"

"Come on, let me see," Toya said, standing in the middle of the floor. I was surprised she was actually talking to me since it always seemed like I was getting on her nerves. I showed her a couple of my moves, and she started laughing.

"What?"

"Why you look so awkward? Stop being stiff. Loosen up." She did a couple of moves and told me to do it, too.

The more she moved her hips, the more I realized it was more about the middle part of my body than anything else. So I did what she did but moved like how I used to move when I was with Dizzle. When I looked at her, Toya's face looked tense. Then she cocked her head to the side. "Are you fucking?"

"Huh?" I said, nervously fixing my shirt.

"You heard me," she said, taking a step closer.

I looked away and rocked back on my heels, swinging my arms back and forth.

"You little tramp," she said.

I bit my lip. Why was she smiling like a witch? She pushed me over to her bed and sat down.

"Okay, so tell me about it! Who? When? Where?"

I looked up at her nervously. "His name is Dizzle. We did it last summer in a motel not far from here."

"A motel?!" she asked, even more shocked, and then she shook her head and looked away. "How you have sex at a age younger than me?"

"You had sex before?"

She nodded. "But I was fourteen, not twelve! Wait, in June you was still eleven then. Dag, girl. Your ass fast. Did you like it?"

I shrugged. That was too hard of a question to answer. In a weird way, I missed Dizzle.

"Where is this Dizzle now?"

"I don't know."

"Niggas," she said, shaking her head. "Well, I hope

you learned your lesson about giving it up. Trust me, I had to learn the hard way, too."

I chewed the inside of my cheek again. I ain't wanna talk about it no more cuz I could tell she wasn't gonna understand nothing about what I had been doing since I last lived with her. If she was this shocked about Dizzle, she'd absolutely die if she knew about all the others. It would be my secret.

About a year after I had been back home, Mommy finally started going out a lot with some of her friends. They went out to eat and for drinks. The more she went out, the more Ryan hung out late with his friends, smoking on the block. Toya began sneaking in her boyfriend Demari from the building across the street when both Mommy and Ryan was gone. She promised to let me wear some of her clothes if I kept Yodi busy in her room. Everything was going good until the time Toya caught Demari playing in my hair in the building stairwell.

"What you doing letting him touch you?!" Toya snapped.

It was something Demari always did when he seen me. He'd crack a joke about something, then play with my hair. I never stopped him. I thought he was just being playful.

"Stop tripping," Demari said. "It ain't no big deal."

"What?" Toya said as she slammed her hand on her

waist. "What you mean it ain't no big deal? That's my little sister and she's only thirteen!"

Demari threw his hands up. "Look, I ain't got time for this shit." He walked down the stairs.

"What else you let him do to you, slut!" Toya yelled and pushed me down the stairs as soon as Demari disappeared. I stumbled down a couple steps but broke my fall.

"You think cuz you got titties now and cuz you fucking, you can have my boyfriend?!" Toya yelled. "Your ass make me sick!"

It wasn't even like that. I mean, I wasn't trying to take her boyfriend. I did like the attention Demari gave me when he saw me every now and then, but he was older and *her* man. I ain't want her boyfriend.

"Toya, it's not what you think it was!" I said.

"Whatever!" Toya shouted back.

"Why you yelling at her for?" Ryan asked, coming up a flight of stairs.

"That bitch messing with Demari behind my back, that's why!"

I shook my head, hoping Ryan ain't believe her, but I could tell by the look in his eyes that he did and he was disappointed in me. I wanted to scream from the top of the building: "I wasn't messing with Demari. He was messing with me!" I could feel tears about to fall.

"Get your ass in the house!" Ryan shouted, pushing

me up the stairs. "Let me find out you in another nigga's face around here!"

Why was he so mad at me for? Mommy noticed right away that Toya wasn't talking to me no more. She tried to get us to be friends, but Toya wasn't having no part of that. Every time she saw me doing my hair in the bathroom, she'd make some kind of crazy comment to hurt my feelings, calling me names like Project Pat Barbie. In the beginning she used to get to me, but after a while I ignored her.

On my way home from school a few weeks after the incident in the stairwell, I was about to cross the street when a light brown–skin guy riding in the passenger seat of a blue Cadillac STS yelled out the window, "Hey, cutie." He was cute, too, with a beard outlining his chin. I smiled when I saw him. His friend pulled over, and then the cutie asked me if I had a boyfriend. I told him no. When he asked me for my phone number, I gave it to him, even though I knew if Ryan knew about it he'd be pissed. It would be worth it just to see Toya's face when this Nut guy called for me. Since her and Demari broke up, she was always in the house, being pressed to answer the phone. I knew she blamed me for their breakup. I stayed out of the house as much as possible so I could avoid her tight face. The angrier she got about not being with Demari, the more she broke out across her forehead and her cheeks. Just about every chance Toya had, she was in the bathroom scrubbing different treatments all over her face to get rid of the acne. Mommy told her to leave it alone cuz it would go away on its own, but no, Toya wouldn't listen, leaving a trail of tiny scars everywhere. That's exactly what she got.

10

Nut reminded me of Dizzle in a way. I never asked him how old he was, but I knew he was about Dizzle's age. Every chance he got he took me somewhere new and bought me something cute to wear. The thing I liked about Nut most is how smart he made me feel I was, like I had the best taste in style ever and that I was willing to try new stuff at least once. He spoiled me in a way. All his friends knew how special I was to him cuz he always had a shopping bag for me whenever he picked me up after school. Bags from DTLR, Rainbow, Fashion Bug, and LVLX. Shoes, cute jeans, and sexy tops. All stuff I hid in my book bag or just left over his apartment around Saratoga.

"You should spend the night this weekend," he said one night.

"I can't spend the night," I said, shaking my head.

"Why not?" he said passing me his blunt.

"My mother would kill me."

"I dig."

We was quiet for a while. I was lying on his chest, listening to his heartbeat and smoking weed with him. Mommy would die if she knew I smoked weed, but I liked it. I could stop focusing on the faces of all those men that kept appearing in my head at night. I could enjoy whatever was happening at the moment with Nut, who was so sweet to me all the time. All he ever wanted was for me to spend the night sometimes. Why not?

"What do you think your mother would say about me if she ever met me?" he asked, playing with my hair.

"Hmmm...she'd say you was handsome. I think she would think you was funny and smart, just like I do."

"Good answer," he said, kissing my lips before he took another hit of his blunt.

I smiled, but Nut already knew he was smart. He always talked about all these crazy ideas he had to make money. Sometimes he'd talk about how he wanted to have his own company and employees. One minute it was a cleaning company, another minute it was a mobile gourmet truck. Other times Nut would find a reason to show me something he read in this old, torn-up Donald Trump book he got from his uncle. I could tell he knew a lot.

"Them niggas ain't getting it, for real," he said about

the corner boys in his neighborhood once when we pulled up in front of his apartment building. "They out here all day long, and the most they might make in a day is a hundred dollars. Them niggas gon' stay broke! For the kind of risks they taking, they might as well work at McDonald's or something. These niggas ain't got no health insurance, no life insurance, nothing. They just standing out here like a target."

He was right, I guess. I loved it when Nut talked like that. It was so sexy. Nut even made me want to be smarter, too. I tried to think like how he thought. When he watched business shows, I did, too, even though I couldn't understand nothing. I would stare at the numbers scrolling across the bottom of the screen and listen to Nut react until I fell asleep. He loved that I was into it...or at least, that I acted like I was into it. I ain't really know how Nut made his money. I just knew he always had it. The one time I asked him how he made money he said he was a hustler and nothing else. He didn't even entertain my confused look.

Whatever that meant, I knew I never had to worry about him having money cuz every time I asked him for something, he made sure I had it. I felt more comfortable over Nut's than I did at home. Ryan and Toya both got on my nerves. Either my brother was telling me what I wasn't supposed to be doing or wearing, where I wasn't supposed to be going, or Toya was busy telling me to get the fuck out of her face. Yodi was the only one who I talked to, but she was so young, wasn't nothing we had in common for real. Mommy just wanted all of us to get along, but I knew it would never be like that.

The craziest thing happened the night I finally decided to stay the night over Nut's for the weekend. We was up all night watching old movies—*Scarface*, *Menace II Society*, *Love Jones*, and *Jason's Lyric*. We was in the middle of watching *Jason's Lyric* when it happened.

Boom. Boom. Boom.

"I know your ass in there, open the motherfucking door!" a girl's shriek voice yelled on the other side of Nut's door. "Trying not to answer your phone. Open the fuckin' door, Nut!"

"Shit," Nut mumbled under his breath before he got up and went to the front room. "Hold on, slim."

I was so confused. Who was at his door? I sat up on one arm and listened. All I could hear was a girl's voice. If Nut was saying anything, I couldn't hear it.

I heard: "Why your ass not answering your phone, nigga?! Who in there?! Let me in . . . No, cuz you do this shit every time I say I got something else to do . . . I'm tired of you doing this to me, Nut! . . . Yeah . . . but still . . ."

I couldn't hear nothing for a few minutes, and then I heard Nut close and lock the front door before he climbed back in the bed.

"You can unpause it," he said before wrapping his arms around me like nothing odd had even happened.

"Who was that?" I asked. It was the first time my heart skipped nervously. Nut had never given me a reason to think I wasn't the most important person in his life. Now I was scared to hear his answer.

"Nobody," he said, taking the remote control and pushing play without even looking at me.

"*Nobody* was real loud and real pissed. Why?" I asked anxiously.

"Don't worry about it," he said, kissing me long and hard. "It's nothing. I'm here with you, right?"

I was confused and scared that whatever the truth might be would mess everything up, so I played the game he was playing and ignored what had happened. Before the movie went off, I climbed on top of Nut and tried to make him feel good. The same way the men used to say I made them feel. Nut seemed impressed cuz of the smile on his face. I ain't want him to forget how special I was to him, so I let him do whatever he wanted to me that night. It was the first time I did more than put him inside my mouth. I wanted him to know that I was better than whoever was on the other side of that door. I ain't wanna share him. Nut held me tight and close the same way Dizzle used to do when he was done. I was hoping from now on I would be his favorite.

The next morning when I woke up, Nut was staring at me like I was a different person. I smiled. He smiled, then kissed me.

"You should be my business partner."

I looked at him, confused, and then he told me he was about to start on his plan to rent and sell houses.

"I really think you'd be slick helping me."

"Me?" I asked, confused.

He ran his fingers through my hair. "Yeah, you. You street-smart enough to make a lot of money."

How could I help him start a business? I was only fourteen.

"I see something in you...You might not know it, but I can see it so clear," he said, smiling.

I listened to his plan. He promised me that I would make a lot of money, that he would help me get my own apartment, and that one day I could own my house, too. My gut said that something wasn't right, but the thought of having my own for a change was too good to pass up, so I told Nut okay. The next night he introduced me to a cute girl with a fly-ass hairstyle named Peaches. After she finished rolling her eyes and sizing me up, she told me all I had to do was help Nut recruit more employees. Sounded too easy. I never knew the taste I gave him the night before would be what he expected me to do for every nigga who was willing to pay for it from that moment on. When Peaches saw my head wasn't into it, she made sure to convince me. "Own them niggas," she used to say just before Nut sent me a new dude to trick. I loved getting the money for a change. Dizzle used to keep all the money.

With Nut, he gave me some to keep for myself. Peaches helped me overcome my fears and reminded me of our goal every chance my mind started to slip. Soon me and her was best friends—closer than my own sisters, even though she made it real clear Nut was her man, even if he fucked me occasionally. For some reason it was fine with me as long as I was a big part of the "business."

Little did I know, the business would be a part of my life for a long time to come.

2009

11

I just couldn't call the police on my brother. A part of me felt like I brought it on myself. Dancing half-naked and grinding on some nigga in front of his very eyes. As hard as it was to digest, I turned Ryan on the same way I did the other dudes at that party. Another part of me felt like it had been a crazy dream, only the bruising and swelling reminded me that it wasn't. Ryan always protected me, even when we was kids. When he snatched me out of that party, he probably just thought he was saving me from harm. Even as shocked as he was to see me like that, I wonder if he thought that's what he was doing, although it still ain't explain what happened next.

I laid there replaying what I remembered in my head. How could Ryan do that to me? There was no way I could tell somebody what he did. I felt sick every time I thought about it. I threw up a lot over the next few days. I skipped classes Monday and Wednesday. I skipped work. I ignored Mommy's texts and Meeka's calls. I was truly sick. The memory of the night was still clear as day in my head. The only way not to think about it was to sleep. I popped more Ambien pills. Once I put a handful in my mouth, but threw it up as soon as the pasty pills touched my tongue. I was too much of a coward to swallow.

So many thoughts clouded my head, but the question "Why?" kept repeating. I couldn't figure out why I cared so much about *why* he did it more than I did about *what* had actually happened. I mean, how can my own brother do what he did? Why did he think he could do it? How could this happen to me? My couch was my new best friend cuz I couldn't sleep in that bed no more. I ain't wanna talk to nobody who knew me. Nobody who could tell something really sick had happened. I just wanted to hide. I wanted to die. How easy would it be to just dissolve all the pills in a drink and sip it slowly through a straw? I stayed in the house watching reality TV and the news, watching other people's misery. I only left the house once to go to the corner store.

At the end of the week, I had a visitor pop up, banging hard on my door. I should've known it was gonna happen sooner than later. "KiKi, I see your car outside. Open the damn door!" I peeked through the peephole. There was Peaches wearing her big Diana Ross wig with Amir. She looked flawless with her lip gloss, peach halter dress, and golden accessories. I ran my hand over my matted hair. I might've brushed my teeth twice the whole week, and that was only cuz I couldn't take the cotton mouth no more. Peaches banged on the door again.

"Come on, chicken!" she sang. I hated when she called me that with a passion, and she knew it. Wasn't no chickenheads around here but her ass. I unlocked the door only cuz she had Amir and I ain't want him to see his mama acting a fool.

"Damn, girl, what happened to your face? You look a hot-ass mess. And what you doing in here? Trash all over the damn place. Is that a hole in your closet? Who did that?!"

"Come here, 'Mir," I said, reaching out for her son. I winced a little when I picked him up.

"Unh, unh. What's wrong with you?"

"I don't feel like talking about it."

"Unh," she said, sucking her teeth and rolling her eyes. Peaches knew the look of a face that had been beaten and the sounds of pain that came with it. I knew she was dying to know but appreciated her more for not even asking. I guess after all she had been through in that department, she remembered what it felt like to have people's harsh comments and relentless questioning when all you wanted to do was hide.

"Well, okay. I'm not gon' get too much in your business. But . . . I am gonna do your hair! I'll be damned. You ain't gon' be representing my salon looking like shit."

I smiled as she went to get her supplies out of the truck. I set Amir up with his toys in the living room. Peaches left Kori and Daneen running the shop for a while just so she could come check on me. She was a real friend who I knew I could count on, but the thought of telling her what my own brother did to me made a nasty taste come to my mouth. I just couldn't do it.

Peaches laced me up with a new do, working her magic, and then she set out on a mission to clean up my apartment. She piled up trash, put all the seasonings and condiments that I'd pulled from the cabinets back on their shelves, swept and mopped the kitchen, Cloroxed countertops, and Febrezed curtains. I merely vacuumed the living room and wiped off the coffee table. Peaches had so much energy, I couldn't keep up with her. As soon as she was finished, she made some margaritas.

"Now, KiKi, you know I ain't gon' rush you, but whenever you wanna tell me what happened, you know I'm here for you. And I'll never judge you," she said over the blender in the kitchen.

I knew Peaches had my back, but this was too much. Nobody could ever understand what Ryan did to me. Shit, I couldn't. I got a headache every time I thought about my tangled, bloody sheets and the sticky semen he left on my body.

"Try it?"

I took a sip of the margarita but wasn't really feeling it.

"Too much ice?"

"Nah. Just don't have a taste for it."

"Oh, okay," she said, rubbing her nose. "You look so down, KiKi."

I gave her a half smile. I knew she was trying to help, but there was nothing I felt like sharing with her.

"I just wanna say one thing. Don't lock yourself up in the house forever. Hey, what if we go visit Camille or Trina Boo? You know, do a road trip. We can go north or south. What you wanna do? It might cheer you up."

While that did sound like a good idea, I really wasn't in the mood. "Not now."

She sipped her drink and kicked her shoes off. I turned the TV to Nick Jr. and gave Amir a napkin with some Cheez-Its cuz clearly they wasn't leaving no time soon. He ate quietly, watching *Yo Gabba Gabba!*

"God, that boy look like his father."

"Tell me about it," she said before taking a long sip. "I dream about that nigga all the time. I be thinking how our life might be if he was still here. Would he be the same type of dude? What kind of daddy would he be to Amir, you know?"

I watched her sip her drink some more, and then all of a sudden she untwisted her golden pendant necklace and put the tip of the undone part to her nose. I watched her sniff what had to be coke. I was shocked but was definitely in no position to judge. No wonder she was always at the shop from the crack of dawn to late at night. She was high out of her mind.

"I don't think I can ever be with somebody else," she said before rubbing her nose. "Want some?"

I shook my head, then took a sip of my drink, which is what I needed after watching her do that. How was she able to maintain everything snorting coke? I tried my best not to shake my head. Hell, I was dabbling in my own self-meds. Peaches swallowed the rest of her drink and popped up to put the glass in the sink.

"All right, Amir. Let's go! Tell Auntie KiKi bye-bye." She was so buzzed and busy like a robot, packing her hair products, gathering his toys, packing his snack, and grabbing his hand.

"You don't have to leave yet," I said, worried about her driving around high and tipsy with her toddler son.

"Girl, I gotta get over to the shop. Who knows what the hell them bitches doing while I'm gone."

"Well, let me keep Amir for a little while. I don't mind. He can keep me company."

She looked at me like I had a third eye growing out my face. "You sure?"

I nodded. "I mean, you came over here to do my hair and to check up on me. I got you."

She took a deep breath like she was near tears, and then she gave me a tight hug. "I love you, Shakira. I

don't know what happened or what's wrong or whatever, but you know you my girl. Fuck, you my sister.
Call me if you need me."

"I know. I love you, too. I'll bring Amir to the shop
a little later."

"Okay," she said, walking to the sofa where her little
man had already sat back down. "You gon' stay here
with Auntie KiKi, Mir–Mir. Give me a kiss."

At the door Peaches said, "But for real. Call somebody, go somewhere, and do something. Even if it's
with somebody you haven't talked to in a while. That
might make you feel better."

I heard what she'd said, but I was in no mood for conversation.

The day after talking to Peaches, I decided to call Yodi
so she could tell Mommy that I had a stomach virus and
was too sick to come visit. That's the thing about Yodi:
She was always home.

"Mommy said do you want her to come stay with
you?" Yodi said.

"No, that's okay. I just wanna sleep. I'm not in the
mood for visitors."

Mommy seemed to buy it cuz she ain't stress me. I
sent Meeka a text with the same lie, though she immediately sent back: YOU SURE THAT'S WHY? I ain't respond
since it wasn't no easy way to answer that question. She
sent: I UNDERSTAND IF YOU NEED SOME TIME TO DEAL WITH THAT SHIT.

I'M HERE TO TALK ABOUT IT, THOUGH. I ain't respond. Kareem's phone calls was being avoided like the plague, too. It was time to just let that relationship fall completely off. Too much had happened since he'd been away in jail, and I definitely ain't feel like the same girl he thought he loved. I packed up all his stuff and dropped them off at his mother's house. She ain't look surprised to see me, either, and didn't even bother asking me any questions. She just pointed to a corner in her living room where she wanted me to drop it.

One night my phone rang, and Mommy's number popped up on the screen. I thought it was gonna be Yodi for Mommy, but when I said, "Hello," nobody said nothing. I said, "Yodi?" but I heard nothing but the TV in the background before the phone hung up. I tried to call right back, but nobody answered. Yodi called an hour later asking me if I wanted something cuz she saw I had called.

"No, I was calling y'all back," I said.

"We wasn't here," Yodi said. "Mommy went with me to take the kids to the doctor."

"Oh," I said, stunned. That had to mean one thing. Ryan.

A few hours of watching TV and lying on the couch had really left me bored after Peaches's surprise visit changed the energy of my apartment. I decided to study for school. Maybe if I focus on my vocabulary and make some flash cards, my mind would stop wandering off. For the entire weekend, I created and memorized all my vocabulary words. I restudied the last chapter and read the chapters Meeka said I missed. It really helped me not to think about none of that shit concerning Ryan.

The next week I decided to go to school. I was sick and tired of being in the house, plus the classes was paid for. As soon as Meeka saw me, she gave me a hug.

"Please, don't talk about it," I said. "Nothing about that night. I don't even wanna think about it."

Meeka nodded, then changed the subject. "Girl, do you know Quentin's father talking about he wanna take me to court?"

I raised my eyebrows. "For real?"

"Yeah, all of a sudden this nigga talking about he want full custody."

"Oh no, Meeka," I said as we walked toward the parking garage.

"Girl, yes. Had the nerve to say he had a better situation than me and the judge would see that clearly."

I shook my head.

"Of course, your ass got a better situation. You ain't have a child on your hip for the last four years slowing you down. Just cuz he gotta job and his own apartment, he think he money now."

"What you gon' do?"

"That nigga better stop playing with me. He ain't getting Quentin," Meeka said, lighting up a cigarette.

I felt a little sorry for her. She was doing the best she could to take care of him. Her mother helped her a lot, but Meeka did make sure her son had everything he needed. The thing is Quentin's father was always on time with his child support and he spent lots of time with his son. They were both good parents. I ain't know how that case might go.

"I think I'm gonna have to stop all this dancing and shit and get a legit job before he try to throw that in my face next."

I understood what she meant. After I dropped Meeka off on Upshur Street, I headed over to the barbershop on North Capitol. I wanted to get a fresh edge up. My barber Rich was happy to see me when I walked in, but he had a client in his seat. I took out my textbook and waited in a chair. I half listened to their conversation about the Redskins preseason training while I studied. Kevin Hart was cracking jokes on the flatscreen, making the shop come alive with laughter. People came in and out, some filling the seats beside me, but I ain't bother to look up.

"Hey, Ms. Royal Blue."

I looked up and saw Audri's pale face, her eyes still hidden behind cute shades. My feelings was hurt that she tried to play like she'd forgotten my name. I nodded. "How you doing? Audri, right?"

She smiled. "I'm good."

This time she was with two girls. The same one with

the boy haircut from last time sat in her barber's seat, and another one with a short, layered cut waited two chairs down. They chatted a little, and then Audri turned to me and said, "You been straight?"

I nodded.

"Good."

"You play any pool lately?" I asked.

"All the time," she said, smiling. "Let me know when you trying to get your ass whipped again."

I winked at her. "Never that."

"Right," Audri said.

My barber was done with his client and signaled for me to come over. I could feel Audri watching as I walked to his chair. She smiled at me as soon as I sat down.

"You want the same thing as last time?" Rich asked.

"Nah, just give me a basic cut."

"You serious? Now, you know you ain't a basic kind of girl, right?"

I smiled. His compliment seemed genuine. "That's all I want this time."

"All right."

He moved faster than he did the last time. I could feel Audri's eyes still on me, but I made sure I ain't look back at her. Didn't wanna give her a reason to talk to me. I just wasn't in the mood. When Rich was done, I paid him, said bye to Audri, and left the shop. Before I could get in my car, I heard Audri say, "Hey, KiKi!"

So she did remember my name. I looked up.

"Um, can I talk to you for a minute?"

I held my car door open with one hand and my keys in the other, waiting for her to come closer.

"I just wanna apologize for how our date ended that time. It wasn't cool how I left."

"That's okay, but I appreciate your apology."

"Um...I wanna cook for you."

My eyebrows rose. Sounded interesting.

"All you gotta do is come by my crib, and I'll make you one of my best meals."

"What's that?"

Audri laughed and scratched her head. "I don't know yet."

I laughed, too.

"What do you like? Fish, chicken, or steak?"

"All of them," I said, smiling.

"All right, well...I'll surprise you."

"Okay."

"Do you still have my number?"

"No," I lied, even though Audri was still the first name on my contact list.

We exchanged information again, agreeing to talk later. I don't know what it was about Audri that made me interested. Of course, I was curious about how she looked—her pale skin and naturally blonde hair—but there was also something else about her. I thought about what Peaches said, talking to somebody who I hadn't talked to in a while or how going somewhere different was both good ways to get over whatever was clouding my head. I mean, I wasn't open for dating, but a new friend wouldn't hurt. I decided that this time I would really try to get to know Audri.

12

The first thing I smelled when she opened the door was barbecue sauce, a sweet, spicy smell that soaked the entire apartment. My mouth watered. It was the first time Audri ain't have her shades on, but a regular pair of glasses. She had the most beautiful gray eyes I'd ever seen.

"Finally, I get to see your whole face. Nice."

She grinned and stepped back so I could come inside. "You look nice, too."

I ain't do much. I mean just a lavender shirt and some gray leggings. I did slip my feet into some cute wedges and threw on some accessories, though. Audri looked cute in her black tank top and carpenter jean shorts. I could tell she worked out. There was a snake tattoo going from her upper left arm across her back to her other shoulder. Interesting. There was a pool table where her dining table should be. No wonder she whipped my ass so bad; she was dead serious. I laughed, and she smiled knowingly.

"What you cooking?"

"Ribs, mashed potatoes, and corn on the cob."

"Nice." I dropped my keys and my handbag on her bar connected to the kitchen.

"It's almost ready."

I walked around, looking at the pictures she had on floating shelves. The decorations was surprisingly cute. Chocolates, dark blues, and creams. Audri used her remote control to turn the music up. Trey Songz was singing his heart out. I took a seat on a bar stool.

"You want something to drink?"

"What you got?"

"I figured you might like wine, so I got pinot noir. But I got some sweet tea in here, too."

"I'll take a glass of wine." I never had that kind before, just Moscato and white zinfandel.

She passed me a glass and made one for herself. It had a rich plum taste.

"So, Miss KiKi, when you eat, I wanna see you eat, eat. Don't try to be all cute and shit. That's why I purposely made ribs and corn on the cob. I wanna see how hard you go," she said, laughing.

"You ain't gotta worry about that. Trust. I gets down. Elbows on the table and all. I hope you got some toothpicks in here. Shoot."

"Yeah, okay," Audri said, laughing. Then she put a plate in front of me. I went to wash my hands in the bathroom. By the time I came back she was sitting on the bar stool, waiting for me.

"Looks yummy."

"Thanks, but how does it taste, though?"

I took a bite of the ribs, careful not to splash sauce everywhere. I nodded. She did a good job. "I ain't gon' lie, these ribs are delicious."

"Good."

We ate without really talking, just listened to the music. I took another glass of wine when she offered, promising myself it would be my last. When Plies came on her iPod, Ryan popped in my head. It's the one artist I knew for sure he liked cuz he stayed blasting Plies in his room behind his closed door.

"Can you please skip this one?" I asked.

"Yeah," she said without asking why. She used the remote to skip it. It's funny how I hadn't thought about Ryan all day, and now I couldn't get him out my mind.

"You all right? Your mood changed like shit."

I nodded and picked over my mashed potatoes. Audri left me alone for a while. I tried to shake off my thoughts of Ryan. "Hey, so what made you get that tattoo?" I asked, trying to change the subject.

Audri laughed and covered her mouth with her hand. "I don't know. Just liked it. Thought it looked slick. You got some?"

I held up two fingers. "Two butterflies."

"Oh, okay. Why butterflies?"

"I like how they start off as caterpillars, then turn into something that doesn't have to crawl no more," I said, never mentioning the fact that one was by choice and the other was by force. Nut made all his girls get tramp stamps etched with the numbers 666 as a way to brand his merchandise.

Our date was going good. We talked, played pool, joked, and teased each other until I finally said it was time for me to go. I ain't wanna be out too late or give her the wrong idea about me. I thanked her before leaving, promising to call her when I got home. On the ride home, I thought about how cool she was and how she ain't push up on me. It had been a long time since someone was genuinely interested in me and ain't expect me to fuck them off the break. It was a nice feeling to have for a change.

A few days after me and Audri hung out, I was on my way home from class when I saw Ryan's yellow ass sitting on the steps of my apartment building, smoking a Black & Mild. My heart jumped, and I froze. *What the fuck did he want?* Thank God, he ain't see me. I sped past my building. I couldn't believe his ass was at my house. I mean, I went out my way not to go by Mommy's house just for that very reason. I ain't ever wanna see him again. How could he just show up like everything was cool? I thought about going back to Meeka's since I just dropped her off, but she had to meet Quentin's father later. I decided to go to Peaches's shop even though I wasn't supposed to work. I ain't know how long he was gonna be lurking around my building, but I ain't wanna give him a chance to say shit to me. *I wish I had some guy friends who could just fuck him up.* I hung out at the shop until it started to get late. After closing, I called Audri to see what she was doing. I asked her if I could come by and was glad she was cool with it.

I sat on her couch an hour later sipping an O'Cup and staring at the TV, still in my uniform and foam clogs. My phone rang, and Ryan's number and face popped up on the screen. *Shit.* I sent it straight to voice mail. I stared at the ceiling and combed my fingers through my hair nervously.

"What's wrong?" Audri asked.

I took a deep breath. How was I gonna explain to her what was wrong?

Audri flipped the TV off and turned to look me in my face. "Look, you all right?" she asked sincerely.

I hadn't told a single soul what happened. Something about how Audri asked made me want to tell her. She ain't know me enough to judge me too harshly, and it was early enough in our relationship that if she had a problem with it, she could walk away and I'd at least have gotten it off my chest. I took another deep breath and blew the air across my lips. "Something happened to me a few weeks ago. Something that I haven't told nobody." I took a sip from my cup filled with cough syrup and a mixture of different drinks.

"You know you can talk to me, right?" she said, shaking my leg that was laid across her lap.

I nodded even though I knew I was about to take a chance that might ruin whatever it was that we had. I guess the doubt was written plainly on my face cuz Audri said, "KiKi, I promise I won't think no different of you. You can tell me anything that's gon' make you feel better."

"Okay," I said before swallowing the rest of the cup, then releasing another sigh. "A few weeks ago...I was raped."

"What? Did you call the police?"

I shook my head.

"Why not?"

I shook my head again and stared at my empty cup. I couldn't tell her why. No one would ever understand why I chose not to snitch on my brother.

"KiKi, you have to call the police."

I shook my head. "I can't," I said so seriously I knew she got the point.

"Was it somebody you knew?" she asked.

I nodded.

Audri stood up and walked around her living room, flexing her muscles. I could tell she was agitated. "Was it a nigga you used to mess with or something?" she asked, looking me dead in my eyes.

I shook my head, and then tears slid down my face. "He broke in my apartment, and I saw him again today smoking a cigarette in front of my building."

"Come here. Stop crying." Audri hugged me tightly the way I wished I had been hugged the morning after it all happened. I cried on her shoulder until I had no more tears. I wanted to tell her it was my brother, but I couldn't. I laid in her arms until I fell asleep. She woke me up a little later so I could go sleep in her bedroom.

The next morning, she sat next to me with a breakfast sandwich and some apple juice. She watched me eat, and then she said, "You can stay here as long as you want."

"Thank you, but I can't do that to you."

"Look, we can go to your crib today. Get some shit and bring it back here. You can't stop your life cuz of that shit."

"But that's too much to ask of you."

"Nah, fuck that...as soon as you finish eating, go shower and throw these clothes on," she said, pointing at the T-shirt and basketball shorts folded neatly beside her. I was so thankful of Audri's offer, but at the same time I felt strange. She barely knew me, and she was being so kind and trusting, offering to let me stay here. After I finished breakfast, I did what she said. Soon we was heading to R Street. Audri parked her Challenger in front and reached between the armrest and her chair and pulled a gun out.

"Fuck that," she said.

I tried not to look shocked, but that's when I knew Audri had some shit with her, too. Next, we headed inside my building. The first thing I noticed was what looked like some kick marks at the bottom of my door. It had to be Ryan. Why was he acting so crazy? My heart skipped as I nervously put my keys in the lock. I knew he wasn't inside, but still, I was really scared now. He obviously wanted something from me and was pissed that I wasn't there. Audri was right; I had to leave.

"You okay?" Audri asked behind me.

I nodded, but my stomach was doing flips. Who had Ryan become?

Audri noticed the hole in the closet door but ain't say nothing. I grabbed a couple duffel bags, pulled clothes off my hangers, dug in my dresser for underclothes, grabbed toiletries from the bathroom, then stuffed shoes and accessories in bags, not wasting no time. Audri helped line bags up at the door. When I grabbed everything that I was gonna need for a while, we headed back downstairs. Safely in her car, I finally took a breath of relief.

"It's all right," Audri said, rubbing my knee.

"Thank you so much..."

She turned and looked at me. "It's all good."

I spent the next couple of weeks at Audri's. She had

some of her cousins help move all of my furniture into a storage unit a couple blocks down the street from my building. I couldn't believe how much she was doing for me without asking for nothing. She flaunted me around her friends and hadn't even done more than kiss me and hold me since she learned about what happened to me.

I had learned a lot about Audri since I started living with her. Number one, she had lied about working for the mailroom. Number two, she really had a couple of hustles going on. Besides being a chronic gambler, between the pool games and crap games, she was also doing something that surprised me but which also made me realize why she was always at the barbershop with different girls. She managed three dancers that did private parties. Who was I to judge?

Audri asked me if any of it bothered me, but maybe that's why I was attracted to her. She had a presence about her. A confidence that even the most sexiest dudes still ain't manage to have. I felt conflicted since that was probably the best time to tell her that I used to do private parties, too. Instead, all she knew about me was that I worked at Peaches's salon and that I went to Everest College. As much as I could use extra money in my pockets, I ain't want her to look at me differently. I kept that part about my past a secret. I was good at keeping secrets. Plus, Audri might've thought I brought that rape shit on myself.

Given the fact that I wasn't in no mood to sleep with

nobody anyway, I just worked as many hours as I could get from Peaches. I was letting the apartment go anyway, even though my lease wasn't up. I couldn't handle no more surprise visits from Ryan. I worried about how I would avoid seeing him for the rest of my life. I spent my money on groceries for Audri and buying a couple things for myself since Audri wasn't being pressed about money anyway. She told me to chill.

I called Yodi a couple times to pass messages to Mommy. One day I heard Mommy yelling in the background that she ain't see me in a month. I promised to take her to get her hair done later, but the whole time I was wondering how I was gonna pull that off without running into Ryan. I knew me ducking him wasn't fair to Mommy, but what else was I supposed to do?

13

It was September when I finally introduced Mommy to Audri. Even though she kept trying to get in my business, I wanted to keep my girlfriend a secret. I mean, Mommy knew that I had moved in with somebody, but I wasn't exactly honest about the fact that it was my girlfriend and not just my roommate. See, the only person I ever let Mommy meet was Kareem, so either way I ain't know how she was gonna act. I invited Mommy over cuz she kept asking me to stop by the house for dinner, but I told her to stop by my house instead. Audri was such a good cook that I knew Mommy would be impressed by her regardless.

Lasagna, garlic bread, and vegetables was Audri's meal of choice. When Mommy walked in the door, she did a good job of not staring at Audri's skin. As a matter of fact, Mommy gave her a hug like she knew Audri for years.

"Such a nice place," Mommy said, walking around. It took Audri a second to understand what Mommy said, but I helped translate. Whenever Mommy asked Audri questions, she turned to look at me to double-check what she had said. I was used to Mommy's broken speech, but Audri not so much. All in all, the night went good. Halfway through dinner, Mommy signed: "She's not just your roommate, is she?"

I blushed.

Then Mommy signed: "No wonder you don't come by no more."

She shook her head. I couldn't tell if that meant she had a problem with it or not. She just let it be. After dinner, I drove Mommy home. I was more nervous about dropping her home than picking her up now that it was late. Ryan was sure to be on the block. Over the past couple months, I had did a good job avoiding him. I would always meet Mommy outside, telling her I had to do something else right after I dropped her off, like meet Meeka for some school stuff or meet Audri.

"So, dis Audri...," Mommy said soon as we got in the car.

"Yes," I said tense.

"Yoo real like hur?"

"I do. She's cool."

"I don't get dis cool stuff."

I smiled. "She's sweet to me, Mommy."

"Okay." Mommy nodded. "Dat's all I wanna know.

You disurv someone who will treat you right for a change."

I smiled.

"I'm not big on this lifestyle, but you old enough to know what you want, 'Kirwuh.'"

I understood how she felt, and I'm proud of Mommy for not trying to tell me how to live, like I expected her to do. For the most part, Mommy had no clue just how crazy my life was. As a matter of fact, the worst thing she thought I had ever done was run away to live with Nut. Her guilt about having us separated and sent to foster care kept her from being the kind of strict parent she should've been. Toya told me that Mommy ain't even go to the police when I ran away, that the police came to her wondering why I hadn't been to school in a week. Mommy got in trouble for not reporting me missing right away, and they had threatened to take Yodi from her again, claiming she was irresponsible for not filing a report. Mommy had a social worker doing surprise visits to monitor Yodi for a while, but everything died down when the police ran into me working Fourteenth Street a few months later. I spent thirty days in a group home before they released me to Mommy. The very next day, I ran away again and back to Nut. Mommy thought it was teenage love and nothing more. And since she was dealing with Ryan's unofficial job of selling drugs, she ain't think there was nothing too wrong with teenage love.

When I pulled up on W Street, my body instantly tensed up. A clutter of niggas stood across the street. Something told me Ryan was with them. I could just feel it.

"Okay, you not gon' come up?" Mommy asked.

"Not this time."

"Okay den, 'Kirwuh. I'll talk to you soon."

Mommy climbed out the car, and I waited for her to unlock the building door and walk safely inside before I pulled off. When I turned back around, ready to go, that nigga Ryan was standing right in front of my car wearing a gray hoodie. My heart jumped. He locked eyes with me and signaled for me to roll the window down. I ain't want to, but the only way to get around Ryan was to hit him. And though the thought crossed my mind, I couldn't do it. I rolled the window down a little.

He leaned down and said, "What's up? Where you been?"

His breath smelled like weed. Was he really this crazy?

"Around."

"I ain't seen you in a grip."

Exactly how I wanted it to be. I tucked my bottom lip under the top one and nodded.

"You still mad at me?" he asked.

I squinted. I couldn't believe he had asked me such a ridiculous question.

"You can't be mad. You a whore, right?" he said

without flinching. "Maybe you pissed that I ain't pay you or some shit. But you gotta give me freebies."

The nerve of this nigga. I mashed the gas, not giving a fuck if I hit him or not. I heard him yell, "Crazy bitch!" as I sped past him. I couldn't stop shaking my head at the sick shit he said. Ryan acted like what he had done was normal.

"It's not fucking normal to rape your fucking sister, you retarded muthafucka!" I yelled in my empty car, hitting the steering wheel. Tears poured down my face. I had to pull over. My hands was shaking so much. I sat in my car on Rhode Island Avenue until I could breathe easily. I drove home and went straight to bed, ignoring Audri's questions.

"Whoa...what's wrong with you?" she asked when she got to the bedroom. "Was it your mother? What? She don't like me?"

I shook my head. "It's not that."

"Then what, KiKi? You can't shut me out."

"You don't wanna know."

She raised my chin from the pillow with her fingers and said, "Don't say that shit...I'm not like other people you used to fuck with, okay? I do wanna know."

I sat up on one arm. That's why I was so into her. She knew what to say to make me believe her. Instead of telling her what was real, I asked her to hand me my cell phone from my handbag. She looked confused, but she handed it to me. I dialed my voice mail and put the phone on speaker. I skipped over recently saved messages from Meeka, Peaches, and Yodi all the way to the one that was left back in August.

"Where the fuck you hiding? Your ass better not think about telling nobody shit, or I'll kill your muthafucking ass."

"Young, who the fuck was that?" Audri asked, her jaws tensing.

A tear rolled down my cheek, and I sniffled. How could I tell her? I shook my head.

"Shakira? Who *was* that?" she asked, looking in my eyes.

"My brother," I finally said.

Audri blinked, then shook her head. She couldn't stop shaking her head as her eyes moved around quickly. What I had said wasn't making sense to her, and I could see the confusion all over her face. "Your own brother did that shit to you?"

I nodded.

She punched her fist in her hand and said, "What the fuck, man?" and jumped up.

As pissed as Audri was, I actually felt better. Finally, someone knew besides me. A weight lifted off my chest, and for the first time since I seen Ryan, I felt like I could breathe. Audri wrapped me in her arms and held me as if she finally understood my pain. I fell asleep soon after.

I was starting to feel like telling Audri was a big mistake. She seemed distant. Sometimes I'd catch her staring at me and not in the loving kind of way she had stared at me before. It was like she was studying me. I could see her mind moving as she looked me over. She ain't touch me like she used to. Just kisses on my forehead. What I had told her had her fucked up. I could see it every time we caught eyes. There was questions that I knew she had, but she never asked them, like, Why did it happen? How many times? How long had he been raping me? Who knew? She was probably even wondering what she had gotten herself into, messing with me.

One day after I finished helping Peaches close the shop, I told her how Audri had been acting different lately. Of course, I ain't tell her what news I had shared with Audri to make her start acting that way, but Peaches told me not to worry about it. She sat in one of the spinning chairs and untwisted the charm on her necklace. Before I knew it, she sniffed coke up her nose again.

"Why you do that shit?" I asked.

"Girl, it just gives me peace. All that shit you talking about, all that shit I had to deal with today with these clients...it just settles me. You don't understand, my nerves fucked up."

"Hmmm..." I heard her, and I could relate to wanting peace, but that shit wasn't for me.

A couple days later, Audri told me she was going out of town with her dancers for some event in Atlantic City. She just straight dropped it on me, like she purposely ain't want me to know until the last minute. Suddenly, she packing an overnight bag and shit out the blue.

"You wasn't gonna ask me to go?" I asked, clearly pissed.

Audri seemed surprised that I was upset. "I ain't think you would wanna be around that shit. You wanna go?" she asked in a way that let me know she ain't really want me to go.

I rolled my eyes and walked in the kitchen for something to drink. Was this a trick question? "No, that's okay. I don't wanna be invited after the fact. You been acting funny anyway lately."

Audri sucked her teeth, then said, "What are you talking about now?"

"Nothing." I poured some cranberry juice in a glass.

"Don't give me that 'nothing' shit. Don't be fishing for answers. What the fuck? Tell me what's on your mind."

I sipped my juice before I said, "Nothing."

"This that shit I can't fucking stand with females. Don't bring shit up, and then say, 'Nothing.'"

"It's just that..." I paused to get my thoughts together. "It seem like ever since I told you about my brother, you ain't been the same."

Audri took a deep breath and nodded. "On some no bullshit...for real...that shit's fucking with my head. I don't understand how that shit even happened. And then to top it off, you ain't even call the police on his ass after that? I don't get it."

I shook my head. I knew I shouldn't have told her. I knew it.

"I like you a lot, KiKi . . . but it's fucking with me."

Audri kissed me on my forehead, grabbed her keys and bag, said she'd call me from the road, then left. I was still standing in the kitchen, trying to understand what she meant by "it's fucking with me." Did that mean she ain't trust me or that I asked to be raped by my brother? That I brought it on myself? That I must not have a problem with what happened cuz I never called the police? If I called the police on my brother, it would destroy my mother and my family. She'd blame herself all over again, thinking about us being snatched from her cuz of her choice in men. It wasn't her fault but wasn't no words I could ever sign to make her believe that, so I'd rather keep my secret to myself. Spare Mommy the pain of knowing her own son raped her daughter.

When Meeka called me later to see if I wanted to go to Ibiza, it was easy for me to say yeah. I begged Peaches to come hang out with us for a change. She said no but that we could come spend the night at her crib later for girls' night. Since I ain't wanna be in Audri's apartment dwelling on our conversation, it sounded like a plan.

I settled on a strapless mustard Tracy Reese dress that showed my firm thighs and my Louboutin Mamanouk booties. I pinned my hair up in a tussled Mohawk.

Did picture-perfect makeup including a splash of MAC's Russian red matte lipstick. Audri was missing it. Shit, I looked like a sophisticated slut. I threw some pajamas, a change of clothes, and some toiletries in my saddlebag. Twenty minutes later I was in front of Meeka's house.

"Audri know your ass out here looking like you on the prowl, bitch?" Meeka asked.

I smiled. "She should've never left me here."

"I know that's right."

We had a ball in the packed club, getting niggas to buy us drinks, dancing on the floor, and joning on bitches who looked set the fuck up. Their asses was dead wrong for leaving the house looking a hot-ass mess. On the way out the club, I bumped into Rich, my barber.

"Hey, shawty."

"Hey, Rich," I said, giving him a hug. He held me tight, making my full body press against his. His neck smelled so good. I was surprised at how much I liked the feel of him and had to pull away before I got lost in his arms.

"Y'all having fun tonight, huh?" he asked.

I nodded, smiled, and waved bye as me and Meeka kept it moving.

"Girl, he look good as shit. Who was that?"

"That's my barber."

"Hmmm. He want your ass," she said, holding my arm, trying to keep her balance in her five-inch heels.

"It's not even like that. I promise." That was just like

Meeka to try and syce some shit up. We jumped in my BMW, and I checked my phone before I pulled off. There was two missed calls from Audri. For a minute, I thought about not calling her but figured it wasn't cool to give her any doubts while I was living for free in her apartment.

"Hey, babe."

"You all right?" she asked.

"Yeah, me and Meeka went to Ibiza."

"Oh, I ain't know you was going out tonight."

"Well, I ain't know you was going to Atlantic City."

Audri sighed. I knew she had just rolled her eyes, too. "Look, I was just checking on you, but since you're good, I'll holler at you later."

"Mm-hmmm," I said, hanging up.

"You need to stop playing games with that girl," Meeka said, shaking her head.

Whatever. I called Peaches and told her we was on our way, then hit New York Avenue, so I could head out to Bowie. I took the Mitchellville exit off of Route 50. She lived in a beautiful three-story brick house surrounded by a wooded area. I mean, her great room was bigger than Audri's whole apartment. The only thing I hated about her house was the pictures of Nut everywhere. I mean, Peaches had a shrine of this man in every corner.

"Hey, girls," Peaches sang from the doorway as we grabbed our stuff from the car. I can tell she had been snorting lines from all her giddiness.

"Hey, Peaches," Meeka said, giving her a hug.

"Hey, what's up? Where's Amir?" I asked.

"Over his cousin's in Greenbelt. Come on inside."

I could hear Keri Hilson singing as we entered.

"I hope y'all want some margaritas cuz I already started making some."

"Hell yeah, I want some," said Meeka, sashaying over to the island and pouring herself a cup.

"Make me a cup, too, please," I said, plopping down on her plush sofa.

"Damn, Peaches. This house is so nice," Meeka said, walking around. Although she had been to Peaches's shop and even went on a cruise with us the past February to Puerto Rico, she had never been to Peaches's house. I watched her walking around, looking at pictures. The big one of Nut and Peaches on top of the fireplace. The one of Amir in the foyer. The wall of framed pictures leading up the staircase. I knew this was all Peaches needed to start going down memory lane. Listening to her talk about Nut was downright depressing. Meeka curled up on the couch across from me with her glass and listened to all the stories I've heard a thousand times. The funny ones that had Peaches's crazy butt up out her seat imitating me or one of my other girlfriends who worked the streets with us and even some of the fucked-up ones that left all of us with watery eyes. By the time she was done, we had been through the whole bottle of margarita mix, two bottles of rum, and a couple glasses of an Amaretto mix Peaches called Alice in Wonderland, swearing she was a bartender. That shit had us so twisted, it took me a second to realize her and Meeka was both snorting lines of coke on her glass coffee table.

Peaches smiled and said, "Here, KiKi."

I felt my body moving toward them. I reached out for the crisp bill she had rolled into a straw and kneeled down to breathe in the magic dust.

14

The first hit made me feel like I could do anything. I kept hearing myself say, "Let's get in the pool, y'all. Come on, y'all, let's get in the pool." Meeka and Peaches just kept laughing at me. I ain't care that it was too cold outside. I had a huge burst of energy, the kind that made me wanna do something not planned. I jumped up off the floor and turned Peaches's iPod speakers up as loud as they could go.

"If you gettin' money/Just throw it in the bag," me and Fabolous rapped.

"Whoa! Whoa!" Meeka and Peaches clapped and danced around me until we had a mini–Soul Train line going and I was pop-locking. I leaped up on her couch and sang some more with the remote control. I felt so free.

"You get it 'cause I got it/I got it, so you get it." I

kept rapping, and then I soared across Peaches's coffee table, just missing the other couch. *Blooop.* The back of my head clipped the coffee table.

"Oh, shit!" Peaches yelled.

"You all right, KiKi?" Meeka said, running to help me up.

My head hurt a little bit, but I still felt like I had eaten a hundred dark chocolate bars. "What we 'bout to do next?" I said, clapping my hands against my thighs.

"Girl, you need to sit down and chill the fuck out 'fore you tear my shit up," Peaches said, giving me a Ziploc bag filled with ice. "Lay back."

I laughed and laid across the couch, holding the bag to the back of my head.

Meeka was laughing, too. "This your first time?"

"I feel like that damn Road Runner cartoon. Meep. Meep." I bounced back up when Ester Dean came on. "Drop it, drop it low, girl/drop it, drop it low, girl."

"KiKi, your ass crazy as hell!" Meeka shouted.

Peaches yanked me back down on the couch. "Come on, KiKi, for real, you doing too much. Chill out."

"All I hear you saying is *wonk-wonk, wonk-wonk, wonk-wonk*," I said, opening and closing my hand to show Peaches what her mouth looked like.

Meeka rolled on her side, laughing.

"Y'all bitches crazy," Peaches said. "I'm taking my ass to bed. KiKi, you know where the guest room is."

Me and Meeka cracked up again as she walked up the

staircase. We both fell asleep soon afterward, right on the couch. The next morning, the back of my head was throbbing like a toothache. Peaches was up before the two of us, cooking breakfast.

"That shit smell good. Okay, Silver Diner," Meeka said, stretching. She got up to use the bathroom.

I laid there, listening to the sounds of the house. The sizzle of the sausage. The water running in the guest bathroom with the jetted tub. The birds outside the window. Fuck! Birds don't chirp outside my muthafucking window. I rolled over on my back and stared at the details of the sage trim on the curtains that matched the faint sage color on the sofas that just so happened to pick up the sage specks in the carpet and the lampshade. This bitch had it made. Living all the way the fuck out here in the woods, just her and her damn son.

"Whenever y'all whores ready, breakfast done!" Peaches yelled.

No, this tramp ain't call me a whore when my fucking twat put the down payment on her deluxe palace. Selfish ass. All this time, she been seeing me struggle and the best she can do to help me is give me a lot of hours shampooing hair? Now that shit don't make sense. I make ten dollars an hour plus tips. And black people never tip the shampoo girl.

Meeka came back out the bedroom fully dressed, so I grabbed my bag and went to the bathroom. Look at this. Plush, creamy towels, scented soap, and candles everywhere like this the W Hotel. I washed up, threw on some black leggings, a fitted red hoodie, some big silver hoop earrings before I headed down for breakfast. Peaches had made pomegranate mimosas.

"You doing the damn thing, I mean, got your own shop, your nice-ass ride, and this place is gorgeous," Meeka said, smiling. "I wanna be like you when I grow up."

Pssst. Peaches smiled and raised her glass. "I'll drink to that." Meeka clinked her glass against Peaches's glass. I rolled my eyes and sipped my mimosa.

"No, for real. I'm glad you like it. It took my interior designer forever to finish, though."

Pssst. Now here she go. Bragging and shit.

"So, ladies, did you have fun last night?" Peaches said.

"I know KiKi's ass did," Meeka said, laughing and pointing at me. Peaches joined in with the cackling, too.

"Fuck y'all," I said, really not in the mood.

"Damn, calm down," Peaches said, still smirking. "Awww...somebody's irritable this morning. You ain't sleep good?"

I rolled my eyes.

"Hey, I got an idea that will cheer you up," Peaches said, her eyes big and bright like a child who just found out they was going to Disney World.

"What?" I said, feeling more annoyed by the second.

"Since Audri just left your ass down here, we should roll up to New York and see what Trina Boo up to.

When's the last time you seen Trina Boo with your shady ass?"

She *would* have to put it that way.

"I'm down," Meeka said, excited. "All I gotta do is tell my mother to keep Quentin another night."

"We should take a picture in Times Square and send it to her ass. Put the word *Naaa* up under it," Peaches said, laughing. "Take that bitch right in front of the Flatiron Building or some shit."

I even had to laugh at that one.

"Wait, let me call Trina Boo first, and see if she's even in town," Peaches said, dialing her number. "I know how her ass like to hop from city to city."

Peaches put the phone on speaker.

"Hey, girl, what's up?" Trina Boo said.

"Hey. What you doing?" Peaches asked.

"Nothing, just waking up."

"Hey, Trina Boo," I said. "It's KiKi."

"Hey, Shakira! What y'all doing?"

"Nothing yet," Peaches said. "You in New York?"

"Yeah, why? Y'all coming to see me?" she asked, excited.

Peaches looked at me, waiting for my answer with a big cheese grin on her face.

"KiKi, you owe me a trip, bitch!" Trina Boo said.

I rolled my eyes and shook my head. They knew how to lay the guilt trip on thick.

"Shit, it's a big party tonight, too. And I'm telling

you, y'all ain't never been to a party 'til you been to one of these kind. Wall-to-wall rich niggas. Rappers, producers, league niggas."

"Hot damn...fuck that, I'ma have to get me something cute to wear," Meeka said. "Hey, Trina Boo. I'm Meeka."

"Hey, girl, nice to meet you. You coming, too?"

"I sure am!"

"Can you get us in the party?" Peaches asked.

"Of course. As long as I bring some bad bitches with me, I can get anybody in. Meeka, you a bad bitch or what?" Trina Boo asked, laughing.

"You best believe it! Bad with a capital B!" Meeka added a snap for extra emphasis.

They all laughed. Now I wanted to go, too. I had never been to one of Trina Boo's celebrity bashes. She had been telling me to come to one for a long time, but I was always too bunned up with Kareem. Camille told me about one she went to in Atlanta, and Peaches told me about the parties she went to in New York, Miami, and Houston. Ever since Trina Boo's name was getting big around the music industry, cuz of all the hot videos she was in, she stayed getting invited to celebrity parties and premieres. Last I checked she was dating a Knick or a Net.

"Please come, KiKi. Your ass be flaking on me all the time," Trina Boo said.

"Okay, okay," I finally said.

"Yay!" Meeka and Peaches sang. I shook my head at Meeka dancing in her seat.

"Let me go pack a bag," Peaches said.

"And let me go raid your closet," I said, racing her up the stairs.

By the time we finally hit the road, it was almost two o'clock. It took us awhile to get there cuz of construction in Philly and in Delaware. We got to Brooklyn at seven o'clock. Trina Boo shared an apartment with a Trinidadian girl named Taryn. They lived in an apartment building on Atlantic Avenue. Peaches said it used to be a Catholic church before they turned it into condos. After Trina Boo buzzed us in the gate, we walked inside the building, then down a long hall, before we stepped out a glass door and cut through a nice-size courtyard in the middle of the building. You would've never thought the courtyard was there from the loud and busy street. I could actually see the sky and where the trees, grass, and plants got its light from every day.

When we rang their doorbell, Trina Boo snatched open the door and gave me and Peaches big hugs. I introduced Meeka to Trina Boo, and then Trina Boo introduced me and Meeka to Taryn. She had pretty brown skin and naturally long, straight hair. She was a dancer, too, under the same Imprint agency Trina Boo was signed with. They was lounging around and not in no kind of rush to get dressed or anything. Free, Trina Boo's little black Yorkie, sniffed our ankles before he went back to his red cushion on the floor. Their apartment was gorgeous. There was higher ceilings than normal, an exposed brick wall, nice hardwood floors, and even a metal spiral staircase that took you to the basement.

"What y'all want to drink?" Taryn asked, going to the kitchen.

"Cîroc and something else," Meeka said.

"You got some Grand Marnier?" I asked.

"Yeah, I'll hook y'all up. What you want, Peaches?"

"Whatever mixed with whatever," she said, plopping down on the camel-colored leather couch. "My feet hurt. We better be catching a cab tonight."

"Of course, we are. About time you finally came here, bitch!" Trina Boo said, squeezing me again.

"I know, I know. I'm terrible."

"Yeah, you are. So what y'all gonna wear?"

We all opened our bags. When I showed the green-and-blue Versace dress I borrowed from Peaches, Trina Boo said, "Oh no. Too many people got that one up here. I've seen it like a hundred times already. You can't wear that."

Damn.

"Let's go check my closet for something else," she said, snatching my hand.

It ain't take me long to find something I liked. Even though Trina Boo had ass for days, everything she gave me to try on hugged my body like it was made especially for me. The one everybody seemed to like the most was an emerald-green Givenchy romper. That shit looked perfect on me.

"Well, we not leaving 'til twelve, so y'all can just chill," Trina Boo said.

"I'ma take a nap," Peaches said, curling up in Trina Boo's sheets. "Uggh, girl. When the last time you washed these fuckin' sheets. They stink."

"Fuck you!" Trina Boo said, laughing. "Ain't nobody tell you to lay in my bed. There's a huge pullout downstairs. I ain't never here anyway."

"Your ass here now," Peaches said, tossing the sheets off of her. "Give me some clean ones, please."

"Trick, this ain't the Holiday Inn. Get your ass up and go to the closet."

Me and Meeka shook our heads, then went to get our drinks from Taryn. I saw her rubbing her nose, the same way Peaches did all the time these days. I knew Taryn had just had a hit, and I wanted one, too. I felt my mouth getting wet cuz I wanted one so bad. I ain't know what had come over me.

"Here you go," Taryn said, passing me a drink.

"Thank you," I said and waited for Meeka to grab hers. When she went back to the living room, I tapped my nose with my finger so Taryn could see me. She smiled and nodded her head to the right. I followed her down the hall and into her white-and-black decorated room. She closed the door behind me.

"You can sit down."

I sat on her bed and waited for her to grab the stash from a drawer. She took out a vial, then passed it to me. I sniffed it and almost immediately felt high. I laid back on her bed and laughed. Before I knew it, I felt Taryn's hands massaging my breasts lightly. Her sexy ass was smiling at me hard. When she leaned closer, I kissed her. Taryn's lips was so soft. She swirled her tongue in my mouth like a snake. She raised my shirt and pulled my breasts out before she flipped her tongue over my nipples. It was feeling so good, but then I heard Audri's ringtone muffled under my butt. I took a deep breath and then pushed Taryn away. *What was I thinking?*

She looked disappointed and then said, "Whenever you want some more, just come see me."

I ain't know if she was talking about more of her or the coke, but I had to leave her alone and answer the phone. I smiled as I walked out of her room, but the music stopped. How crazy was it that Audri chose to call me now but ain't call me all day? I dialed her back.

"Hey," I said, walking to the living room. I climbed down the metal staircase so I could have some privacy in the basement.

"Damn, you wasn't gon' call me all day?" Audri asked.

"You just thought about calling me, I see." I sat on the plush chocolate couch.

"Man, whatever. What you doing?"

"Nothing." I decided not to even mention that we was in New York. "What you doing?"

"Getting ready to get outta here. The party's in a suite upstairs and shit."

"Hey, Audri...have you ever fucked one of your dancers before?"

"What? Where the fuck is that shit coming from?"

Now she's stalling. "I just wanna know."

"You ain't never 'wanna know' before."

"Have you or not?"

"No! I don't mix business with pleasure. Ever. Why the fuck you asking me that shit?"

"You sound guilty," I said.

"Man, I don't have time for this."

"Are you lying? Which one you fucked?"

Audri sucked her teeth, and then she said, "I'll talk to you later."

She hung up the phone. I laughed at myself for what I had just did. I picked a fight with her on purpose, and Audri fell right into my little trap. It's true. I never even cared if she had gone there with any of them little hood rat hoes cuz they was there before I had even stepped in the picture. But now she was making me wonder. Hell, she never even brought them broads around me, and since she ain't invite me to Atlantic City with her or any of her other little road trips, maybe it *was* more to their relationship than I thought.

I climbed the stairs to see where everybody was.

Meeka had fallen asleep on the couch. Trina Boo was on the phone, and Peaches was curled up in her sheets snoring like shit. I decided to go see what Taryn was up to. My pussy was still wet from earlier, but when I tapped on her door, there was no answer. Maybe it was for the best. I went back to the living room and tried to fall asleep on the couch across from Meeka.

15

We ain't show up to the rooftop party until after one in the morning, but you couldn't even tell it was that late since everything was still popping around the city. They never lied when they said New York never sleeps. When we stepped off the elevator, the DJ was pumping a Pharrell and Clipse song. The crowd was still packed and celebrities was everywhere. Trina Boo gave me and Meeka a little pep talk in the cab ride over, reminding us not to act starstruck when we saw celebrities.

"The trick is to treat them niggas the same way you'd treat a nigga who wants to smash. Period. They ain't nobody for real," she had said.

And I tried my best not to do double-takes when I saw them, either. Taryn took me to the bathroom once to do a few lines, and that was just what I needed to give me that extra boost to work the room. Competition for attention was fierce. A girl stepped on my fucking foot with that same green-and-blue Versace dress I left back at Trina Boo's, and I wanted to kill her ass.

"You all right?" Meeka asked when she saw me bend over to check my foot.

"Yeah, I'm okay."

"Girl, look. You see who that is on the couch?" Meeka said slyly, talking with a glass in front of her lips.

I looked over to where she was staring. "Who is that?"

"That's the dude that just got traded to the Giants from the Redskins. I can't remember his name."

I knew exactly who she was talking about cuz his face was all over the news in D.C. Not only was he and the owner not getting along, but the dumb muthafucka put his credit card inside a waitress's shirt at a bar downtown and she sued his ass. "Are you sure that's him?"

"Girl, that's him."

I stared at the dude and knew that if nothing else I recognized his face. I followed Meeka over there since he was chilling by hisself and my foot was still hurting.

"Thank you for saving these seats for us," Meeka said, squeezing in on his left.

He looked at her like she was crazy. I sat on his right, sandwiching him in, and then I took my shoe off and rubbed my foot. That shit still hurt.

"Why you looking like you lost your shih tzu?" Meeka asked.

His forehead folded up as he stared at the crowd. "I don't know what you talking about."

"You miss D.C., don't you? Tell the truth," Meeka said.

He snorted and shook his head. "Fuck D.C."

"Damn. Like that," she said, her neck snapping back and her top lip curling up.

"Yeah, like that."

"What's in your cup? I'ma get your ass another drink. You want something stronger?"

He laughed and shook his head.

"Now that's better...I'm Meeka, and this is KiKi," she sang and fluttered her thick lashes.

I flashed him a fake smile and rubbed my toes.

"You look like you in pain," he said to me.

"Some stupid bitch stepped on my fucking foot, and it hurt like hell."

"And she probably still dancing, while you sitting over here crying like a baby," he said with his country accent before laughing.

I rolled my eyes, then smiled. "What's your name again? I'm not even gon' play like I remember."

"X," he said, showing us his tattoo with his bama-ass.

"Oh, that's right." Xavier Moreland. Mr. Million Dollar Man himself. He threw away a blank check with the Redskins when he cursed the owner out in the locker room while a reporter was still around, and then he turned around and pulled that dumb stunt with the waitress. I bet we could trick his stupid ass out of some money if we wanted to.

We sat on the couch with X, watching people plot, then pounce on different celebrities, just as we had. Everybody tried to play it cool, but it ain't take much to notice vultures in the room, swooping over from one failed opportunity to the next. Meeka gave me a look that let me know what she was trying to do. I gave her a not-so-sure look back. Then she said, "Don't you wanna leave this joint? It's the same old, same old. You look bored anyway."

I knew she wanted to pull a stunt with this dude, but I wasn't really up to doing all that. The last party I did was the one uptown when Ryan walked in, but Meeka still ain't know what happened after that, so she had no idea that I wasn't even feeling doing this shit. But when X said, "Yeah, let's go," I ain't have no plans to let Meeka go by herself. When X stood up, me and Meeka followed him. While we waited for the elevator, I sent Peaches and Trina Boo a text, telling them what was up.

Peaches sent: SEND ME THE ADDRESS AND BE CAREFUL.

Trina Boo sent: BE CAREFUL AND CALL ME LATER.

X called his car service. As we waited for it to pick us up, he asked us where we was from.

Meeka said, "The District, baby!"

Then he smiled. "I should've known."

"Yeah, you should've known. We got the baddest bitches, right?"

"Yeah, y'all bad. I like your little thick ass," he said, slapping Meeka's butt.

It didn't take us long to get to his hotel of choice on Fifth Avenue after we climbed in the town car. We ordered drinks at the bar, then headed upstairs. As soon as we got in the room, I sat on the couch. I ain't want no part of their little excursion. Meeka pushed X to the bed. For her to be so much shorter than him, you'd think she was the one who was taller and stronger by the way he fell on the bed. I had never seen Meeka so excited before. It had to be the dollar signs in her head. Don't get me wrong, X was sexy as hell, but I knew she was more turned on by the possibility of what she could get out of him. She took his clothes off, and I couldn't believe how sick his body was. Arms and legs like Bamm-Bamm. His stomach was cut like a statue.

I sent Peaches a text with the address I found on a notepad beside the couch, and then I watched Meeka straddle him. My finger accidentally hit the video recorder button. Before I knew it, I was sitting on the couch making a bunch of mini-movies of Meeka's performance. Hell, if nothing else, I was gonna have something to show Peaches and Trina Boo when we got back. I smiled to myself.

"Hey, KiKi, come here," X said breathless. I walked over to the bed. "You don't want none of this?"

"Not this time," I said.

"Not this time?" he repeated, smiling.

He did have a massive penis. I recorded Meeka sucking it.

"What you doing with your phone?" he asked.

"Nothing, I just sent a text to my girl so she could know where we was at and that we was safe. I'm putting it up now," I said, making sure I got X's face clear as day before I put the phone down.

"Come here," he said again, but I smiled and walked back to the couch. I ain't want none.

When Meeka was done, she climbed on top and gave X a joyride, the kind where she put her ankles under his shoulders and leaned back to hold his ankles. I smiled at her using one of my favorite moves. I went to the bathroom. By the time I came out, they was done. *Damn. He couldn't hang?*

Meeka winked and then went to the bathroom.

"Your girl good," X said, knotting the condom and then wiping his dick with the sheet.

I shook my head as he went to the bathroom behind Meeka. I saw his jeans on the floor by the bed. As soon as the door closed, I checked his pockets. His dumb ass left his wallet. I took a picture of his ID with my phone just in case Peaches and Trina Boo ain't believe it was him. Even though I could've easily taken his Black Card, I took all the cash out and stuffed it inside my bra. I stood up when I heard them laughing in the bathroom, then Meeka moaning. They was making me horny, but I wasn't gonna break. I rubbed my nose and went to the wet bar. I opened a small bottle of tequila, swallowed it, and sat back on the couch. I knew Meeka was doing him, but now I was ready to go. That shit was sounding too good in there.

I closed my eyes and took another sip. My phone rang. The screen said, "Unknown." I ignored it. When it happened again five minutes later, I started not to answer it cuz I ain't do unknowns, but since it was after four in the morning, I knew it wasn't a bill collector.

"Hello?"

"KiKi."

I was shocked to hear Audri's voice. "Hey, babe. Where's your phone?"

"Hey . . . I'm in the hospital," she whispered.

"What?" I said, standing up.

"Some niggas robbed me. Beat me like a dude and shit, too."

"Oh my God, Audri," I said, sitting back down. I felt so guilty for picking a fight with her earlier. I felt guilty for cheating on her with Taryn. I felt guilty for not even telling her I made a trip to New York with my girls. I just felt like shit. "You okay?"

"I had to get twelve stitches on my forehead cuz they pistol-whipped me, broke my arm, and bruised my ribs, but other than that, I'm all right."

"Where are you?" I asked, shaking.

"At AtlantiCare."

"Oh my God. I'm coming as soon as I can, okay?"

I said, rubbing my forehead, wondering what happened and just how bad she was. Audri gave me her room number and told me the address, and as soon as she hung up, I looked up the directions on my phone, and then I called Peaches. She tried to calm me down.

"We can leave first thing in the morning, KiKi. Ain't nothing gon' change between now and a few hours."

That wasn't what the fuck I was trying to hear from her. I hung up and knocked on the bathroom door.

"Hunh?" Meeka said, sounding winded.

"My bad, Meeka, but Audri just called me from the hospital. We gotta go."

"Oh, shit. What happened? Wait, I'm coming out."

Ten minutes later, she came out and put her dress back on, leaving X in the shower. I told her everything Audri said as we walked to the hotel elevator and that Peaches said we could leave later in the morning.

"Well, what you wanna do?" Meeka asked. "She's our ride."

Meeka was right. I guess we just had to wait. I felt so helpless and wanted to get to Audri as soon as I could. We took a cab to meet the girls back at the party. Peaches and Trina Boo came down soon afterward. Taryn had left earlier with some of her girlfriends. I was pissed at Peaches for not wanting to drive through the night so I could see my girl.

"Well, at least I got Xavier's number," Meeka said. "I know that shit by heart: 646-555-3303."

"Y'all bitches crazy!" Trina Boo said.

Even I had to smile at that. "Wait until you find out just how crazy we are."

I showed them the videos I made on the phone. They cracked up laughing at Meeka giving him the best that she had.

"Damn, look at Meeka go. Go, shawty, it's your birthday, it's your birthday. You should post that shit up on the Internet," Peaches said. "Or you could blackmail his ass for some more dough."

"No, don't do that. You gon' mess up my good thing," Meeka said.

"Oh yeah . . . I took some money from his wallet, so I don't know about all that . . . ," I said.

"Damn, bitch! Where's my cut?" Meeka said, laughing and holding her palm out. "All that work I did."

I gave her half and said, "Job well done!"

"Damn, I miss y'all," Trina Boo sang and gave out hugs.

16

We ain't get to the hospital 'til eleven cuz of a big-ass accident on the turnpike that had traffic backed up all the way to the Verrazano Bridge. It ain't help that we ain't leave Trina Boo's apartment until nine o'clock. Bitches talking 'bout they had to eat and shit. *Was my baby eating?* When I walked into Audri's room, she was sleeping peacefully.

"She probably high as hell right now," Peaches said. "You know they got her on some pain medicine."

Meeka said she wanted something to drink so the two of them went to go find a vending machine. I kissed Audri on her cheek and then sat with her for a while. When she woke up and saw me, she smiled.

"How long you been here?" she whispered.

"For a little while. How you feeling?" I said, kissing her.

"Sore as shit. Them niggas beat the shit outta me."

I wished I could take her pain away. Audri told me how she was in the parking garage at one of the casinos when some dudes attacked her, stole her wallet, phone, and her car. She told me Myra, Cha-Cha, and Whitney was on their way back to D.C. in a rental now that their pockets was full from the party where they performed in the wee hours that morning.

"The doctors said I can leave today, though."

"Good," I said.

"Hey, you're up!" Peaches said, walking inside the room.

"Hey, Audri," Meeka said, following her.

Audri smiled. "I ain't know they came up here with you. Wassup?"

"You all right?"

"Just a little fucked up, that's all," she said, smiling.

"Yeah, we came to check on you," Peaches said.

Everybody knew that I ain't plan to tell Audri that we was in New York, so it all worked out. After they discharged her, we all piled in Peaches's truck. Audri was confused about the luggage in the back when we put her suitcase back there, but she ain't say nothing about it since it was Peaches's truck. Audri was quiet the whole ride. I knew she was in a lot of pain, but she just seemed like she was in her own space. I sat in the back with her and pushed the front passenger seat up so she could have plenty of space to stretch her legs. It ain't seem like there was nothing I could say to make her feel better. After a while, she fell asleep.

When we stopped at a rest stop in Maryland to use the bathroom, I asked Peaches if she had some coke with her. She looked at me sideways, then took her necklace off and handed it to me. I went in a stall and took a couple hits. It was just what I needed. Back at the truck, Audri had turned to the side so that most of her body was stretched across the backseat. I ain't wanna wake her up, so I let her stretch her legs across my lap. I felt guilty about the thoughts I had earlier about Peaches. I mean, maybe she ain't realize just how bad my situation was. She was always there for me when I was in a bind, like now.

When Peaches dropped us off at Audri's, I helped Audri up the stairs and to the elevator, taking tiny steps cuz it seemed every move she made brought her more pain. We walked to our bedroom, where she collapsed on the bed and went back to sleep.

Over the next few days, the pain medicine had Audri like a zombie. When I came home from work or school, she was laid up, looking depressed. One time I saw her using her free hand to knock balls around on the pool table. I guess I hadn't even thought about how blown she must've been not being able to play pool. Then out of the blue, Audri confessed the true story about what happened that night in Atlantic City. She said that she had got caught cheating.

"They threw me out, and then them motherfuckers beat me up and stole my car."

No wonder she was so fucked up about it.

"Now, I'm losing money sitting up in here with a arm that don't work."

"You gotta stop feeling sorry for yourself," I said. Her depression was blowing me.

"You don't understand . . . the kind of work I do can't be done from home. Ain't got no ride. My dancers talking about finding another manager and shit . . . You can't really help me."

She rolled the ball across the table, knocking the yellow one down a hole. Ain't this a bitch? After all I been doing around here, trying to nurse her back to health. Spending all my pennies to make sure we had food in here, to put something on the bills even if I couldn't pay the whole damn thing, and she had the nerve to say I wasn't really helping.

"You know what? Fuck you!"

I grabbed my leather jacket and stormed out. *Just cuz your gambling ass fucked up, now it's my fault?* In the car outside, I called Meeka to see what she was doing, but she said she was helping her mother rearrange some of the rooms in their house. I called Yodi to see if Mommy was around. She said Mommy was gone somewhere with her new boyfriend, Isaac. Damn. I ain't feel like going to Peaches's shop. Then I thought of my sister Toya. Even though I ain't hardly fuck with her, she lived less than ten minutes away in a towering building over on Columbia Road. I bit my lip and looked upstairs to Audri's window. I ain't feel like going back in there with an apology right now. I dialed Toya's number. She answered on the second ring.

"Hey, sis. You busy?"

"Hey, Shakira. Not really. What's up?"

"I just wanted to come by and say hi. I'm not too far."

I could hear the shock in her voice, but Toya just said, "Okay."

I headed over and found a spot to park. Once inside, she seemed happy to see me, which was strange. She even gave me a hug.

"When's the last time we seen each other?" I asked, sitting on her couch. She had a simple apartment, no lavish decorations or anything, but you could tell she definitely wasn't struggling and that shit wasn't cheap. That's always been Toya.

"Had to be the spring, I think."

"That's fucked up. You know I live right around the corner?"

"I didn't know that. You want something to drink?"

"Yeah, what you got?" I knew she had a nice selection with her alcoholic ass. I followed her over to the kitchen where she had a mounted wine rack. All types of wines. Since I was having a hard time deciding, Toya opened the refrigerator and took out a bottle of white wine.

"Here, try this."

"Sau-vig-non blanc," I sounded out.

"Girl, it's so good," she said, untwisting the cork.

"We'll see. Sound like some bourgie shit to me."

She laughed and poured two glasses. She seemed in a good mood, unlike her usual self. I took a sip of the semisweet wine and sat back down on her couch.

"It taste all right."

"I love it," she said, smiling like a cheerleader.

"You love wine, period."

She laughed again.

"Why you in such a good mood? I hope this wine make me feel like you."

She smiled and shook her head. "Girl, I just got a promotion today!" she said, doing a little dance.

Damn. "Congratulations." I couldn't help but feel a little jealous. Good shit always landed in Toya's lap. Even though she seemed like she had an attitude most of the time, I knew it was cuz Toya was frustrated about not getting something she wanted, especially when she thought she had worked hard to have it. I mean, on some level, I guess I could understand it, but on the other hand she just seemed like she was always trying to be something she wasn't meant to be. On top of that there had been a wedge between us since that incident happened with her ex-boyfriend Demari back when we was young.

"Thank you," she said before taking a sip. "But what's up with you?"

"Nothing much."

"I'm glad you called me. Sometimes, I be thinking that it's not right that me and you never really hang out."

She was right. Me and Toya acted more like distant cousins than sisters who had the same parents. But let's be honest, that's probably all we've ever had in common. If I told her about the kind of shit I had to deal with in my life, she'd treat me like a stranger with the quickness.

"It ain't too late," I said before swallowing the rest of my wine.

"You're right. Oh my God," she said, slapping my leg. "Alvin Ailey is in town. We should go see them!"

"Who in the hell is Alvin?"

"No, it's a dance company. You still like dance, right?"

I nodded.

"Oh my God. We gotta go see them." She jumped up and grabbed her laptop and sat back down. In a few seconds, she had a clip of the dance group on the screen. I was so mesmerized by the way they moved. There was so much passion. Every movement seemed like it represented a word. Almost like sign language, I guess.

"I'm booking us some tickets now. And you can't say no!" Before I could stop her, Toya had whipped out her credit card.

I felt weird. I mean, I ain't never been to nothing like that before. I wouldn't even know how to act. The Kennedy Center ain't seem like a place meant for me to be.

"Okay, we can go Friday. Do you have to work?"

"I mean, I can switch days with somebody." I figured I can at least do that if Toya was willing to buy the tickets.

"Good. Done," she said, closing her laptop.

I gave her a closed-mouth smile. How bizarre was this? Me and Toya going to the Kennedy Center. Toya gave me a hug to make the situation even more weird.

"Here, drink some more," she said, filling my empty glass to the brim.

And I did until I was finally ready to go home and face the music with Audri.

"MADNESS TO MAGNET KEEPS ATTRACTING ME"

—kid cudi, "day 'n' nite"

17

I was so excited the day of the show. I felt like I was going to the prom. After I got my mani-pedi, Peaches hooked my hair up. She even let me borrow her fly-ass black Zac Posen dress that I was gonna rock with my Prada slingbacks. She seemed just as excited for me, slipping it in a wardrobe bag so I could carry it home. That's the thing about Peaches, she always had the real nice shit. I mean, I had a couple nice things, but I found most of my stuff at Filene's Basement. Or if it wasn't a gift from whoever I was dating, I'd take a few dollars and splurge at Nordstrom or Lord & Taylor every now and then. I loved that Peaches was never stingy with her clothes.

"I'm glad you and Toya finally doing something together. You know? I don't know nobody who ever been inside the Kennedy Center before, and that's a damn shame," she had said before giving me a black-and-silver necklace like it was a corsage. Peaches winked, and I knew it had exactly what I wanted. She also gave me a tiny coke bag of my own. Guess I had said one too many times how nervous I was.

After I left her house, I headed over to North Capitol Street so Rich could hook up my taper. There was three dudes ahead of me, but every time I jumped up to get in another barber's chair, Rich warned me how fucked up they was gonna cut my hair. I laughed nervously and decided to wait for him.

"How you been?" he asked when I finally sat in his chair.

"I been all right. What about you?"

"I been good. You and your girlfriend have fun the other night?"

I smiled and said, "Yeah."

"You looked like it."

"Did you and your boys have fun?"

"It was all right. Too crowded for me. I don't like going out to shit like that, though."

"For real? Why not?"

"It ain't my style. Plus, whenever I got a girl, ain't no real reason for me to be at no damn club."

"Unh. But you don't like the music?"

"Hmmm . . . yeah, but it ain't like you really dancing in a place like that. Too packed for dancing. Just a bunch of drunk niggas trying to catch chicks slipping."

I laughed. "I guess you right."

"I'd rather do something different."

"Different like what?"

"I don't know. I like doing *real* shit."

"Real shit, like what?"

"I think I'll keep that to myself for now," Rich said with a smile in his voice. "Who knows, maybe you'll find out one day, maybe not."

"Hmmm...," I said. Let me find out Meeka was right, that Rich *was* feeling me. He was sexy as shit, and I liked that he stayed low-key in the store. I could tell niggas respected him. They always asked his opinion, made sure he was good when they went to get something to eat, or checked to see if he was watching something on the TV before they messed with the channel. After Rich brushed my shoulders off and I paid him, he asked me if I had a boyfriend. I shook my head but wondered why it was so easy to dismiss Audri. Maybe cuz of how stank she had been acting ever since her little incident in Atlantic City. Instead of asking for my number, he just nodded. I was surprised he ain't ask me for it.

Later, when I was getting ready at home, Audri kept shaking her head from across the room.

"What?" I said finally. I mean, it seemed like she wanted my damn attention so bad.

"Just funny how you seem to have money for going out and shit when they 'bout to cut the damn cable off."

Tssk. Ain't this some shit. "I told you my big sister bought these damn tickets."

"Right. Your big sister," Audri said, trying to scratch inside of her cast with an unraveled wire hanger. "I thought y'all ain't get along."

"We don't," I said, irritated that she was even suspecting anything different.

"Like I said, that shit is funny."

I sucked the back of my teeth again. She was blowing the fuck out of me. I wasn't letting her ruin this night. First of all, my makeup looked too damn good to be frowning and rolling my damn eyes. Secondly, just cuz she feeling like shit don't mean I have to. She been moping around too much. In the house all the damn time, questioning my comings and goings, hating on my outfits, just overdoing it all the time.

"You know who I talked to today?" she asked.

"No, who?" I said, fixing my strapless bra.

"Cha-Cha," Audri said, talking about her dancer with the short, fire-red boy cut.

"Oh, yeah?"

"Yeah. We spoke for a minute. She told me some wild shit that shocked the fuck out of me."

"Oh, yeah. What's that?" I asked, spraying on some perfume.

"That not only did my *girlfriend* used to do parties before I met her, but that she *used* to work the strip, too."

Fuck. I dropped the bottle on the dresser. Glass and perfume flew everywhere.

"It's true, huh?"

I was quiet and kept my back to her.

"Well, goddamn. I'll take that as a yes. Funny how you never told me that shit... Make me wonder, though. Like who are you really?" she asked with anger in her voice. "Why you with me? Huh?"

I stayed quiet. Wasn't nothing I could say that was gonna make her back down.

"Shiiiit... and tell me, what was really up with you and your brother?"

"What?" I was up on the bed and in her face before I knew it. My fingernails clawed at her cheeks, but Audri was much stronger than me. She knocked me to the ground with one arm, like I was a feather.

"KiKi, calm your ass down. I should be the one who's pissed the fuck off! I gotta find out from somebody who used to work for me that you did that shit! How the fuck you think I feel? How that shit make *me* look?"

I sat on the floor, livid. My leg shook nervously. I felt sweat dotting my forehead. Leave it to a money-hungry bitch to throw salt in my shit. Jealous heifer.

"I mean, on the real... I guess I can understand why you ain't say nothing," Audri said, shaking her head like she didn't understand. "I can't believe you keeping secrets from me. Why?"

I blew out a breath. Why we have to have this conversation tonight? Finally, me and my big sister was gonna bond, and Audri wanted to ruin it. Light scratches left her cheeks red. Audri took a deep breath, then said, "I'ma apologize for what I just said about that situation with your brother. I fucked up. I should've never even went there."

Audri reached for my hand. I hesitated, but soon she interlocked her fingers with mine and pulled me up off the floor.

"Shakira, my bad, all right. You forgive me?"

I rolled my eyes and let her kiss my lips. She pulled me in her arms, and soon I was kissing her back. I hated being mad at her, but this was too much. Audri kissed down my neck, ran her tongue behind my ears, across my shoulders, and even traced my underarms. It felt so good, my nipples tingled and my coochie throbbed.

"You still my boo, though," Audri whispered. She laid back on the bed and pulled me on top of her. Before I knew it, my bra and panties was on the floor, and I was riding the hell out of her face. Arching my back the same way I did when I rode dick. She loved how I moved my hips. Shit, I tried to write cursive letters on her mouth with my pussy lips. Back and forth I rocked so she could get all this sweetness. For some reason, I always squirted whenever Audri ate me. The shit she did with her tongue—like she knew me better than I knew myself—was unreal. I collapsed on the bed, exhausted. Audri smiled and pulled me close to her.

"You good?"

"Always," I said, smiling.

"Good." Audri was quiet for a while, playing with

my sweated-out hair. Then she said, "You know I'm sorry about what I said earlier, right?"

"Mmm-hmm."

"You know that Ryan shit fucks with me still," she said, rubbing her forehead. I looked into her gray eyes and wished she ain't look as conflicted as I felt about what happened to me. If I spent time thinking about all the bad things that happened to me, I knew I'd self-destruct. It was easy to just move on to the next thing that would take my mind off of Ryan, just like how Nut helped me to forget about Dizzle and how Kareem helped me forget about Nut. It was how I coped. Doing a party for a nigga who ain't mean shit to me was just that . . . a party for some dollars. Sleeping with dudes for money all these years numbed me from being able to feel what Audri must've felt when she learned I had been keeping secrets from her. I couldn't help it that my past seemed to follow me around like a shadow.

"When Cha-Cha told me that shit, it just made me feel like you wasn't being honest with me. Your past is your past, but you gotta always be honest with me. You understand? You got my heart, man."

I nodded. I wanted to be honest with her, but guilt washed over me. How could she forgive me for lying to her? Why did she still treat me this way? The feeling was overwhelming.

"I gotta use the bathroom," I said, kissing her lips and pulling away.

I needed to do a line. Bad. I emptied some of the coke Peaches gave me out on a hand mirror, and then I used a book of matches to slice up the powder and make three neat rows. I snorted a line.

"Hey, want me to...," Audri said, barging in the bathroom. "What the fuck!"

I tried to hide the mirror, but it was too late. Audri tried to snatch it from me, and the mirror fell on the floor.

"Oh, shit! Look what you did!" I dropped to my knees and used my acrylics to sniff it up. "Look what you did!"

I could feel Audri's eyes drilling into my skull, but she was crazy if she thought I was gonna waste it.

"KiKi...you gotta go. You gotta pack your shit and get the fuck up outta here. Tonight."

"No!" I blocked her out as I scraped the powder up.

"I want your scheming ass to get the fuck out my house!" Audri said, jerking me up off the floor. She tossed me out of the bathroom, then grabbed a handful of my clothes out of her closet and threw them on her bed.

"No, Audri. I don't wanna leave!" I begged. When she went to grab more clothes from the dresser, I hurled the ones she threw on the bed back toward the closet.

"KiKi! I don't give a fuck where you go, but you gotta get the fuck outta here. I don't know what new shit I'ma find out about your ass!"

"But, Audri...," I cried as I dropped to the floor. I couldn't believe she was putting me out. For snorting coke? Come on now. It wasn't like I was stealing from her or lying to her. She was putting me out for absolutely nothing. I could stop if I wanted to, but she ain't even give me a chance to say I'd quit it. "Audri, you want me to stop? I'm not gon' do it no more. I promise. Audri, you hear me?"

But she ain't say nothing. She just kept throwing my shit on the bed. Shoes, shirts, belts, bags.

"Audri!" I shouted. "Stop! Look, Audri...I only do it cuz I can't handle it by myself. You don't know about me. You don't know all I been through!"

Audri shook her head and sat down on the edge of the bed.

"Baby, I ain't mean to lie, but I knew you would leave me if you knew," I cried. "And I don't want to be alone."

Audri rubbed her hands over her face. I knew she was trying to hear me out, but from the twisted look she gave me, I must've been asking a lot. "Coke, though?"

I wiped tears from my cheeks and nodded. "Baby, I need it...cuz it makes me forget about what Ryan did to me...and about all the other shit I wish I could forget."

Audri shook her head again, either not believing me or not understanding what I was going through.

"When I take a hit, you just don't know...I feel so good. Wanted. Loved," I whispered.

"See, KiKi, that's the problem...I should make you feel that way."

Her words took my breath away. Ten minutes later, Audri stuffed all my shit in my car.

"I wish you the best."

"But I thought you loved me!" I cried.

"I did...but I can't be with a cokehead."

Her words stung so bad, I shook. I flung her keys out the car window and cried.

When I pulled up at Toya's, I was a mess. My eyes was swollen, my face bloated from crying so much, and my car filled with balled-up clothes, shoes, handbags, and makeup. I wiped my face and sat outside wondering what I was gonna tell Toya. So much had happened tonight. I just wanted to forget it and enjoy whatever was left of it. I couldn't have Toya's judgmental ass talking shit about me, too. Since I was supposed to meet her at her apartment so I could ride with her to the Kennedy Center, I called her from downstairs to see if she had a steamer. She said she did, so I grabbed my shoes and the Zac Posen Peaches let me borrow and ran upstairs.

As soon as Toya opened the door in her gorgeous body-hugging red dress, she said, "Did you forget we was going? Cuz you look horrendous."

If I hadn't just went through what I went through, I would've told Toya she looked beautiful, that her makeup was on point, and that her hair was stunning. But at that moment I wasn't in the mood. "Look, I just broke up with my girlfriend, and I wanna forget about it, okay? Can you help me do that?"

Toya shook her head like she was the one who got put the hell out. "All right. Hurry up! We gon' be late."

She steamed my dress for me while I jumped in the shower. I took a hit before I did something to my face and hair. Forty minutes later I felt like I was in Hollywood, walking on the red carpet at the Kennedy Center.

A slew of nice town cars were dropping people off in the front. Everyone was dressed real nice. As soon as we was inside, I went to the bathroom. I had to take another hit cuz it seemed like everybody knew I ain't belong.

When we left the bathroom, I felt like I could do anything. "Toya, watch this." I stretched my arms high over my head like the dancer on the banner hanging from the wall above us. I walked on my tippy toes and raised my leg out. Fuck, I could do that shit, too. When I jumped up, Toya looked at me like I had just pissed on her leg.

"Stop embarrassing me, Shakira!"

"What? I can do it, too," I said, jumping again but landing awkwardly. My heel bent the other direction and broke. I grabbed her so I wouldn't fall. "Oops."

"Get off of me!" Toya said, yanking away. "You're such an embarrassment."

I laughed until I realized I was standing by myself. Toya left me in the lobby and went inside. I had to find my seat by myself. It was already bad enough I had to carry my broken shoe in one hand. The usher asked me for my ticket stub, but Toya had it. The usher told me to wait until more people took their seats, and then she'd let me peek inside to see if I could find Toya. But them people was taking forever. I couldn't wait that long. I pushed pass the usher and screamed, "LaToya Scott, where the fuck are you?" as loud I could. Everybody turned around to look at me, and none of those faces was Toya. "Toya! Where you at?" Before I knew it, security snatched my arm and led me out of the theater and then all the way out of the building.

"Shit," I shouted in front of the glass doors.

I walked with one shoe, feeling the cool stone beneath my bare foot. Then I flagged down a cab with the broken shoe in my hand. I couldn't help but laugh at my situation. I fell asleep in the back of the cab. The driver woke me up when he got to Toya's house. I paid him and climbed in my car. I looked around at all my stuff and knew the only choice I had tonight was to sleep in my BMW. I drove to Rock Creek Park and pulled into an empty parking spot, then closed my eyes, hoping the police would be merciful and leave me the hell alone.

18

Tap. Tap. Tap. I opened my eyes, damn near forgetting that I fell asleep in my car, at a park no less. A Park Police officer was standing at my window, pointing his flashlight at me. I rolled the window down. He said, "Sorry, but the park is closed." I nodded, then looked at my clock: 6:18 a.m. At least the sun was gonna be up soon. I backed out of my parking space and drove down Beach Drive. When I came past the bridge near the National Zoo, I thought about Daddy. It was here that the evil tree branch snapped and crushed him to death. Wonder what he'd say about my life? How different would it be if that shit would've never happened? Mommy would've never had a dude with a crack habit. None of us would've been split up. I wouldn't have met Dizzle or Nut, and Ryan probably would've never did that disgusting shit he did to me.

I drove to McDonald's, got a breakfast sandwich and some orange juice, and then I ate in my car, listening to the radio, thinking about what I was gonna do next. I couldn't believe Audri threw me out just that quick after telling me I had her heart. That shit was confusing. I only had enough for some gas, not enough for a motel room. Maybe Meeka's mother wouldn't mind letting me crash on her couch for a while. But then how was I gonna explain why I wasn't staying on Mommy's couch? Meeka ain't know about that Ryan shit, and I ain't have no plans to tell nobody else about it. Peaches popped in my head, but she had never offered a place for me to stay before, I ain't wanna ask her now. I took a deep breath and started my car. I was gonna have to face Ryan. Wasn't no other way. Wasn't nowhere else I could go. And like the devil had read my thoughts, the first person I see when I got on W Street was Ryan. He grinned when he saw me get out the car. I rolled my eyes and made a beeline for the building.

"Aye, KiKi, what's up, sis?" he yelled across the street.

I ain't say nothing, just went straight through the front door and hopped on the elevator. As soon as I unlocked the apartment door and walked in, Yodi said, "Hey, girl, you all right?"

"Yeah, why?"

"Toya called last night, saying you was acting real strange."

"What?"

"No, she actually said you looked like you was tweeking and shit."

"Man, fuck Toya, bourgie ass!"

"I'm just saying..."

"Where Mommy at?"

"Her and Isaac went to IHOP."

I shook my head. I guess Mommy was really digging this new dude. She been spending so much time with him lately. Ryan walked in the door and went to the fridge. "What's up, KiKi? What you been up to?"

I rolled my eyes. I couldn't believe he was gon' act like we was cool. Chrissie started crying down the hall, and Yodi disappeared. Ryan sat across from me with a tall glass of milk.

"You been hiding from me and shit," he said before taking a long swallow. I was so heated. I flipped my phone around in my hand. "You don't never come through no more. You don't return my calls."

I shook my head and stared at the TV. *What the fuck he think?*

"I see your ride about to burst at the seams. You got all your shit in there? What? You looking for somewhere to stay?"

I cut my eyes at him, then looked back at the TV.

"You can come share my room," he said, laughing.

"You foul as shit!" I said through clenched teeth. "Should've had your bitch ass locked the fuck up for what you did to me!"

He leaned forward with his half-empty glass and whispered, "But you ain't do it, did you? You liked it, didn't you?"

I couldn't believe him. He stood in front of me. "Here, drink the rest of this."

"No," I said, rolling my eyes, disgusted that his deranged ass thought I would ever drink behind him.

He shoved the glass in my face. I twisted away. "Stop, Ryan!"

"Drink it!" he yelled and gripped the back of my neck tight. Since I still ain't look his way, Ryan pressed the glass against my mouth. I pushed him backward, making him spill the milk all over the dress Peaches let me borrow.

"You stupid muthafucka!" I yelled, jumping up. "Stay the fuck away from me!"

"That shit look good on you," he said with a wicked smirk.

I knew I could never stay there, no matter how desperate I was. I grabbed my bag and left the apartment. Fuck that. Peaches owed me.

She opened the door just as I was about to ring the doorbell. Peaches's security system must've alerted her that I was on her property.

"Hey, girl! Dayuum. What the fuck you do to my dress?"

That's all she worried about? "Peaches . . . I need a place to stay for a little while. Can I stay here with you until I can get shit straight?"

She looked at me like a deer staring at some head-lights.

"What? Cat got your tongue, bitch?"

"What happened with Audri?"

"She kicked me out."

"Why?"

"Don't worry about why! Can I stay here or not?"

Peaches shook her head and let out a deep breath.

"See, that's the shit I'm talking about. You don't want nobody staying up in this castle but you. What? Did you forget where you came from? The fire I walked through with you so you could have this shit?"

"What the hell are you talking about? You act like I ain't never fucking help you! I drove your ass to Atlantic City so you can get your girlfriend," she said, counting her fingers. "I cooked for you and cleaned your nasty-ass house after you barricaded yourself in there for a week. You sound dumb, KiKi. Listen to yourself!"

"You only wanna help me the way you wanna help me, not the way I need to be helped! Your selfish ass done forgot that I helped you get this muthafucking house selling *my* ass for your sick-ass husband!"

"What!" Peaches said, jamming her hand on her hip. "*I* paid for this shit. My salon keeps the lights on. I gave your no-skills-having ass a job when you couldn't find one. I tried to talk sense into you when you was still out there selling your ass when you ain't have to. Don't tell me I ain't never help your ass out!"

"Whatever, Peaches."

"Get the fuck off my stoop with your ungrateful bird ass!"

"Arrgh!" I screamed before jumping on Peaches and yanking the wig off her head. We wrestled in the doorway until I ended up in her foyer, knocking furniture and vases over. She ripped the dress she let me borrow into shreds.

"Mommy, Mommy!" I heard Amir shrieking behind her.

All of sudden Peaches got real strong on me. She rolled me over and pinned me on the floor, her eyes bigger than I'd ever seen them before.

"You bring this shit to my muthafucking house, disrespecting me...in front of my son?" A razor blade appeared in her hand from nowhere. "I oughta cut your ass a new fucking smile."

I flinched and fought to pull away as she pressed the blade against my cheek.

"No, Peaches, don't do it...I'm sorry, I'm sorry," I begged, tears streaming down my face as I squirmed.

She stared at me for a while, knowing she had won, and then she said, "Get the fuck off my property! All this time and your ass still ain't learned shit. You can't bite the hand that feeds you. Don't even think about showing up at the shop, bitch!"

I pulled myself off the floor, limped to the doorway, and walked out the door.

"You can have that nasty-ass dress, too!" she yelled to my back.

I cried until I got inside my car. I cried while I drove back to D.C. I cried at the light on New York Avenue. Seem like everybody hated me: Toya, Audri, Ryan, and now Peaches. I ain't have nobody in my corner. I wiped my eyes with the back of my hands, sure the face crossing the street was one that I knew. It was Kareem, and he locked eyes with me, and then just as quickly he shook his head and kept walking. I could see the pity oozing from his skin. I felt so embarrassed. My tearstained face, ripped dress, overcrowded car. Could I look any worse? I looked away.

The crave for a hit built up. I pulled over to an empty parking lot, no longer able to fight the urge. Who knew how I was gonna get more? I snorted the last of it and closed my eyes. About fifteen minutes later, I pulled up to Meeka's mother's house on Upshur Street down to my last few drops of gas. As soon as Meeka saw me, she let me in without even asking no questions.

I had no idea just how trifling Quentin's father had become. Since the judge ain't give him full custody like he thought he deserved, this nigga had straight stopped giving Meeka any money. Actually told Meeka's mother, Ms. Kathy, once when he dropped Quentin off while we was at school that she needed to make a list of what Quentin ate so he could buy it for him. Meeka damn near lost it with him after that and wrote him a note that said: *Quentin's Grocery List—ones, fives, tens, twenties, fifties, etc. Stupid Ass Muthafucka! Your son needs money! If you knew him well enough, you'd know what kind of food he eats, too, by the way.*

"What the fuck he think this is? What about the lights that his son needs, the heat, the muthafucking clothes that keep shrinking every other month?" Meeka complained.

As messed up as it was, it was a chance for me to convince Meeka to start doing parties again. I mean, we both needed the money. I knew Meeka ain't wanna jeopardize her court case, but now that she still had full custody, it was easy for me to get her to see the benefit. She called up her girlfriend Quita to see if she knew about any parties we could do. She said no but that Macombo Lounge on Georgia Avenue was looking for some new girls.

"What you thinking?" Meeka asked me. "You wanna do it?"

What the fuck, man? I wasn't tryna be on nobody's payroll and work a schedule doing this shit. I just wanted the cash.

"Come on, KiKi. We ain't gon' have to worry about needing no security and shit."

I twisted my lips to the side and walked back and forth, fumbling with my hands. She was right. It *was* much safer, I guess. All I kept thinking about is the blow I needed to cop. "All right. I'll do it."

Meeka smiled and got the information we needed. She told us we had to do an audition at noon the next day. I needed to get it together because I looked and felt like shit. I needed to feel sexy, so I borrowed forty dollars from Meeka and went to see Rich. I had this urge to be somebody else. If just for a little while. He was all smiles when I walked in the door. He was coming from the back of the shop.

"What's up, beautiful?" he asked.

I gave him a half smile. "Nothing much. How you doing?"

"Good, now that I see you."

I smiled again. I touched my hair, knowing it looked crazy and said, "I want you to cut it all off."

He looked puzzled. "Why you wanna do that for?"

"Rich, just cut it off."

He shook his head, then said, "Okay."

I sat in his spinning chair, let him put the cape on, then closed my eyes when I heard the buzzing.

"You sure you wanna do this?" he asked.

"All off."

"You got it. Your sexy ass will still look dope. My sister came in here just the other day asking me to do the same shit. You women be killing me."

I smiled and waited for him to cut away. Gobs of honey-blonde hair fell around the black cape. The vibrating metal felt cool against my scalp. Rich was done in no time.

"Here's the mirror, sweetheart."

I looked and for the first time, felt like crying at what I saw. The tip of my nose looked unusually red. Dark rings was around my eyes. I shook my head to stop the tears I felt growing. *What the fuck was I thinking?*

"What's wrong with you? Don't get all sad on me now. You came in here, going all hard and shit. Fuck that. You better work this fly-ass haircut. Your ass look *good*!" Rich said, trying his best to cheer me up.

"Thanks," I said, wiping a tear away and handing him twenty dollars.

"Nah, this shit on the house."

I nodded and excused myself out the shop. I wished I had some coke. I felt so weak right now. As soon as I got in the car, I took out my compact and dabbed the dark splotches under my eyes. When that ain't work, I drove to the nail shop and got some new lashes. That helped me feel a lot better. After I got back to Meeka's, she suggested I dye my hair. It wasn't a bad idea, but I decided to wear a wig. A blonde one still short as hell, but slightly styled with soft bangs. It made me feel sexy.

"Your ass definitely look fuckable!" Meeka chanted.

I winked cuz that was actually the point.

The next day the audition went smooth. It wasn't like I was an amateur. The manager hired both of us and told us we could start the same day. Good cuz I was broke as fuck, and strip clubs always paid in cash. When we came back to Macombo later, the first person I see as I walk in the dressing room was Cha-Cha's redhead ass, looking me over. She laughed at me and said something to another dancer. *Still hating*. I gave her the finger and waited for her to say some shit.

"Who that?" Meeka asked.

"That trick bitch I told you about who told Audri everything."

"Unh," Meeka said, rolling her eyes at the skank. "You know she can't wait to text Audri, right?"

"At this point, I could give a fuck!" I shouted, even though I really did.

"I know that's right," Meeka said.

Audri was the first person who loved me for me and not for something I could do for them. I was hurt that she wasn't in my life no more, and now I knew she was gonna find out I was back using my body for money. When we both finally got dressed, somebody called my new stage name, Kharisma.

"Aye, get your ass out here!" the dude yelled after I threw back two shots of Hennessy.

I fixed my thong and headed to the stage. The speakers thumped a Gucci Mane song I ain't never heard before. It was so dark in the audience, except for the light by the bar and the one light on the stage. I let my hips ride the thick bass beat. I did some of the tricks I remembered seeing Quita and Marcha doing, and then

I squatted on the floor, holding my knees apart with my hands, giving them a sneak peek at my freshly shaved kitty. I looked in the faces of some of the dudes greedily eyeing me and moved my body like a snake. It was so easy, and the dollars rained down on me in waves. I had to put a payment on my R Street storage unit and save some money toward a new apartment, so the more it rained, the more I gyrated.

The next night I did pretty much the same routine, but this time when I looked around the room, my eyes locked on Rich's. *What the hell was he doing here?* He smiled and winked. For some reason, I ain't feel embarrassed, though. When Plies's "Plenty Money" came on, instead of being pissed cuz it was one of Ryan's favorites, I moved to that shit like I was the dirty, bad girl Ryan must've wanted me to be. I watched Rich hard, like I was dancing just for him. I laid on my stomach so that my ass was in the air. I twirked each cheek just for him. He licked his lips. I crawled toward him and straddled his lap. Rich wanted me bad, but not more than I wanted every single dollar in his hand.

After I danced, I was supposed to go work the floor for lap dances. Hell, anything to get more tips. I was on a mission to find Rich and his money-having friends but was blown when I ain't see him nowhere. I felt a little crushed that he ain't wait for me. I focused on the task at hand, working the club, giving lap dances to a handful of dudes scattered around the room until the night was finally over. Five hundred and twenty dollars richer, I packed my bag and waited for Meeka so we could head out the door.

Once we walked out, Meeka lit a cigarette and handed me the lighter so I could light mine. Two seconds later, a sleek black S-Class Mercedes sitting on spit-polished twenty-sixes pulled up. The passenger window rolled down. I looked at Meeka, who smiled at me.

"Aye, KiKi. Come here real quick." It was Rich.

Meeka mouthed, "Who is that?"

"My barber, girl."

She pressed her lips tight like she was impressed. One look at his ride, and I knew Rich had more paper than I thought he'd had. I swished my hips over to his Benz, the same way I used to do back when I worked the Fourteenth Street strip. "Hey, Rich."

"What you 'bout to do?"

"You," I purred.

"That's a bet," he smiled. "Get in."

"Can you drop my girl off first? I was her ride tonight."

"No problem." Upshur Street was only like ten blocks away.

"Okay. Come on, Meeka!" I called over my shoulder.

She sashayed over to the car like she wanted to hit Rich, too, but that shit wasn't even happening. "He said he'll drop you off for me."

Meeka looked hurt. I gave her a look that said this

was personal, not business, and no, she couldn't have none. She nodded and relaxed. Once we dropped her off, I looked over at Rich and smiled innocently. He shook his head and smiled back.

"Damn, KiKi. I ain't know that's how you rolled."

"What you mean?"

"You know exactly what I mean."

Of course, I did. I laid my head against his plush leather seats and watched him drive downtown. The music and the lights from other cars forcing me to stay awake. Rich lit a blunt, took a hit, then offered me some. I took a pull, hoping it was laced with something stronger. But this was nice, too. 'Dro would do just fine. My face instantly started feeling numb. Rich headed toward the Third Street Tunnel, and soon we was pulling up to one of the brand-new apartment buildings near the Nationals baseball stadium.

"You live here?" I asked.

He nodded and drove into the Axiom parking garage. My mind was running a hundred miles a minute. On the elevator ride up to his apartment, I studied Rich's face. Even though I always thought he was handsome, I wouldn't have put him in the same category as Kareem with his Laz Alonso pretty-boy look. Rich had a smooth brown complexion, a strong jawline, and lots of confidence like he dared somebody to cross him. He kinda reminded me of Amar'e Stoudemire, except he was about six feet even.

"What you thinking 'bout?" he asked.

I raised my eyebrows. "Just surprised I'm here with you right now."

He nodded. "I don't bring just *anybody* to my domain, either," he said, winking.

Rich led me out the elevator when the doors chimed open, and then he walked to the end of the hall and unlocked the door. I followed behind him and couldn't believe how laid out his apartment was. I mean, straight-out-a-magazine nice. The view was to die for. From one room, you could see the Capitol building, and the other, you could see the peak of the monument. Rich was really surprising me with every step.

"You want something to drink?"

"Yeah. Whatever you got," I said, admiring his taste.

Charcoal gray, plum, and buttery yellow was everywhere. He had a pool table in his living room like Audri had, but it was much larger. Everything was plushed out like his huge charcoal-gray sectional sofa that faced the gigantic flat screen on the wall. I was too confused. As soon as Rich handed me a Long Island iced tea, I had to get in his business.

"Okay, Rich, wassup? I'm stuck. How the hell can you afford this?"

He smiled. "See...you all in my business. Ain't nobody ask you why you stripping at Macombo."

Well, damn. He had me on that.

"But...since I fucks with you...I do all right. Me

and my partners own a couple businesses, including the shop."

I hadn't even realized that. I mean, I thought he might've been a manager or something, but I ain't know it was his spot.

"I own Diamond Kutz on Minnesota Avenue, Rough Edges on Martin Luther King Avenue, a Laundromat in Capitol Heights, and a car wash in Hyattsville."

Jackpot. "For real? You seem too young for all that. How old are you?"

He sipped his drink, then said, "Twenty-nine. How old are you?"

"I'll be twenty-one soon." I took another sip, still confused. I was too impressed. "And you still cut hair, even though you own those businesses?"

"I like cutting hair. I get to be creative and talk shit with my friends. It don't even feel like work for real. Shit, I only work three days a week." He sat his drink on a coaster. "Let me ask you something since we doing interviews and shit."

I prepared myself to talk about the elephant in the room.

"Why you come in the shop yesterday and have me chop all your hair off?"

He surprised me with that one cuz I just knew he was gonna ask about me dancing at the club. I shook my head, not sure how to answer. "For a lot of reasons, I guess."

"Name one."

"Um…" I paused, wondering how deep I wanted to go. "I got a lot of drama going on right now, and I just wanted to feel like I was starting off with a fresh slate, but I think it backfired. I look crazy."

"Take that shit off," he commanded.

I froze, feeling insecure but knowing Rich had already seen my hair, I pulled the short blonde wig off and ran my fingers over my low cut.

"Come here."

I stood up and walked over to where he sat. He took my hands in his, and then he said, "Why you keep looking away when I look at you?"

I shook my head. He was making me feel nervous. He stared at me for a long time.

Then finally he said, "You are beautiful. I tell you every time I see you cuz I mean it. Shit, I been feeling you ever since you came in my shop. I was rushing like shit to get you in my chair," he said, smiling. "And then that day I saw you leaving Ibiza…man, I wanted to leave behind you, too. I told my boys, 'The chick I want just left.'"

I blushed and looked away. He turned my chin back to look at him.

"I know I don't know much about you, but I'm trying to get to know you, you feel me?"

I smiled, even though it wasn't the first time somebody said those words to me. I had so much shit with me. Rich ain't want no part of Shakira Alexis Scott for real. That was just his dick talking. I kneeled down in front of him, then ran my hand across his rock-hard dick and squeezed. Rich pushed it away and lifted my chin with his hand.

"Nah, KiKi. I want you to believe me," he said, locking his eyes on mine. "Trust me."

I was speechless.

"The more I look at you, the more I just wanna protect you. For real, you look lost and like you on the brink of doing something real stupid to yourself."

A tear slid down my face. How could he know all that?

"I don't want you to add me to whatever drama you dealing with. You hear me?" He wiped away my tear with his thumb. "Starting right now. I don't even wanna know about your drama. All you need to know is that the drama stops here and now, okay?"

I nodded, and then he pulled me up from the floor and sat me across his lap, my legs outstretched on the long, luxurious couch. He kissed my forehead, and I buried my head in his chest. Tears came from nowhere. I tried to sniff them back, but they just kept falling. For the first time in a while, I ain't feel like I had to worry. Rich rubbed my arm and hushed me to sleep.

19

The next day after breakfast, Rich drove me to Meeka's so I could get whatever I wanted. He told me that he ain't want me working at Macombo's ever again, that I should just focus on going to school, and that he would take care of me. For the life of me, I couldn't understand why Rich wanted to do so much for a girl he barely knew. I ain't feel like I deserved it. I tried to ignore the urge to snort. Part of it was cuz I ain't know where to get none from besides Peaches. The other part was cuz I ain't want to ruin whatever it was me and Rich was starting. Coke was what destroyed me and Audri. Wasn't no way I was gonna let it spoil this new thing with Rich.

Over the next few weeks, Rich took me to all the best places to eat across the city, Lauriol Plaza, B. Smith's, Citronelle, and Adour for dinner, and shopping in Georgetown, Arlington, and Bethesda. Him keeping his hands off me only lasted two full weeks. All it took was for him to find out I loved sleeping naked, and he was up inside me with my legs on his shoulders. After messing with Audri, I had forgot just how good dick was, especially the way Rich hit every corner and curve inside me. He paid attention to my every need and watched me as he stroked in and out. He asked me how I felt in a way that made me know he cared that I was satisfied just as much as I wanted to make sure he was, too. Rich was the first guy I ever squirted with, and he killed me at how *unsurprised* he was that he made me do it.

Rich was spontaneous enough to keep my mind from wandering to the dark places that usually left me thirsty for coke. I noticed him staring at me once when I felt a little antsy and was digging through all of my old purses, hoping I could find a vial that I had somehow forgotten about. It was almost like he knew there was something I wanted that he couldn't give me, but instead of asking me what I was looking for or what was wrong, Rich told me to hurry up and get dressed. "We're going to a cabaret so put on something sexy," he said. I ain't wanna disappoint him, so I stopped searching long enough to pick out a cute black dress. Rich looked sexy as hell putting on his fresh black button up. I threw my arms around his neck and gave him a kiss.

"What was that for?" he asked, smiling.

"Just because," I said.

Rich kissed me again, then said, "Hurry up and get five starred up." He smacked my butt and turned me toward the bathroom. An hour later we was dancing our asses off to the Lissen Band out Lanham. We had met a couple of his friends and their dates there, too. I felt so happy.

After a few weeks, I realized pretty quickly that Rich's businesses wasn't as legit as he had made it seem. Him and his partners met up way too much in the parking lots behind the businesses. I sat in his car watching them swap packages out their trunks, wondering what was in them. Things started making more sense about where he lived, the cars he drove, and the money he spent. Of course, I never asked him no questions. Hell, since Rich never asked me questions about my past, I wasn't gonna ask him questions that ain't concern me. I figured the less I knew, the better off I'd be.

One weekend in October, Rich drove me to southern Maryland so I could taste what he swore was the best crabs ever. He said it was in a place called Solomons Island, and I remembered Peaches telling me about it before. There was lots of shops, spas, and bed-and-breakfasts, but people mostly loved the marinas. Rich said him and his boys came down a lot to go crabbing and fishing. I couldn't believe he said that he actually owned a boat. I had to see what all the fuss was for.

Our first stop, though, was in Calvert County. The

orange, gold, and burgundy leaves of the different autumn colors looked so pretty. I was surprised when we drove down a dirt road, and Rich pulled up in front of a tan house with a big porch and a white fence going around it. There was a blue-and-white boat attached to a red Ford F-150. It was parked beside a pearl Cadillac. Rich parked and opened the car door for me. I never asked questions cuz I felt safe with Rich, but I was tense when I noticed the floor mat outside the door said THE MALLOYS. Rich's last name. As soon as the door swung open, I saw a slim woman with gray-streaked hair waiting with a big smile on her face.

"Boy, come on and get in here. It's a chill in the air," she said.

"Hi, Aunt Pat," he said, giving her a hug.

"Hey, Richie. Why, hello," she said to me.

"Hi. I'm Shakira."

"Girl, you need to give me a hug. You know how many times Richie brought somebody to meet me?"

I blushed and shook my head.

"I can count on two fingers and that includes you so you must be some kind of special."

And I still had no idea what he saw in me. She hugged me tight with the type of hug Mommy used to always give when I first came home after being separated for so long. My nerves started to get the best of me, but I fought the urge that had been calling me for some time.

"Come on in. I done steamed a heap of crabs for y'all."

I gave Rich a playful pop. He could've told me I was coming to meet some of his folks. She was so funny, telling me we couldn't sleep in the same room and that she had a nightgown for me to wear.

"I'm just teasing, baby," she said two seconds later. "When I was your age, a lot of things was different. Make yourself at home."

Rich clearly did, popping open bottles of beer and carrying them to the table. We broke into those juicy crabs and loved every bit of the lump meat spilling out of each one. Aunt Pat even got busy. She was a pro. There was stories she told me about Rich, him learning about crabbing and fishing with his uncle Roy, and about the summers he used to spend with her. In between bites, she told me to look at pictures she had around the living room of all her grandkids. In just about every picture where Roy or Pat was, kids hugged all over them. I thought that was sweet. After Daddy died, me and my family never really had that kind of affectionate relationship.

After we ate, Rich led me to the backyard where there was a lighted stone path that snaked down to a small pond, carrying two beer bottles in his other hand. We sat on a bench and watched the turtles, goldfish, and frogs play around while we sipped.

"Is that your boat?" I asked.

He nodded. "Yep, *Bonita Applebum*. Me and Ty come down here like twice a month."

I was surprised. Not too many people I knew even knew how to fish, let alone owned boats. We sat quietly for a while sipping our beer, and then to break the silence that made me nervous, I said, "Can you tell me one thing?"

"What's that?"

"Why me? I mean, after you seen what I was doing in that strip club . . . why you still want me?"

Rich swallowed more beer before he spoke. "I guess cuz I knew you before I saw you there. I wanted you way before I knew that part, and for real, that shit just turned me on a little bit," he said, smiling.

I pushed his leg away playfully. I was truly confused. Out of two girls, I happened to be one he introduced to his aunt. I still ain't understand what he saw in me. I mean, with all the shit he had going for him, I had to keep knocking bitches back. Thank God, Rich ignored all the late-night phone calls here and there and bitches grinning in his face at every shop he rolled up in. What was it about me that was so damn interesting? "I still don't get it," I said, shaking my head.

"KiKi, you act like something wrong with you," he said, looking at me suspiciously.

I looked at the bottle.

"I'm not the first person who's dated a stripper before," he said, looking me directly in my eyes. Thank God that was the only part he knew about me.

"Okay. Fine. Since you gotta know...I like that every time when you used to come to my shop, you had your head in your textbooks. That you ain't pay no attention to none of the niggas trying to get at you or none of the bullshit going on in the shop. I like that you out here trying to make it on your own. I like the way you treat me and the way you let me treat you. You never complain when plans change. You never doubt what I say. I like that you're open to doing new shit. That you take chances."

I smiled a little.

"I like how you don't blame your mother for what happened to you when you was younger and how you make sure she's straight before you do anything else with your day. I just want you to feel like you deserve every good thing that comes your way. Just because you're you and not for nothing else. Baby, please just stop asking why I'm with you. Just know that I am cuz I wanna be. You feel me?"

I smiled, even though I still ain't feel so sure. I knew I had a habit of ruining relationships when I felt like they was too good to be true. It drove me crazy that I did that in spite of myself. Rich rubbed my knee and took another sip of his beer. "Now, you know where my aunt lives, you know where I live, you know where I work. You starting to learn way too much about me.

You know if you hurt me, I'ma have to hurt you, right?"

I looked at him crazy, and then he smiled and kissed me. "I'm just playing with you, girl. I'd never hurt you . . . even if you hurt me. I'll walk away first. You understand me?"

I believed him so I nodded and let him kiss me even though I was more worried about me hurting him. I closed my eyes and prayed that I never did.

The next morning we woke up early to go for a ride in *Bonita Applebum*. It was cool. He showed me how to crab, using a metal crab trap, a thing he called a dip line, and pieces of chicken and turkey necks he got from Aunt Pat. It was weird seeing how the crabs latched on to each other, snapping arms and legs off of other crabs, fighting not to get pulled up. Those suckers was not coming at their own free will. After we caught a crateful, we rode the boat back to the shore and headed to Aunt Pat's house. By the afternoon, we showered and changed into different clothes before heading to Eagles' Landing Gun Range. Rich was a trip, laughing at me every time I jumped cuz of the gunshots going off around me. The people running the joint made me get internal and external headsets to muffle the loud noise.

"You supposed to be from the hood. How you gon' be jumping every time you hear gunshots?" he teased. But my nerves was bad fucking with that place.

"When I hear gunshots in the hood, it's cuz they

meant to kill somebody. Not to be shooting at no damn paper man," I told him. I looked around at the other people shooting. They was so at ease, taking their time to aim and hit their paper targets. "Look at how relaxed they is. They be shooting deer, they don't get shot at."

He just laughed and tried to show me how to hold the gun the right way. As sexy as he said I looked, that part of the day wasn't fun to me at all. *What the fuck I need to know how to shoot for?* Rich took me to Solomons Island Winery. He bought me two bottles of that Sauvignon Blanc that Toya let me taste at her apartment that time I visited.

"Look at you, knowing your wines," he said, surprised. "And you not even legal yet."

I stuck my tongue out and sashayed to the truck. Before we went back, he took me to a restaurant on the waterfront and then for a walk on the boardwalk. I was having so much fun, but I was so exhausted from the long day since we had been up at the crack of dawn to hit the bay. On the ride home Rich told me to listen to some old-school hip-hop song he loved. He turned it up:

> *There are times when you'll need someone, I will*
> *be by your side.*
> *There is a light that shines special for you and me.*

It was sweet, and I was surprised Rich was digging it. He winked and rapped along with Common. By the time we rolled back to his aunt's, I was too tired to even get out of the car. Rich parked, then carried me from my seat to the doorstep.

"And just think, I was gonna take you to see the wild ponies in Assateague last weekend. You wouldn't have been able to hang," he whispered in my ear.

I curled closer to his neck and held tighter. "Maybe next time."

He kissed me, then opened the door.

20

A week before Thanksgiving, Yodi called me to see what I was gonna bring for dinner and if I was coming by early to help cook, but I told her I wasn't coming at all. Mommy went off in the background. I told Yodi to tell her if Ryan was gonna be there, then I wasn't gonna be there. Yodi seemed confused but passed the message on.

"Mommy said, 'What that got to do with it? Ryan lives here,'" Yodi said.

"Yodi, tell Mommy that I'm not coming!"

"Why not?" Yodi asked.

"Ask Ryan why I'm not coming!" I said, hanging up.

When Yodi called me back, I sent the call straight to voice mail. Rich came home just as I opened my book. I blinked away the drama that just happened and painted a smile on my face. I ain't want him to think something had pissed me off. It was him and his stocky best friend, Ty. Rich kissed me and went to the fridge to get a root beer. He said it reminded him of when he was a kid and it kept him grounded.

"What's up, Miss KiKi?" Ty asked, stealing my book.

"Stop playing, boy!" I said, tossing a throw pillow his way.

"What's this . . . let's see. *Medical Billing Level I.* Let me test you," Ty said, laughing.

I rolled my eyes. He always wanted to play around. "All right. Chapter nine."

"No, let's go back to chapter eight, and see if you still know it."

"Stop playing, Ty. Rich!"

"Ty, stop fucking with my girl," Rich called from the kitchen.

Ty laughed and handed me back the textbook. I stuck my tongue out.

"You just mad you don't remember it," Ty teased.

"Whatever."

It was fun being around the two of them, but I did miss hanging out with my girls. I wished Peaches could see me now. Rich had me in the same shit she flossed. Moschino, Gucci, Dior, and Zac. And the best part was I ain't have to shop off the clearance racks no more.

"You got a passport?" Rich asked, sitting next to me. I shook my head. "Why?"

"We never stay here for the holidays," Ty said.

"So that mean you can't go with us to Martinique, babe," Rich said.

"Why not?" I asked, pissed.

"It takes too long to get a passport," he said.

What? Why he ain't tell me before now?

"Don't look so disappointed. You can have one in time for Christmas, though," Ty said, flipping through another book.

"Where y'all going for Christmas?" I asked, excited. I had never been out of the country.

"Costa Rica," Ty said, smiling and nodding.

Nice. Even though I was pissed I couldn't make the other trip, too. *What was Rich gon' do without me?*

Rich picked me up and carried me to the bedroom. "You mad, ain't you?"

Of course, I was. He started peeling my clothes off while I was standing, and I ain't stop him. He always made me feel better.

"I just wanna look at you," he said, looking me over from head to toe.

I tucked one foot under the other. It's funny how uncomfortable I felt with him staring at me naked when I let so many guys see me that way before. His eyes looked at every inch. I smiled nervously, and then he laid me back on the bed.

"You are so beautiful. Turn over."

I rolled on my stomach. Then he kissed the back of my neck, across my shoulders and on my tattoo, and down my back to kiss the other tattoo. I felt wetness in between my legs as he kissed my butt and licked down my crack, and then he slipped inside me. It felt sooooo good as he stroked and held on to my hips. In the middle of his thrusts, Rich twisted my body around so that I was facing him. "You trust me?"

I nodded.

"Good, cuz I trust you, too."

My pussy tightened, and I held Rich inside me until I felt him cumming. His body rocked hard against mine before he went limp from exhaustion. He held me against his chest.

A couple days later, me and a bunch of Rich's friends was up Adams Morgan, barhopping through the night, bouncing in and out of overcrowded bars and clubs, getting white boy–wasted. When we was coming out the Sutra Lounge, some dude snatched Ty's watch off his wrist and sprinted up the block. Before I knew it, Ty, Rich, crazy Ed, and Donte was behind the dude, stomping his ass in the middle of the street. Ed was like a live wire attacking the dude. I was scared to death. Donte kept lookout. When Ty leaned down to get his watch back, the dude on the ground stabbed him in his side. I couldn't believe my eyes. It had all happened so fast. All that blood gushed over his shirt. I screamed at the top of my lungs. Rich was holding Ty while Ed and Donte went berserk on that thief-ass nigga. Soon the street was so crowded with the people watching, and then the police and paramedics came. I ain't know which way was up and which way was down.

Ty was released from the hospital two days later, and Rich wasn't letting him stay nowhere else cuz he wanted me to make sure he got better. I loved the way he looked out for Ty. He told me they had been friends forever, and I could tell it wasn't nothing he wouldn't do for him. I had thought about hooking Ty and Meeka up cuz they was both wild and funny, but Rich told me not to do it. "Meeka would end up getting hurt," he said, and I took his word for it and let that idea drift away.

The day they was supposed to fly out, Ty said he was in too much pain and wasn't gon' have fun. He couldn't drink and couldn't hit the beach. Rich understood and asked me to take care of his friend for the three days he was gonna be away. I felt weird agreeing to do that. I mean, Ty ain't have no female friends who could nurse him back to health?

"I trust you," Rich said before he left with his boys Ed and Donte.

On Thanksgiving Day, since I wasn't going to see my family, Ty asked me to drive him over his family's house in Fort Washington. I mean, how could I say no? As soon as we walked in the door, they all rushed him with hugs. I couldn't help thinking why Ty ain't stay over here with them. As soon as he got in the door good, I told Ty I'd pick him up later.

"Sweetheart, you can stay and get something to eat," said some guy who looked like Ty.

"No, thank you," I said stepping back out on the porch. "But happy Thanksgiving, everybody."

"Shawty baaaad," the guy said to Ty.

Ty pushed him in the house. "Thanks, KiKi. You sure you good?"

I nodded and headed back to Rich's Benz. I really felt lonely. Here it was the day for family, and I was hopping into my boyfriend's car without him. I drove around, even past Peaches's salon and then by her house but didn't see no Infiniti truck nowhere. I drove pass Mommy's apartment building and saw the light on in the living room. Did anybody even miss me there? Toya and Ryan was probably talking shit about me right now. I stopped to buy some cigarettes and then headed back to the apartment.

A few hours later, Ty was knocking on the door. His cousin had dropped him off.

"Here, I brought you a plate back."

Yes! All I'd eaten was junk food the whole day. I tore into the turkey, mac and cheese, yams, and collard greens. Ty sat on the couch and flipped the TV on to football. Before I knew it, he was cutting coke on Rich's coffee table like a pro. My eyes grew wide and my mouth got a little watery. I sucked, then bit my lip. Before I knew it I was like a magnet to Ty's side. This was exactly what I needed. How did Ty know I felt like shit today? Ty looked at me, then smiled and handed me the rolled bill. I felt so guilty sitting here, staring at the neat lines on Rich's table. It had been nearly two months since the last time I got high. I rubbed my elbows and looked away for a couple seconds. Then like the coke was calling my name, I turned back around and stared at the fine particles. "You first," I said, smiling.

He snorted a line, then gave it to me. I hit the next line, feeling like a spark among a whole batch of fireworks. I was so hot. I took my cashmere sweater dress off.

Ty smiled again and said, "I know a secret," before he hit another line.

"What?" I asked.

"You a bad girl, for real."

I laughed and danced around the room in my bra and panties. It had been so long since I had a line. I forgot how good it made me feel. I laid across the big couch and stared at the ceiling. I ain't wanna move.

"Damn, girl. You gon' make me lose my best friend fucking with you. Your body's sick."

"You can look but don't touch," I said, giggling.

When I sat up, I saw Ty massaging his thick dick with slow strokes. It made me horny, but I would never do nothing to hurt Rich. I felt ashamed cuz he trusted me so much, and here I was arching my back for his best friend. I jumped up and hit another line. I leaned back to enjoy my high. When I opened my eyes, Ty was standing on top of me, pumping nut over my face.

"Stop it! Stop, Ty!" I screamed and pushed him away before running to the bathroom.

"Girl, you can't be teasing me and shit," he said, breathless. "What the fuck you thought I was gon' do? Damn!"

I shut myself in the bathroom and climbed in the empty bathtub. *What was wrong with me? Why did I let him see me like that?* I cried until I couldn't cry no more.

21

I avoided Ty as much as I could until Rich came back from Martinique. Neither one of us ever spoke about what happened that day on Rich's couch, and Rich ain't pick up on shit, either. Whenever he went to meet Ty for something, I stayed in the car to avoid all the chitchat, and if he wanted us to double-date with some new girl Ty found, I told Rich I ain't feel good. The truth was I *wasn't* feeling good. I wanted more coke, and since I ain't have a connect, I knew I needed to make friends again with Ty. He could at least put me in touch with somebody who could get me what I needed.

On the flip side, Rich was so sweet to me. He couldn't wait to take me to Costa Rica. He took me shopping for some fly shit to wear. He was big on seeing me in white. He bought me two white bikinis, one white Roberto

Cavalli dress, and a white Stella McCartney short shorts outfit. I was letting my hair grow back. Fuck what Rich said about me looking beautiful, I felt my flyest with hair. In fact, I was going to Peaches's spot to get my lace front done. I wanted to surprise her, let her see how sweet my life was now. I even borrowed Rich's car so she could see me pull up in it.

As soon as I got to the door, Peaches cut me a look that almost made me turn back out the door. But fuck that, I wanted her to know just how good I was doing. As soon as Kori and Daneen seen me walk in, they both shook their heads.

"What you want?" Peaches said, clearly irritated, but out of respect for the woman in her chair, she ain't curse me out.

"I need you to do my hair, that's what."

Peaches laughed in my face and kept doing her client's hair.

"Can I talk to you for a minute, for real?"

She sighed and sucked her teeth, like I was asking her to open an account for me in her name or some shit.

"Excuse me for one minute. I promise I won't be longer than that," she said. When her client nodded, she said, "Thank you," then walked to the back office. I followed closely behind her. As soon as I shut the door, Peaches said, "You got some fucking nerve showing up in my salon, talking about getting your hair done after all that shit-talking your ass did!"

"You want this money or what?" I asked, showing her a fat knot.

"Do I look like I need your money?" she said, crossing her arms over her chest.

"Okay, Peaches. Damn. You right. I'm not here just to get you to do my damn hair. I miss your ass, and I'm sorry for all that shit I said."

"Your ass better be muthafucking sorry! After all I did for you, and you tried to throw shit in my face like I wasn't nobody to you. I ain't appreciate it at all!"

I looked down and played with my fingers, feeling like a child again. I knew Peaches needed to know all that led me to lashing out at her that day. My back was against a wall, and I wanted her to save me, but she turned me down when I was at my lowest point. I took a deep breath and then blew the air across my lips. "I have to tell you something...," I started. Then I told her how Ryan raped me. By the time I was done with my story, Peaches was passing me tissues to wipe my face and giving me a hug. I felt better telling her. Relieved. Almost like I had actually told Mommy, even though I knew I'd never, ever tell nobody in my family.

After Peaches finished her client's hair, she hooked me up with a two-tone do. One-half black, the other half blonde, a cute bang and all. I loved my super-hot look, especially with my favorite red lipstick. It looked like something Fergie would wear. Peaches left Kori in charge so we could go get lunch from Chipotle and catch up. I was happy Peaches was on my side again. I needed her in my corner. She knew me almost as much as I knew myself. I told her how me and Audri ended, then about my sweetheart Rich. I even told her about the dumb shit that went down with Ty.

"Be careful with your heart, KiKi. That's all I ask."

"What you mean?"

"Sometimes, you do too much."

I ain't understand what she meant, and I guess it showed on my face cuz she said, "I know how...sometimes you gotta do what you gotta do to make sure you got a roof over your head and everything, but Rich seem like he want what's best for you. Why you gon' fuck it up for some coke from his greedy-ass friend?"

I already felt like shit for what happened. Why she have to point out the obvious? "Tell me something..."

"Okay." Peaches took a bite of her burrito bowl salad and waited for my question.

"Can you be honest with me?"

"Of course."

"And I'm not trying to be disrespectful, either."

Peaches looked at me sideways and pressed her lips together, like she knew I was gonna ask something disrespectful anyway.

"How you get Nut to do so much for you? I mean, when he met you, you was already hooking. How you get him to marry you and keep you up?"

Peaches shrugged her shoulders. "I don't know. I

don't think I was trying to get him to marry me in the beginning. I just loved him. Everything about him. All his imperfections, and I ain't judge him for it. I think he loved that about me. He knew I'd do anything for him. Nut could trust me with his life, and I proved it to him every time he tested me."

I ate a bite of my burrito and thought about what she said.

"Why you ask?"

"I mean . . . Rich is so sweet to me. I ain't never have nobody treat me like he do, not since my father did when I was a little girl. Sometimes it makes me feel uncomfortable, you know? Like I ain't supposed to be getting the extra attention."

"You just forgot, that's all. I forgot for a long time, too. I'm still learning how to make sure people respect me. Nut definitely had his days when he treated me like shit," Peaches said, shaking her head and sipping her lemonade. "Rich sounds good for you, though, KiKi. You need to appreciate him every chance you get."

I kept replaying what she said in my head while we finished eating. When I dropped her off at the shop, I leaned over and gave her a hug. She squeezed me tight and said, "Don't ever let us fall out over some dumb shit again, you hear me?"

I was so happy we was able to squash that bullshit before I left the country.

"Love you, girl, and no, you can't have your job back."

I laughed and told her I loved her, too. "Merry Christmas, trick!" I yelled out the window.

"Same to you!"

After I got my hair done, I drove to Mommy's job. I hadn't seen her in a while. As soon as I walked in the cafeteria, she frowned. I knew she was still pissed about me not coming to Thanksgiving dinner and for trying to show off Rich's car when I took her to the doctor once. She told me I was being too busy and that I needed to focus on finishing school. Of course, I told her I was, but for real, after winter break, I think I was going to skip a semester so I could spend more time with Rich.

"What you doing hur?" Mommy asked, stacking plates.

"It's good to see you, too!" I signed and gave her a kiss.

"Who did your hair?" she asked.

"Peaches, you like it?"

"It's okay. So wot's up?"

"I just wanted you to know that Rich is taking me to Costa Rica for Christmas, and I'm not gonna be around."

Mommy shook her head and kept stacking plates.

"What?"

"'Kirwuh, I don't know why you stay so busy chasing love."

"What you mean, Mommy? You not happy for me?"

Mommy sighed and went to grab silverware. "'Kirwuh, go and have fun. Okay? Is that wot you want to hur me say? This the second time you not home for the holidays, and I jus don't understand why."

And she wasn't gonna ever know why I couldn't be around Ryan if I could help it.

"You weery me, 'Kirwuh."

"I'ma be fine, Mommy. Don't worry." I kissed her on the cheek and headed back out of the cafeteria.

I couldn't believe who met us at Reagan National Airport. Haitian Smurf. The same blue-black nigga I fucked twice about five years ago when I was at a party with my girl Camille. Everybody knew Smurf had something to do with Nut turning up in two pieces. Smurf and Rich dapped each other up, and then Smurf smiled when he saw me. I smiled and acted just like I had never met him a day in my life. I wasn't sure if he recognized me, but I knew how to play dumb with the best of them. Smurf was so caked up and so respected on the streets that I knew for sure now Rich was definitely in the game. I was a little hurt that Rich ain't introduce me to Smurf as his girlfriend, but just his friend. If Smurf did remember me, I wanted him to know that I wasn't a tramp no more.

Ty brought a dark-skinned, model-looking chick named Jacylyn. Ed and Donte had some eye candy with them, too, who acted like they was too fucking cute to speak. Nakeeda was about my complexion and Yenee was a dark honey color. Smurf came with two dudes I ain't recognize. We all rode in first class, sipping champagne. I felt like I was in wonderland.

From the moment we stepped off the plane, I felt a new energy. I could smell the salty but fresh scent of the ocean. The jungle heat laced my skin, making beads of sweat rise up. Rich grabbed my hand and our luggage with the other. Then our whole entourage headed to the cab area. Ty and his girl, Jacylyn, climbed in the same one with me and Rich. We drove a little ways down a parkway that curved around thick green trees and beautiful mountains. I was so excited when I finally seen the beach. Rich kissed the back of my hand and smiled. I saw a sign that said GANDOCA-MANZANILLO WILDLIFE REFUGE. I couldn't believe that just this morning I was in freezing-ass D.C. and now I was in the steamy jungle with gigantic leaves the same size as me, sprouting from trees just as tall as city buildings. As soon as the cab pulled up to a place called Almonds and Corals, I saw two black monkeys run across the wooden path lit by two dozen torches. My heart jumped.

"This is so nice," I said before kissing Rich. "Thank you for bringing me here."

"You supposed to be here."

There was cottages that looked like tree houses cuz the roofs was covered by huge palms and they was raised high off the ground. It seemed so peaceful back here.

We all went to different tree houses. Me and Rich's tree house had a Jacuzzi built in the floor. Red, pink, and yellow flower petals floated in the water with candles. A hammock swung near the Jacuzzi in front of a huge window. The beds was all covered in crisp white linen. White fabric hung around the bed to keep mosquitoes out. This was really paradise.

Rich laid me on the soft sheets and planted kisses all over my body. He pulled my halter dress over my head and took off my panties.

"You smell so good," he whispered, but I felt a hot, sweaty mess from all that traveling and the jungle humidity. "Let's get in the Jacuzzi."

He carried me over and helped me get in the warm water. I took the candles out of the tub while he took off his army-green linen shirt and dark-blue jean shorts. He stepped out of his boxers. I smiled as his dick stood at attention. Then he slid in with me.

"I can't believe you brought me here with you," I said before wrapping my arms around him.

"Believe it, girl."

I rubbed the head of his dick before I put it inside of me, the thickness filling me up. He held me close to his chest as I worked my hips. I wanted to make him love me. I closed my eyes and imagined this was our honeymoon and my last name was Malloy. I thought about what Peaches had told me about appreciating Rich every day for the special way he treated me, even if I didn't feel like I deserved it, and then I rode him the best way I knew how. I rocked my hips slow and hard, making sure each stroke meant something to Rich. We stared at each other for a few moments until Rich's eyes closed so he could enjoy every inch of me. Water splashed over the wood floors in a rhythm, but I ain't even care. I wanted him to know that I loved him.

The next morning after we ate breakfast, we all headed on a safari deep in the jungle. Smurf and his friends brought some Costa Rican girls they must've snagged the night before for the ride. We was in three different Jeeps before we climbed out with our tour guides to take us on a walk through the rain forest. We saw all kinds of birds—big pelicans, hummingbirds, parrots, and even the rainbow-colored birds like the kind on the Froot Loops box. I saw a blue frog for the first time in my life. Rich told me it was poisonous, so I stayed the hell away from it. I saw a hairy-ass, two-toed sloth, and there was monkeys galore, too. Brown, yellow, gray, and black monkeys leaping from one tree to another. Huge iguanas and all different types of colorful snakes at every other turn we made. By the time we pulled up to a steamy lagoon with a waterfall pouring from the rocks above, I was damn near scared to hop out the Jeep cuz of all them wild animals on the loose.

But since I looked much cuter than the other girls in my white bikini, I had to stunt for Rich. He knew I couldn't get my hair wet so he carried me around the lagoon on his back. Then suddenly he dipped me underneath and ruined my hair. I was so heated. All he did was laugh and tell me to take my wig off, but it was a full-laced wig. I couldn't snatch it off that easily. Thank God, it was human hair, and I could just blow-dry it back at the villa.

It was kind of weird around Ty. Since he had Jacylyn with him, it was easy to keep the convo light. I don't even think Rich noticed since I was so stuck on stupid with all the newness I was experiencing on this trip. We stayed at the lagoon well into the afternoon before heading back to the villa to shower and change for lunch. I put on a bad-ass light floral Anna Sui dress, and Rich had on a cream linen shirt and beige khaki shorts with these dope-ass Lacoste sneakers. The trendy restaurant was in an open-air courtyard in the middle of a hotel in San José. We sat around a long wooden table with each guy and their date sitting beside them.

"I'd like to propose a toast," Smurf said with his thick French accent. Everybody raised a glass of something, including me with my bubbling champagne.

"To my man Richie Rich, for all your hard work. That shit don't go unnoticed, son," Smurf said, smiling. His dark skin shined under the lights. "Maybe I can finally get this dude to quit cutting niggas' hair."

The table laughed, and Rich shook his head.

"All right. We'll see, my nigga," Smurf said. "Cheers."

"Cheers," everybody said as they clinked each other's glasses.

I felt so proud to be Rich's girl. I rubbed his knee underneath the table and leaned over to kiss him. I was so excited about all of this that I half ate my stuffed fish, string beans, and sliced carrots. I felt like somebody needed to pinch me cuz this had to be a dream.

22

The next night after a long and exhausting, fun day of ziplining through the rain forest (which really means it rains all the time, by the way), chilling at the beach, snorkeling around the coral reef, and on the lookout boat for pools of dolphins, me and Rich got a couples massage where they put steaming hot rocks all over our backs. That shit felt so good. He was so quiet the whole time, though. I thought he had a lot on his mind cuz his mood was so much different earlier. When we got back to our tree house cottage, we both collapsed in the hammock and took a long nap. When I opened my eyes, Rich was staring at me. He had been watching me sleep.

"Hey," I said, smiling.

"Hey. It's something I wanna ask you."

I smiled, wondering what that wonderful question could be.

"Today at the beach, Ty told me something that I ain't wanna believe, and I need to know if it's true."

What the fuck? All of a sudden I felt a stack of bricks drop on my chest as I tried to breathe. I gasped for pockets of air. *What was happening?* Tears slid from my eyes, and I couldn't breathe.

"Whoa, KiKi, breathe, girl," Rich said, trying to sit me up.

I tried to inhale again. Suddenly my lungs opened up, and I could breathe better.

"You okay now?" he asked, wiping my face.

I nodded even though I couldn't remember ever hyperventilating before in my life.

"So tell me...everything. Right now."

More tears slid from my eyes as I thought about what he might've already known. I ain't wanna tell him everything. There was no way I could tell him about the coke or what Ty did to me or my part in what Ty did to me.

"Stop thinking about *what* to say and just say it," he said with his patience obviously thinner than before.

I shook my head and wiped my own tears, sniffling the whole time.

"All these tears can't just be about no damn coke," Rich said before stepping out of the hammock.

I sniffled again, closed my eyes, and tried to swallow the truth that was stuck in my throat.

"Just fucking tell me," Rich said, pissed.

"Um . . . um . . ."

"Don't give me that 'um' shit!" Rich barked and paced the wood floors. "Just spit it out. Did you fuck him, too?"

I shook my head cuz I couldn't speak. My mouth had gotten too dry. He had never been mad at me before.

"KiKi, I love you, man," he said, pausing and shaking his head. "This shit is hurting my heart."

"I didn't touch him, baby, I promise. And he ain't touch me, either. I swear to God," I cried, knowing that it took a lot for him to admit his feelings for me. I felt so low. Rich looked at me with doubtful eyes and shook his head.

"I was hoping you was gonna tell me he was lying about the coke or some shit, but not . . . not this."

"I was high, Rich."

The look on his face told me that ain't make a damn bit of difference.

"Why can't you see what I see in you?" he said with a look I had never seen on nobody's face before when they looked at me. "I'll be back."

Rich headed out of the cottage. I ran behind him, but he pushed me toward the bed. *How could I disappoint the one person who loved me without any questions?* I stayed in the room, crying in a ball on the bed until I heard him come back in the early hours of the next morning. He smelled like liquor when he climbed in the bed. I reached out to him, but he pushed my hand away and kept his back to me. I felt so pitiful. I cried into the pillow, feeling like somebody else's trash.

When Rich had fallen into a deep sleep, I crawled down his thighs and put his dick in my mouth. I sucked until I felt him getting hard. Rich put his hand on the top of my head as I licked and sucked until every inch of his entire body lurched awake. He moaned as I deep throated and swallowed every single drop that flowed from him.

When I was done, instead of Rich kissing and holding me like he usually did, he rolled back over and went to sleep. I felt like a failure. Like I couldn't make him see that what happened with Ty wasn't on purpose. Some of this was his fault, too. The tears wouldn't stop, no matter what I did. I had to get out of this tree house. It was choking me. I climbed out of the bed and headed to the bathroom. I threw on some jeans, a tank top, and some flip-flops and went outside for a walk on the lighted wooden path. I could hear frogs croaking, crickets, and whatever other creatures lurked in the darkness on both sides of the jungle. I felt stupid for being out here alone, but for the life of me I couldn't breathe in that room. I smelled a thick whiff of burning cinnamon in the air. I turned around to find Smurf walking behind me, smoking a cigar. I jumped and froze.

He smiled before saying, "Don't be scared. Why you out here all alone?"

I gave him a half smile and rubbed my shoulders. "Couldn't sleep. What about you?"

"Couldn't sleep, either. Uneasy lies the head that wears the crown," he said before offering me his cigar.

"No, thank you."

"Rich know you out here?"

I ain't know how to answer that cuz I ain't know what Smurf was getting at.

"Miss KiKi, you know, I remember you, right?" he said with a huge smile.

I shook my head. Not this tonight. Not on top of all this other shit.

"You came to my house before in Upper Marlboro... years ago."

"Nope. Wasn't me."

He snorted and took another pull from his cigar. "That's what your mouth say... but I'll leave it at that if that's what you want."

Thank God. I told him good night, and he gave me a gentle salute. I couldn't believe he remembered me after all this time. I felt like my past was catching up with me at the worst time ever. Not when somebody loved me for me and not for how I made them cum. I walked back to our cottage, stripped naked, and climbed in our soft bed. I wrapped my arms around Rich, pressing my breasts against his solid back. Even if he ain't hold me back, I wasn't letting go.

I woke up with him pushing deep inside of me, wondering how he found it in his heart to forgive me. But when he was done, he ain't kiss me. He simply climbed off and went straight to the shower. I felt like shit. Later at breakfast, I ain't feel no better. Ty gave me the eye, like "yeah, I told my man about your trick ass," and Smurf gave me the eye, like "you know I know that was you at my house." I ain't wanna look up from my plate no more. Hell, I ain't wanna look at nobody no more. As beautiful as Costa Rica was, I ain't wanna be there. After breakfast, all the guys was getting ready to go for a ride to a tiny island on a fishing boat. When I ain't see them taking fishing gear, it ain't take a genius to know it had something to do with some bricks. I had noticed the little petite airplanes that kept buzzing by while we was on our safari and wondered if one was meeting them on that tiny island they was headed to.

All the girls wanted to head to San José again to go shopping. Even though I ain't wanna go with these fake-ass broads, I definitely ain't wanna be stranded at the villa all day lying out on the beach. Thank God, Rich left me some money to buy some souvenirs and stuff, but he ain't even kiss me good-bye when him and the fellas left on the fishing boat.

Me and the girls caught a shuttle to Avenida Central so we could walk around the market and buy some things to bring home. Smurf's three Costa Rican girls (who the rest of us called the triplets)—Malia, Caterina, and Adriana—was leading the way. I stayed to myself since

I ain't feel like I had much in common with the other chicks. One seemed okay, I guess. Ed's girl, Nakeeda, had graduated from Roosevelt in D.C. but went to Temple University in Philly. The other girls wasn't truly from D.C. Donte's girl, Yenee, was Ethiopian, and Ty's girl, Jacylyn, was from the suburbs in Montgomery County some damn where. She kept correcting everybody who called her Jacqueline by mistake. Her and Yenee was more stuck up than Toya's ass ever could be.

The downtown scene was pretty busy. You could smell charbroiled chicken, corn on the cob, and potatoes. Strong peppers and seasonings filled the air. Costa Rican people tried to sell everything for "bargain prices," but I only bought a couple things. Some coffee and a cute dress for Mommy, a necklace with matching earrings for Yodi, and even a set for Toya's bourgie ass. I bought some Costa Rican rum for Peaches and Meeka and a flask with the symbol from the Costa Rican flag etched on it for Rich. After everybody finished shopping, we went to a tiny restaurant for lunch and ate something called arroz con pollo, but just tasted like good-ass chicken with rice and beans.

Since the guys was still gone on their "fishing excursion" by the time we got back to the villa, we all agreed to get dressed and head back to the city so we could see some of the nightlife. I put on a lime-green maxi dress I actually found at BCBG and some fabulous gold heels that made my legs look like I borrowed Amerie's. After adding my accessories and grabbing my clutch, I headed to Nakeeda's tree house to see if she was ready. She was stepping out just as I got close. She ain't look bad in her turquoise dress from last season's Zara collection.

"You look cute," she said to me.

"Thanks. So do you," I said, fanning a colossal mosquito away and doing a two-step to dodge his ass.

She giggled and helped me get away.

"Girl, these bugs love my AB positive," I said, walking fast.

We headed to where we planned to meet the other girls. When they came, we all piled in a shuttle van back to the city. We stopped at Castro's. Smurf's triplets said we had to go cuz that's where you see the true salsa and merengue dancing. We could hear the trumpets, trombones, congas, and cowbells as soon as we pulled up to the door. A live band was doing they thing and I loved live music, so I was psyched. My hips started to shake just like I was at a Go Go. I couldn't wait to get inside.

We ordered two rounds of shots of Patrón before Nakeeda and Yenee grabbed my hand, cha-cha-ing to the dance floor. It was so much fun, seemed like everybody was celebrating their birthday. Even me. I nearly forgot about the drama that went down between me and Rich, I was partying so hard. Later when the DJ played Daddy Yankee, it seemed like the dance floor shrunk two sizes. It got too crowded way too fast. Me and the other girls worked our way back to the bar, where Smurf's triplets paid for a round of drinks. We all bobbed and swayed to the beat. Before we knew it all of us was back on the overcrowded floor, moving to the wave of the other partygoers, smiling from ear to ear. Soon I was so sweaty my dress stuck to my body like I had jumped in a pool with my clothes still on. I felt tipsy as I bounced with the crowd. Malia passed me and Yenee a drink, and Caterina passed Jacylyn and Nakeeda drinks. It ain't matter what kind of drink it was. I was so hot that I downed mine in one swallow. The dance floor was way too hot and packed. When I started seeing double, I had to get out of there. Nakeeda, Yenee, and Jacylyn looked just as ready to leave as me. Smurf's triplets led us out of the club and into a minivan. I fell asleep as soon as I laid on the backseat.

When I cracked opened my eyes, I had no idea where I was. It smelled foul like a stuffed toilet and rotten fish. The room was lit by a small lightbulb hanging from the dingy ceiling. My head throbbed, and when I tried to sit up, I felt a pressure forcing me back down. I knew I had a hangover, but I felt like I had been drugged, too. I rubbed my body and felt relieved that my dress was still on, but where was my clutch and what was the weight around my ankle? From the corner of my eyes, I could see Nakeeda lying next to me. Yenee was on a bed across from me. I could hear weak groans on the other side of a dirty sheet that separated the room like a curtain and raspy voices speaking in Spanish. Again, I

tried to sit up. I pushed against whatever force was trying to keep me glued to the sheetless mattress and sat all
the way up. I looked down to see a handcuff latched to
my ankle and connected to a long chain that led to the
bedpost. *What the fuck?* I looked around the room and
saw Yenee had a bloody nose. My eyes grew big. Where
the hell was we? All I could think about was Rich. I
needed him.

"Why can't you see what I see in you?"

I heard his voice in my head.

I tried to shake Nakeeda, hoping she ain't get loud
when she saw me. When she cracked open her eyes, I
whispered, "I don't know where we at, but we gotta get
outta here."

She wiped her eyes and sat up. When she saw the
chain on her ankle, the fear settled in her face the same
way mine did.

"What we gon' do?" she whispered back.

I pointed to Yenee and said, "We gotta wake her up
and get outta here."

"Where's Jacylyn?"

That's when it dawned on me. *Oh no.* The groans
from the opposite side of the hanging sheet must've
been her.

"We can't leave without her," Nakeeda said.

But nobody was gon' leave with chains on our legs.
I tried to pick up the chain without making noise, and
then I slowly folded it up. The key had to be somewhere

in the room. Had to be. Tears crawled down my cheeks.
I could feel my mascara clumping up. Where was we,
and what was happening to us?

"Look who's up, finally," said a voice with a rich
Spanish accent from over my shoulder.

I froze.

"Venir aquí novia," said a fat, oily-haired man with a
beard before he yanked Nakeeda up with one hand. She
screamed before I heard him slap the shit out of her
twice. I closed my eyes, relieved that he ain't choose me
first to do whatever he was doing on the other side of
the sheet. I looked around the room for something to
hit him with so whenever he did come for me I'd have
something for his fat ass. But there was nothing. Just the
two filthy mattresses, two gigantic bottles of water, and
a large trash can.

I could hear gurgling and groaning. My chest got
tight. *What in the fuck was going on?* I looked at the chain
on my leg, then picked it up with two hands. Maybe
I could choke him with it. Just as the thought entered
my mind, I heard chains hitting the floor, and then a
skinny man, with a teardrop tattoo and dozens of tattoos
snaking his arms, pulled Jacylyn from behind the sheet
and then dumped her on the mattress with Yenee. She
never looked me in my face, and she was still groaning.
He smiled at me, showing two rotten bottom teeth.

"¿Estás lista, mami?" he said before walking toward
me and yanking me up.

I dropped the chain that was in my hands. I was too scared to move.

"¡*Vamos!*" Skinny Man said as he pushed me toward the sheet.

"No!" I screamed.

He pushed me harder. On the other side Oily-Haired Man was stuffing a thick tube down Nakeeda's throat. Her eyes was closed, but she still looked like she was out of it.

"*Sientate,*" said Skinny Man, shoving me into a chair. He took a syringe from the table and stuck it in my arm before I could prepare myself.

I watched Oily-Haired Man attach a funnel to the tube before pouring a bottle of clear liquid down Nakeeda's throat. I felt groggy from whatever Skinny Man put in my arm, but I could see him reaching for a tube like Nakeeda's before my eyes closed completely. The next time I opened my eyes, Oily-Haired Man was leading me back to the mattress. My stomach grumbled and rolled in waves. I groaned as I laid down beside Nakeeda on the dirty bed. I felt nauseous and closed my eyes.

When I woke up again, I heard chains scraping the floor and Yenee's voice.

"I can't stop shitting," she was saying to Jacylyn.

"Me, either," Jacylyn said, pacing back and forth.

I looked around the room. The sheet was gone, and Yenee was coming out of what must've been the bathroom. She was holding her stomach. Where there used to be windows was bricks blocking out any light. I couldn't even tell what time of day it was. "What happened to us?" I asked groggily.

"All I know is whatever they put down our throats keeps making me go to the toilet," Yenee said.

Nakeeda woke up beside me and rubbed her eyes. She popped up and ran toward Yenee. Her chain scuffing the floor as she dragged it across the concrete, Nakeeda slammed the bathroom door shut.

"It's so rancid in here. They barely left us anything to wipe ourselves with," Yenee said with her heavy Ethiopian accent, like we all knew what the hell *rancid* meant.

"And there's nothing in here to eat, either," Jacylyn said. "Just bottles and bottles of hot water."

"I can't believe this," I mumbled just as vomit rushed up my throat. I ran over to the huge trash can and let everything pour out. The trash can was disgusting. The smell was so trifling, I threw up again. Jacylyn gave me a bottled water.

"Where are we?" Nakeeda asked when she came out the bathroom.

Yenee shrugged.

"The last thing I remember was getting into that minivan," Jacylyn said.

"Them Costa Rican bitches set us up," Yenee said.

We all nodded cuz the triplets knew what they was doing the whole time. My stomach tossed and flipped like I was on a cruise. I rushed to the bathroom, squatted, and let everything out. By the time I was done, I felt so weak. I dragged my chain back over to the mattress and laid down. I swallowed the rest of the water.

"What the hell do you think they made us swallow?" Jacylyn asked as she pulled the doorknob on the locked door in vain (cuz it didn't budge an inch).

"Can't be but one reason I can think of," Yenee said, worried. "They must be getting us ready to put something inside us."

"How do you know?" Nakeda asked.

"My brother used to tell me these crazy stories about how a gang in my old neighborhood back home used to stuff drugs down the throats of girls, then send them to the UK. He told me how they had to get the girls ready. Flush them out first, so there's room on the inside. Then stuffed them like turkeys."

I couldn't believe what I was hearing.

"Stuff them? What you mean stuff them?" I asked, sitting up.

"I don't know for sure," she said, shaking her head.

"Oh my God," Jacylyn said. "What if something goes wrong?"

Yenee and Nakeeda shook their heads.

"I tell you one thing, I'm not letting them use me however they want to without a fight," Yenee said sternly. No wonder she had a bloody nose already.

This was a nightmare. Of all things that could happen

to me, I'm here? In this situation? How could paradise turn so quickly to hell? It couldn't be really happening. I closed my eyes and opened them again.

Then Yenee said, "No, KiKi. I am sorry...You are not dreaming."

"...IT'S WHEN YOU'RE IN THAT VALLEY YOU CAN SEE BOTH SIDES MORE CLEARLY"

—india.arie, "back to the middle"

23

I t seemed like forever had come and gone by the time we heard someone unlocking the door. The muggy heat seemed to make the dingy walls let out a deep breath when the door swung open. We all was too drained and hungry to even sit up to see who it was. Just an hour earlier, a gigantic jungle fly had squeezed through a vent, and instead of killing it, we all welcomed its company. It gave us something new to watch as we waited for whatever was gonna happen next. It was Skinny Man. He stood over my bed smiling, showing his disgusting brown teeth. Then he squeezed my breasts like it was mangoes on an oxcart in the market. I was too exhausted to even fight him off. I guess he got bored with me cuz he went over to Yenee. I watched him run his hands up her thighs, then underneath her skirt. She screamed and pounded on his chest.

"Get off of me, you filthy dog!" she yelled as loud as she could, straining her already hoarse voice.

Skinny Man punched her in the face. I looked away cuz I couldn't bear to watch him beat her. But the sound of her crying didn't stop, and it was just as painful as me watching him smash her face up. Finally, Skinny Man shouted, *"¡Silencio, punta!"* then he walked back out the room, slamming the door and locking it behind him.

That's when I noticed Jacylyn and Nakeeda had been covering their eyes, too. Nakeeda went over to Yenee first with toilet paper from the bathroom so she could wipe her eyes. Yenee cringed. Jacylyn and I looked at each other. I could tell she felt the same way I did—clueless about what we could say or do to make her feel any better. I shook my head and sat beside Yenee, rubbing her thigh. Nakeeda tore off a piece of her dress and damped it with water. She laid it across Yenee's forehead.

"Why? What did I do to deserve to be here?" she cried.

"None of us deserve this," I said. I couldn't believe what we was going through. We couldn't even give her ice for her swelling eye.

"I can't take being here!" Yenee cried.

"Shhhh. It's no need for you to scream now. You've already lost your voice. Just catch your breath now," Nakeeda said, trying to fan her with her fingers. "It ain't nothing we can do but sit here and wait for whatever they brought us here for."

"Maybe they want to make us prostitutes," Jacylyn said, twisting her face up and shaking, like she was disgusted. "I could never, ever do that. Please God, don't let that happen to us."

"As gross as it might sound, if that's all they want, they can have it. Just let me go back home when they done," I said, shaking my head.

They all looked at me like I was crazy, but it wasn't nothing worse than what I had ever done before.

"I am not a whore," Yenee snarled at me. "I will not let them have me as they will. My parents did not raise me to be a whore, and nobody with any self-respect would let anyone use them. I don't care if it's for sex or drugs."

I rolled my eyes cuz being a whore is what saved me from a lot of shit. But that wasn't none of their business.

"Who am I kidding? My parents would disown me if I slept with anyone who was not my husband," she said, half laughing. "They'd kill me if they ever knew I was even dating a guy like Donte."

"Why do you say that?" I asked.

"Because number one, he's not Ethiopian, and number two, he's not Ethiopian." Yenee laughed again.

"Well, at least you're laughing," Jacylyn said with a slight smile. "I am so hungry. How long are they gonna let us starve in here?"

"I wonder what time it is," Nakeeda said.

"Do you think we're in a house or an apartment?" I asked, walking to the walls and touching it. When I knocked, it felt hard like cement and not the weak stuff they used for walls at any apartment I'd ever lived in.

"I think we're in a warehouse or something," Nakeeda said.

"I still don't know why we're here," Jacylyn said. "My mother is going to go ballistic when she finds out."

"You better hope we get out of here alive," Yenee warned.

I hadn't even thought about the possibility that we might not make it out of here. Fear crawled down my back like cold air had just entered the stuffy room. I wondered if Rich was worried about me. He had to be back from his meeting by now.

The locks on the door was being unbolted. We all froze. My eyes went from Nakeeda to Jacylyn and then to Yenee. Skinny Man and Oily-Haired Man walked in with bowls. *Finally, we could eat.* When I got mine, I saw a few spoonfuls of beans with red and green peppers. *Was this it?* They walked back out and locked the door. Everybody but Yenee dug in and ate like it was the best thing we had ever had.

"Look at you . . . licking your bowls like the dogs they're making us out to be," Yenee whispered.

I rolled my eyes. She must've bumped her head if she

thought I was gonna let myself starve to death on top of all of this other shit.

"You really need to eat, Yenee," Nakeeda said. "You don't know when the next time they gonna give us something."

"I am not an animal, and I will not live as one," she mumbled. "This squalor is for pigs."

Jacylyn snorted and shook her head. "Leave her alone then. I'm getting sick and tired of all these African proverbs."

Yenee grunted. "It doesn't surprise me that you feel that way. The first day we met at the airport, you looked down your nose at me the moment you heard my accent."

Jacylyn said, "No, I didn't. You were seeing things."

Yenee coughed, then said, "Like I saw you take my bag off the conveyor belt and leave it on the floor when you saw it wasn't yours?"

"What does that have to do with anything?"

"You're selfish," Yenee said bluntly. "Yesterday at the market, you only bought yourself things. You come all this way and you only think about yourself as you shop, didn't even buy anything for the person who brought you here."

Jacylyn rolled her eyes. "It ain't none of your damn business what I do!"

"You two stop!" Nakeeda said, trying to be a peacemaker.

"Maybe that's why you're here," Yenee said, coughing more. "So you can learn about yourself. This is a perfect time to reflect, don't you think?"

Jacylyn stood up and snatched Yenee's bowl of food from off the mattress, and then she dumped it in the trash.

"That's taking it too far, Jacylyn," I said.

"Again, selfish," Yenee said. "You could've at least offered it to one of them."

Yenee was right about that part, but I couldn't understand her. After that incident, we all stayed to ourselves for a while. I could tell Jacylyn was still mad at what Yenee had said. Her forehead was crinkled up in rows. Nakeeda tried to get Yenee to drink some water, but she said she wasn't taking nothing from the men who had her locked up like a beast. I watched Yenee bend the spoon back and forth until she finally got the round part to pop off. She put the handle inside a hole in the mattress. What she was doing or thinking about doing seemed too crazy to even ask her about.

An hour went by, and me, Nakeeda, and Jacylyn had each gone to the bathroom at least once. Soon Oily-Haired Man came back to collect the bowls and spoons.

"*¿Donde son su plato y cuchara?*" he asked Yenee.

She pointed to the trash can and smiled. The trash still reeked from my throw up and whatever else was in there before I hurled in it. Oily-Haired Man made a face and stormed back out the door.

"So even they think it's revolting in here, too!" she giggled in a hushed tone.

More time seemed to slowly tick away. A gigantic chocolate cockroach slid between the crack in the door. At first I wanted to kill it, just like I would do if I saw one at home, but it ran up the wall and waited for a while, like it was watching us. The antennas moved back and forth like it was shaking its head. I watched it run across the door and over to the bathroom, then disappear. I shut my eyes and thought about Rich. The last kiss he gave me. The couples massage we shared at the resort. How he looked at me like he never wanted me to be somewhere without him. I thought about the last time he fucked me like he loved me. I could feel the tears sliding down my face, but I wasn't gonna open my eyes and let the memory disappear. I wanted to forget where I was and be back in the tree house with my man, making love. The tighter I closed my eyes, the more I really felt like Rich was touching me. His strong but gentle hands rubbing my body. I felt his warm kisses all over my neck and down my belly, then down my thighs. It felt like butterfly wings flapping against my skin. It felt so real I opened my eyes.

"Aiiii," I screamed at the gigantic cockroach that ran down my knee. I jumped off the mattress and grabbed my shoe. "I'ma kill your nasty ass!"

"No, don't kill it," Nakeeda said.

"It's all that perfume," Yenee said, laughing. "What is it called?"

"Le Funk Couture," I said in my best French accent.

"What I would do to take a bath right now," Jacylyn finally said.

Yenee sucked her teeth. I laid back down on the mattress beside Jacylyn and practiced my sign language alphabets.

"You know how to do sign language?" Nakeeda asked.

I nodded.

"Wow. I've always wanted to learn how to do that. I think it's so amazing that people can have full conversations without saying a single word."

"I would've never thought you could do that," Yenee said.

"Why not?" I asked.

"You just don't look like the type," Yenee mumbled.

"And what type is that?" I asked, confused.

Yenee ain't answer me; she just looked away.

"Why don't you just say it?" Jacylyn said, rolling her eyes. "'You look too ghetto to know anything.'"

"Is that what you meant?" I asked Yenee.

Yenee was quiet, but tucked her lips back like that's what she wanted to say but was choosing not to.

"Can't get her ass to shut up no other time, now the bitch can't talk," Jacylyn snapped.

"Yenee, is that how you see me?" I asked, sitting up on my elbow.

She looked away. *I guess if you ain't had nothing good to*

say, don't say nothing at all. I shook my head and looked the other way.

"I guess you got flaws just like I do," Jacylyn snarled. "Bourgie-ass bitch."

"Y'all need to stop being so damn catty," Nakeeda said, looking back and forth from Yenee and Jacylyn. "The last thing you need to worry about is who we was before we got caged up in this room. What matters is who we are now—four women with nothing but the slightest bit of hope—and who we gon' be when we get out. Survivors."

"I don't know about hope. I have my dignity, not hope," Yenee corrected.

"No, you have too much pride if you ask me," Jacylyn cut in.

"I have hope, Nakeeda," I said. Maybe only a little bit, but I had it. Wasn't no way in hell I was gonna give up after all the wild shit I been through in my life.

"Good," she said, giving me a tight smile.

We was all quiet again for a long time, and then soon I fell asleep.

The next time the locked door opened again, someone hurried over to the lightbulb and smashed it. Pieces of glass rained to the ground, and it became pitch-black in the room.

"Get off of me!" Yenee screamed out. "I can smell your rotten breath, you dirty dog!"

I was too scared of what was going on to move. No

one moved. It sounded like a lot of commotion. Yenee fighting back maybe, but her screams was muffled under something. I thought about Ryan and what happened to me. I shook my head to erase the memory. I wanted to help her even though she thought so low of me. I wondered if Nakeeda was gonna jump in it. She seemed to want to be peacemaker so bad, but when she ain't move, either, I rolled over and covered my head with my arms, trying to block out everything but the sound of skin slapping on skin and the groans coming from the throat of Skinny Man.

When I woke up a few hours later, the room was still dark. I heard Yenee's soft crying. I tried not to feel guilty for what had happened to her earlier. I wondered why none of us had jumped the Skinny Man. We probably all could've taken him if we wanted to. Two of us could've held him down while the other one wrapped our leg chain around his neck. I never even seen him or Oily-Haired Man with a weapon. Yenee sniffled more. The sounds of her whining in the dark like that made me feel sick to my stomach. It seemed like she cried for hours. I tried to block it out as best as I could. Then like she was reading my mind, Jacylyn said, "Shut the fuck up!"

Yenee sniffled again and then was quiet for a while. I wondered why she ain't use that broken spoon she had stuffed inside the mattress. After several long, quiet minutes, Yenee started crying again. I knew what she was thinking about. Her parents. What people was gonna say? She seemed to feel more guilty about what had been done to her than sad.

"Shut the fuck up!" Jacylyn shouted again. "You brought that shit on yourself, running your damn mouth!"

This time I ain't agree with Jacylyn. Ain't nobody deserve to be raped.

"That's enough," Nakeeda said. It was the first time I had heard her voice in some hours. I wondered if she still had hope.

Time kept going by, at least an hour or two, cuz I practiced signing "The Pledge of Allegiance," "Twinkle, Twinkle, Little Star," and every song I knew by heart. I thought about Mommy and what she'd think of me being here right now. She kept telling me to slow down. I guess she was right. Soon I heard someone messing with the locks on the door.

"¿Que pasa con la luz?" Oily-Haired Man asked. He shut the door and locked it again before coming back, this time with Skinny Man. One of them put another lightbulb in the light. As soon as they cut the lights on, Nakeeda let out a high-pitch scream. I looked at what she was looking at and couldn't believe the bloody red mattress. Blood was even on Nakeeda's dress. Oily-Haired Man and Skinny Man seemed to go crazy, speaking in tongues at one another. Yenee had cut open her wrists. Who knows how long she had been bleeding out. Her eyes was slightly open.

"*¡Está muerta!*" Oily-Haired Man shouted.

"Oh no," I said. I felt another chill take hold of my body, even though it was steamy hot in the room. I ran to the trash can and threw up. Yenee had definitely been right about one thing—I wasn't dreaming cuz this nightmare wasn't ending.

24

After they took Yenee's lifeless body out of the room, we ain't say nothing to each other. Jacylyn even seemed to be deeply fazed by what happened. I couldn't believe they left the mattress right where it was. My soul felt empty. Yenee's spirit seemed like it was hovering in the rank room, still judging us. Even though I knew she'd rather die fighting, in the end, killing yourself still meant they won. And as much pride as she seemed to have in herself, I couldn't believe she chose to go out like that.

We all tried to flip the mattress over cuz it hurt seeing Yenee's bloodstains there. The other side was just as trifling as the front. It made me think there was a lot of other girls here before us, doing God knows what. My mind went back to the triplets. Where did Smurf meet them? Was they some random girls he and his two friends happened to run into somewhere? Was they hookers trying to make a dollar out of fifteen cents? I just couldn't understand how they could let these men have their way with us.

Nakeeda had squeezed on our full-size mattress cuz nobody wanted to sleep on Yenee's deathbed.

"It's starting to get to me," Nakeeda admitted.

"Don't give up. We gon' be all right," I said, surprised that I had said it.

"Think so?" Nakeeda asked.

I nodded. Hell, if I couldn't believe that, I might as well kill myself, too.

"Have y'all ever thought that maybe they had something to do with it?" Jacylyn asked.

"They who?" I asked.

"Our boyfriends," she said. "Ty, Ed, Rich...Donte."

"No, not my Ed. No," Nakeeda said, shaking her head. "I'm not even trying to hear that."

"Why you think that?" I asked Jacylyn.

"Cuz it's yayo," Jacylyn said. "Think about it. They went to a meeting on some island. Probably met some people who flew in on some crop duster, and now suddenly we're here."

"Not my Ed, honey. I'm not even going to believe that," Nakeeda said, shaking her head some more. "We been together too long and through too much for him to even consider making me do that."

"Hmmm...." Jacylyn sighed, sounding doubtful. "What you think, KiKi?"

I took a deep breath. I could only hope my Rich ain't set me up like that. Even though I could see what Jacylyn was getting at, my heart said Rich would never do that to me. True, we hadn't been together long enough for me to think that he wouldn't do it, and no, unlike Nakeeda, we hadn't been through a lot. I just ain't think he would do me this way. He told me he saw something in me that even I hadn't seen in myself. I knew smuggling drugs back home wasn't what he saw for me.

"Niggas will do anything for money," Jacylyn said.

"So will bitches," I said. "Trust me on that one."

"Well, this ain't the first trip that he's taken me out of the country," Nakeeda said. "We just came back from Martinique for Thanksgiving."

"Oh, I was supposed to go, but I needed my passport," I said.

"Wait, was Ty there?" Jacylyn asked with an attitude brewing in her voice.

Nakeeda was quiet for a while. She gave her that innocent church girl look that I'd come to notice about her ever since we'd been stuck in this room. The kind of look that said, "I might think dirty thoughts, but you'd be the last to know."

"Nakeeda, tell me the truth!" Jacylyn said angrily.

"Yeah, he was there," she said.

"He brought another girl, didn't he?" Jacylyn asked.

"Why are you worried about that right now?" I had to ask.

"Cuz that motherfucker probably set me up to be in here right now! You should wanna know if Rich took another girl."

"Did he?" I asked.

"No, he was the only one by hisself. Even Donte brought another girl, too."

I felt relief wash over me.

"See, is that what they do? Bring chicks out of the country and turn them into...mules or whatever it is they call them?" Jacylyn asked.

"Was Smurf there?" I asked.

"Yeah, he was. I think it was their first time meeting Salvador," she whispered.

"Who's that?" I asked.

"I'm not supposed to say."

"Fuck that," Jacylyn said. "Who is it?"

"It's Smurf's connect," Nakeeda whispered.

"See, all this shit just seems too fishy. I promise, these dudes set us up," Jacylyn said, clapping her hands for more effect.

"Not my Ed," Nakeeda said without flinching. I admired how secure she seemed about her boyfriend.

"How long y'all been together?" I asked.

"Since I was a freshman at Temple. This is our third year together."

"Oh, for real?" I said.

"Yeah, he would never do anything to hurt me," she said. "Ever."

I wished I could make Rich feel that same way, but I had betrayed his trust. He never even asked me details about what happened with Ty. Just the thought of me and Ty doing something that I would ever consider keeping a secret left him hurt. I thought he'd be pissed about the coke, but me and Ty's incident was worse. My heart still told me he'd never hurt me, especially not like this.

I stood up to get another bottled water. As soon as I went back to the bed, I heard the door unlock again. This time they shoved another girl in the room. She was Hispanic. I could see how afraid she was. I couldn't believe they replaced Yenee like it wasn't no big deal. We ain't know what to say to her, and since she only spoke Spanish wasn't nothing we could say to each other. I understood tears, and I understood fear. I even tried to use sign language, wondering if she might recognize some of the letters, but I found out real fast that was a dumb idea.

The two amigos came in later with needles. They poked each of us, then gave us a glass of clear liquid to drink, except for the Spanish girl. It tasted like lemons and vinegar. It had to be the same stuff Mommy gave me when I was little, constipated from eating too much cheese or something. They made us drink it all. They used the tube and funnel to force the Spanish girl to swallow. The drug they stuck us with made us all groggy and sleepy. When we finally woke up, it was a fight to the bathroom. Later, I tapped the girl and pointed to myself. "KiKi," I said. Then I pointed to Jacylyn and said her name and then to Nakeeda and said her name, too.

I could tell she understood cuz she said, "Elena." I smiled, hoping she wouldn't feel as afraid as she did before. Elena smiled back even though it wasn't a true smile. Who could really smile in a room as trifling as this?

A couple hours seemed to pass by before the door unlocked again. I could smell burning cinnamon as soon as the door opened. Instead of it just being the fat oily-haired man with the scruffy beard and the skinny man with all the tattoos, Smurf walked in, smoking a cigar. My mouth fell open. It *was* him. Elena jumped off Yenee's mattress and stormed toward the door. Skinny Man punched her until she collapsed on the floor.

"Calm that bitch down," Smurf said, his Haitian accent strong.

Skinny Man picked her up off the floor and threw her on the bed. Smurf plucked his ashes on the floor just where Elena had been lying. He said, "I see y'all been giving them problems. That's why I had to come down here myself to see what's going on."

I couldn't believe he was standing there.

"Look at you, KiKi. You look bad. Real bad. All of you do. But it won't be for long, ladies. I just need you to do something for me. Something really, really important."

We all was too stunned to speak. My ass was still on fire from the last trip to the toilet. I ain't even wanna wipe my butt cuz it was hurting so much, and here he was walking in here smoking a cigar, like he was on vacation.

"Well, don't look so happy to see me."

Yenee had killed herself cuz of *him*. Her blood was still on the mattress across from me, and her spirit was still in the air. We been starved, beaten, chained, and locked in here like animals, and he was standing there with a grin on his face like this was just another day at the beach.

"In a few minutes, you're going to swallow something important for me. KiKi, you should be good at that," he said, smiling. My eyes grew small at his cheap comment. "In exchange for your service, I'll let you go home. If you fuck up in any way, you'll be carried out of here in a trash bag, just like your girlfriend was."

Nakeeda winced. I covered my mouth with my hand, closed my eyes, then shook my head. I couldn't believe he had said that so easily. I couldn't believe he was someone who I'd had sex with before.

"But why us?" Jacylyn had to know.

"Why not you?" he said. "You enjoyed yourself in Costa Rica, right? Did you pay for anything?"

Skinny Man laughed, making me realize he understood English the whole time.

"I have your passports. I have your IDs. I know

where you live back home. I know who you live with. I know who you love and who loves you. If you want to fuck with me, try me now."

I thought about Mommy and Yodi. That was the address on my license. I thought about Rich.

"Come here," he said, looking at me.

I stood up and reluctantly walked toward him. He put his hand on my stomach and kneaded his knuckles. "Nice."

"You come here," he said to Nakeeda.

I hadn't noticed until now that she was crying. Smurf rubbed her stomach, too, then he did the same thing to Jacylyn. "They're ready now," he said to the two Spanish dudes.

After Smurf left, I watched Oily-Haired Man fill the fingertips of latex gloves with the packets of white powder. Then he cut and knotted it with a plastic string. I couldn't believe how simple they made it look and that the thin casing was supposed to be strong enough not to tear inside of me. I think all of us was terrified that one would leak. Elena was the only person who wasn't gonna have to swallow the packets now. Next, Oily-Haired Man made me swallow three pellets straight. He gave me bottled water to help them get down. By the fifth pellet, I was already starting to feel full.

Oily-Haired Man shouted, *"¡Tragarlo! ¡Tragarlo!"* and moved his hand back and forth, showing me to hurry up.

I drank more water and took the next pellet from his

hand. It hurt to swallow, and the water wasn't helping. By the time I had got to eight, I wanted to lie down. My stomach felt so tight, but Oily-Haired Man looked angry. He said, *"¡Tragar mas! ¡Tragar mas, bonita chica!"*

I walked around in tiny circles to see if the packets would settle in my stomach. I put my hands on my hips and blew air in and out. My stomach hurt more when I did that. Tears slid down my cheeks. I couldn't squeeze no more pellets inside of me. I couldn't, but I could tell Oily-Haired Man ain't wanna believe it. How did it come to this? He gave me another packet and waited. I looked at Nakeeda. Skinny Man was giving her more packets to swallow, too. Jacylyn had already reached her max and was laying on the mattress. I took the packet from Oily-Haired Man, rolled my eyes, and threw my head backward so that the packet would fall straight back without hitting any teeth or even my tongue. Then I shut my mouth and tried to swallow. It felt like it was stuck in my throat, so I took a long swig from the water bottle and tried to suck it down my throat for a second time. Wasn't no way in hell I could ever snort this shit again. I wondered if people who snorted it knew this was how it had to come in the country first.

The two sweaty men made sure that the number of pellets they wanted us to smuggle in was inside each of us before they left. Jacylyn had eleven. I had twelve, and Nakeeda had managed to swallow fourteen. She wouldn't stop crying after they had left.

"You not losing hope, are you?" I asked.

She sniffled, then said, "I think this is karma."

"What do you mean?" I asked.

She just shook her head and kept her mouth closed for a while. I could tell her mind wasn't in the room for a while. Then she said, "When I was a freshman, I did something bad." Her eyes was in a far-off place.

"Don't start talking crazy, Nakeeda," I said, but even Jacylyn had sat up to hear what she was saying to me.

"Ed got me pregnant. I don't know what happened. I was on the shot. Well...I forgot to get another one when I was supposed to. I lied to Ed and told him that I did. I was being selfish. When I found out I was pregnant, I was devastated. I had just got to college. My parents had sacrificed so much so I could be there. Neither one of them had ever gone to college. I was the first one of their kids to go. Plus, with the grades I had in high school, it seemed like I could really graduate and be something they could be proud of." She paused for a while before saying, "I wasn't ready to have a baby. I wasn't ready to deal with it."

"What happened?" I asked.

"You had an abortion?" Jacylyn asked.

Nakeeda shook her head, then wiped new tears that had just as quickly fallen. "I was four and a half months when I found out I was pregnant. My periods was coming on but real faint. Ed couldn't believe it. He said he wasn't ready to be a parent, either. I knew I couldn't.

How was I gonna disappoint my mother and father? Daddy had been dropping dollars in a savings account ever since I made the honor roll twice in a row in fourth grade," she said, smiling. "Mommy told all her coworkers I was gonna be a lawyer or a reporter. How could I disappoint her by dropping out to be a mommy instead?"

"What happened already?" Jacylyn asked, clearly annoyed.

"Me and Ed went back and forth about what to do. He said give it up for adoption. I said abortion. I ain't want my child finding me later, making me feel terrible about what I decided to do. I just couldn't do it."

"So you was selfish, too?" Jacylyn asked.

"Yes, I was," Nakeeda said with no feeling in her voice. "I was selfish. I wanted to make my parents proud. I wanted to have a career and be more than what my brother and sister had ended up becoming, and I ain't want no baby to tie me down."

Nakeeda's eyes swelled up with more tears. "I hid the pregnancy cuz I had missed the cutoff time. I ain't go home for breaks. I told them not to come visit me. I wore big clothes, did whatever I had to. Five months was too old. I could feel the baby moving. Kicking and twisting around, but I ignored her."

"Her?" I asked.

"The baby was a girl," Nakeeda said, wiping tears.

"Every time I felt her moving around, I told myself it

was gas or cramps or something crazy like heartburn to keep me from calling it a baby. Ed acted just like I wasn't pregnant, too. He never touched my stomach. He never asked questions about anything. He actually up and disappeared for a while. Not answering my calls. Sending them straight to voice mail. With him not being around, it made everything easier for me to ignore my baby, too. I treated my stomach like I had a tumor. I got bigger clothes and acted like it was gonna be removed one day."

"How could you be that selfish?" Jacylyn asked, disturbed.

"Stop cutting her off!" I shouted.

"One day Ed showed up, saying he had an idea." Nakeeda whispered the last few words. She shook her head like the memory was too much for her to think about. "I agreed with his plan."

"What was it?" Jacylyn asked.

Nakeeda wiped her face with the back of her hand. "I didn't even know what contractions was. I hadn't read a thing about giving birth. Never went to a single class. I didn't want to know. Knowing would've made the pregnancy real. I ignored the pulsing happening in my stomach. I ignored it until I couldn't no more cuz they was coming too hard and too quick. I called Ed. I was scared. He told me to get a motel room and that he'd meet me as soon as he could. He drove from D.C. to Philadelphia. But by the time he got there, I had already had the baby. She ain't even cry when she came out. She just looked at me. I can still see her innocent face." Nakeeda broke down crying. I rubbed her shoulders and let her cry it out.

"What happened to her?" Jacylyn asked.

Nakeeda took a deep breath and drank some water. Then she said, "I ran the bathwater. I wanted...I wanted to clean her off. I wanted her to cry, to smile, to do something, but she didn't. She didn't even seem to hear the water running. She didn't move, she just stared at me. I held her over the water, thinking I could keep her. I could do what I was supposed to. I could forget about what people thought about me and just raise her. I don't know how long I held her there, but she looked like an angel looking back at me. Soon my arms felt heavy, and I let them fall a bit. My hands had grazed the water, and soon I was letting her slip into the tub. I closed my eyes and ran out of the bathroom!" Nakeeda wailed. "I stayed on the, on the bed...until Ed finally showed up. Blood was all over the sheets, the towels, and the mattress. When Ed walked in, he hugged me first and let me cry until he finally said, 'Where is it?' 'She. Where is she?' I corrected him before pointing to the bathroom."

I couldn't believe church girl Nakeeda was the person telling me this story.

"Unh, unh, unh." Jacylyn shook her head.

"When he went inside the bathroom, he stood at the door for a long time. Then he ran back out and left the

room. He came back with a duffel bag. He stripped the
sheets, stuffed them plus the towels in the bag, and then
he took it in the bathroom. When he came out, he told
me to get dressed before he carried the bag to the car.
The scariest thing was taking the water out of the tub so
I could wash off everything. I knew it was the water in
the tub that killed her."

"No, *you* killed her!" Jacylyn said, putting her
straight. "And here I was thinking you was Miss Sweet
Perfect!"

"Shut up, Jacylyn!" I yelled. I was getting sick of
her shit. She loved to stomp on people when they was
down. The last thing Nakeeda needed was our opinions.
I got up to get her another water. When she seemed
ready to talk again, I asked, "What happened next?"

"Me and Ed bought a trunk from a thrift shop. Then
we found a small storage place off of some back road in
Lebanon County and rented a unit. We still make pay-
ments on it the first of each month," she said sadly.

"So not only did you kill her, but every month you
pay to keep your secret a secret," Jacylyn said. "You dis-
gust me."

"Stop. That's enough!" I said. Even if what Nakeeda
did was wrong, wasn't nothing our words could do
to bring that baby back. We still had to deal with
each other and our crazy, fucked-up situation now. This
wasn't the time to beat her up for that horrible decision
that obviously still ate at her mind.

"You should've put yourself in that goddamn trunk, you stupid bitch!" Jacylyn shouted.

Instead of attacking Jacylyn back, Nakeeda just cried, "I'm sorry. I'm so sorry."

"And you still think Ed ain't have nothing to do with setting you up? He can't stand your ass for what you did to his baby. You're right, this is karma for you," Jacylyn added.

"So if it's karma, then what the hell did *you* do?" I snapped.

Jacylyn cut her eyes at me and said nothing. It couldn't have been karma. I wasn't gonna believe that Nakeeda being trapped in this room had something to do with choices we made or the men we loved. If it did, what did I do so bad? Why didn't Donte, Ty, Ed, or Rich show up with Smurf? I needed to believe that Rich ain't have nothing to do with it. That he still wanted to protect me. It was the only thing that kept me from losing it like the rest of them.

25

Nakeeda coughed and twisted back and forth all through the night. Even though Jacylyn went off on her, she still slept in the full-size bed with us while poor Elena slept on Yenee's mattress. Oily-Haired Man came in with cold cups of orange juice filled with that pulpy stuff I usually hated. But now it was the best thing I ever had. Skinny Man came in the door with a gun in his hand. He told us to stand up. When Elena stood up, he pushed her back down on the mattress. Oily-Haired Man unlocked our legs from the chains, and then he made us hold each other's hands before they led us down the hall. None of us had our shoes on, and the ground was wet and smelled like urine. We had been in an old warehouse that stored tires and car parts. I felt so weak. My legs was so wobbly cuz it was the most steps I had taken in a long time.

Skinny Man made us climb inside a dirty yellow minivan, and then they drove out of the building. The sunlight was too much for my eyes. I blinked until they adjusted. We was still in the city. I couldn't believe it. We drove past tourists and merchants buying and selling like it was a normal day. I saw a flashing sign on a bank that had the temperature at 92 degrees, the time at 3:17, and the date at December 26. We had been in the room for three days. Except for a small bowl of beans, we ain't have nothing to eat. I wanted to scream out the window. I wanted to let somebody know that we wasn't supposed to be here. I wanted to jump out of the van and make a run for it, but I couldn't get my arms to reach the latch. Maybe I was too scared to try it.

I looked over at Nakeeda. She had her head leaning against the window and her eyes closed. Her hand rubbed her stomach. I wondered if she was thinking about her daughter or if she just didn't feel good. Jacylyn was looking at all the places we passed like she was trying to spot something she recognized. I knew I couldn't. Everything looked the same to me. Pink, yellow, peach colors swirling into one another. I closed my eyes and opened them when I heard the screechy brakes come to a stop.

"*Vamos,*" Oily-Haired Man said. We was at a motel. They made us hold hands again, and then we walked into a room. There was clothes and shoes for us. Oily-Haired Man pointed to the bathroom, then threw a towel and some soap at me. I was delighted all of a sudden. I could finally scrub off the gross funk that layered my skin. I could try to erase Yenee from my mind. I could erase the disgusting memory of that hideous room. I grabbed a green Costa Rica T-shirt, a pair of jeans, and a clean bra that was way too small from off the bed, then headed to the bathroom. I couldn't wait to lather the soap over my skin. I even washed my hair. I wanted to take the lace front off completely but couldn't. The hot water and the lavender soap was a dream. I watched the brownish-gray sludge fill the tub and leave a cakey line around it.

"Hurry up!" Jacylyn yelled on the other side of the door. She was right; now *I* was being selfish. I hurried and dried off before throwing a towel around my head and sliding into my clothes. As soon as I opened the door, Jacylyn flew inside. The tub still had a nasty ring around it.

Skinny Man sat in a chair at the door, watching us with his gun on his thigh. Nakeeda was lying on the bed, curled up in the blanket. I could tell she wasn't feeling well. She was shivering, but there was sweat on her forehead.

"You okay?" I asked.

"I think something went wrong," she whispered.

I looked confused.

"I feel terrible," she said, trembling.

"Hey, she need some water!" I yelled at Skinny Man. "*¡Agua rápido!*"

Skinny Man smiled and didn't move an inch.

I grabbed a plastic cup and went to get her some water from the bathroom. When I came back, Nakeeda said no.

"You need to drink this," I said.

"That's okay," she whispered. "Look, I need you to do something for me."

"What?"

"If something happens to me and I don't make it, I want you to promise me something."

"Don't say that. We're gonna make it. You sound like you've lost hope."

"KiKi, promise me... when you get back home that you bury my daughter. Her body belongs in a grave and not how I left her," she cried.

"Nothing's gonna happen to you. We're gonna make it, Nakeeda."

"She's in Lebanon," Nakeeda said in a low voice. "Lebanon Storage. Unit 111A. Promise me."

"We're gonna make it."

"Promise me."

"I promise," I said.

She was good for a while. I kept wiping her sweaty forehead with tissues from the nightstand, and she kept shuddering. After a while Nakeeda shook even more than she did before, like she was having a seizure. Hard shakes that made her shoulders rise off the bed. Her eyes rolled to the back of her head.

"Keep your eyes open!" I yelled. "Hey, Nakeeda!"

She just kept shaking harder, and white bubbles foamed at her mouth.

"Oh my God, she needs help!" I screamed at Skinny Man, but he ignored me.

"Hey!" I screamed again, but when he didn't jump up quick enough, I smacked Nakeeda hard until she opened her eyes, but the look staring back at me was empty.

I cried out at the top of my lungs. Jacylyn ran out the bathroom. "What's wrong?" she screamed.

"She's . . . not breathing," I cried.

"Fuck!" Skinny Man finally shouted, and then he said something in Spanish. He took out a cell phone and spoke Spanish to whoever was on the other line. I stayed with Nakeeda and rocked her in my arms as the tears ran down my cheeks until Jacylyn peeled my fingers away.

"Oh my God, oh my God," Jacylyn repeated over and over, walking around in circles.

I wiped the foam from Nakeeda's mouth with my thumbs, then rocked her some more. *How could this happen?* I cringed knowing that one of the bags must've burst inside of her. I looked at Jacylyn, who looked just as scared as me. "What's happening to us?"

An hour later, Smurf came to our motel room with the two crazy-looking goons that had been on the trip with us earlier standing behind him. One look at Nakeeda's body under the blanket and he said three words I'll never forget: "Cut her open."

I blinked back the shock of what he said, and then I felt my lungs closing up, just like they did when Rich found out about me and Ty. Short, quick breaths lurched out of my throat. I was hyperventilating again.

Pop.

The sting of Smurf's smack ain't change my breathing to normal. He was a monster in a nightmare that was never ending. I rubbed my burning cheek and blew a long breath across my lips.

"Calm the fuck down!" Smurf barked. "You two will keep your mouths shut about this, or I promise you, I'll kill you myself!"

With horror, I watched Skinny Man and Oily-Haired Man yank Nakeeda up and carry her limp body to the bathroom. I was too shocked to keep looking.

"Let's go!" Smurf said before standing back so his goons could push me and Jacylyn out the door and into their minivan. Inside, Smurf showed us our passports and licenses. He showed me a picture of Mommy and a picture of Yodi with Chrissie and Kamau that was in my wallet. My body shuddered nervously. Smurf showed Jacylyn a picture of a baby. *Wow, she had left a little boy at home?*

"Tyrelle Elijah. Six months," Smurf read from the back of the picture.

She had a baby by Ty? Now I understood why she was so pissed off. If he had set her up, then what would that say about their relationship? Jacylyn's tears streamed down her face. I squeezed her leg. Maybe she felt guilty about being selfish coming on the trip without him.

"Do you bitches understand how serious this is for me?" Smurf shouted, staring at each of us long and hard. "I don't eat, I don't sleep until I get back what's mine!"

I felt like I was in a movie. This couldn't be happening for real. People was dying left and right. Guns in my face. Threats on my life and my family's life. I knew what Smurf was capable of cuz of what happened to Nut a couple years ago, but this was too surreal. Instead of enjoying my last ride in Costa Rica, looking at the beautiful sights, I felt horrible as Smurf's goons drove to the airport. I wanted to erase every memory from my mind of this foreign place. Yenee. Nakeeda. I thought about jumping out of the moving minivan again but couldn't will myself to do it.

Once we got to the airport, Smurf's goons took suitcases from the trunk, gave me and Jacylyn one, and then took one apiece. They left the car in the parking lot. It wasn't my suitcase, and I knew the one Jacylyn had wasn't hers, either. They felt pretty light. When we walked inside the airport, I felt strange. We went from being trapped in a filthy, tiny room with four girls to being in a huge, busy place with hundreds of people. So much chatter, so much noise, so much confusion. I wanted to tell every person who made eye contact with me what Smurf was making us do. I saw security walking around looking like they wanted me to confess our crime, but I was too scared of what it might mean for my family. When it was time to go through customs, I wanted to shout out as loud as I could "I have drugs inside of me!"

After all the questions that I said no to, they just let me through. Tears swelled in my eyes. I thought about Yenee and Nakeeda cuz they should've been leaving with us. How could we leave here without them? What was their family gonna think about them vanishing into thin air like that?

"That went smooth," Smurf said. "Y'all hungry?" We both was starving so we nodded. Then Smurf said, "Too bad. You think I want you fucking up my shit!"

Him and his goons that he called Gorilla Zoe and Green Mile bought arroz con pollo, torturing us while we waited for our flight. Their food smelled so good. My stomach burbled. When Smurf heard it, he looked at me crazy.

"Here," he said digging in his pocket for money. "Go up there and buy you and her some orange juice. Nothing more, nothing less. And your ass better not even think about running."

I rolled my eyes and took the money. Of course, I was thinking about running. But to where? Was Rich still at the resort waiting for me to show up? Was he looking for me around the city? I walked over to the Tampico counter and bought two large orange juices. I looked around the airport while I waited for the drinks. Maybe

I could reach the security guard standing by the coffee counter. I bit my lip as I thought about how everything would happen. What if the guard only spoke Spanish or just a little bit of English? Would he understand me? What was I thinking? I could never do it.

"*Gracias,*" the girl at the counter said as she handed me the two cups.

I walked back to Smurf and sat down feeling defeated. Smurf smiled. He seemed beyond relaxed for what we was about to do.

"Did Ty have something to do with this?" Jacylyn asked.

Smurf grinned. "Is that what's worrying you, sweetheart?"

Jacylyn nodded. I was surprised she had the courage to ask.

"And what if he did?" Smurf asked. "Would you be really pissed at him?"

Jacylyn picked at her straw. I knew sarcasm when I heard it, and I kinda felt bad for her. Wasn't it obvious that she wanted to know so she could have peace of mind?

"What difference does it make?" Smurf asked, like he was thrown off by her direct question.

"It makes a difference," Jacylyn said point-blank.

He finished eating his food, wiped his hands, and drank his soda. Maybe he was wondering if it was worth even saying. A family walked by, and they was laughing at the silly way one of their kids was walking. We watched them until they found a seat. All of a sudden Smurf said, "No, not in the way that you think he did. He brought you here for a vacation, knowing we came here to conduct business. That's just as bad, don't you think? It's disrespectful. If you meant something to him, he should've left your ass at home for this trip."

Gorilla Zoe and Green Mile nodded like the shadows they was. Jacylyn pressed her lips together and rolled her eyes.

"I had to make an executive business decision," he said, smiling. "This shit is better than FedEx."

I wanted him to tell us more, but I knew he wouldn't volunteer the answers I needed. Despite his little sarcastic comments, I did feel a little relief spread over my body, though. Rich ain't know about Smurf's plan. I watched Jacylyn breathe a little easier, too, knowing her baby father ain't plan to use her to smuggle in dope.

"You girls are ride or die bitches, though, right?" Smurf asked, smiling. "This should be easy for you. I know it's easy for you, KiKi. You used to doing what you gotta do to survive, right? Sucking dick, eating pussy, swallowing packets?"

I wanted to tear his face off. I ain't wanna hear the trash spilling out of his mouth. Not now. Not when I was being forced to use my body and risk my life for him. Jacylyn looked at me and shook her head. I sipped my juice and looked away. A few minutes later, he told us to toss our empty cups and follow him. We stood inside the smoking area so he could smoke his cigar. I'll never forget that burning cinnamon scent for the rest of my life.

When we boarded the plane, I was surprised he had us in first class still. Later I figured it was cuz we had a little more space not to be cramping up his packets and it wasn't that many people around us to be all up in his business. My stomach felt so full and tight. I ain't want the packets to burst. The minute the plane took off, I fell asleep.

As soon as we landed in D.C., I woke up like I knew I was finally home and safe. I felt my energy come back. Smurf gave me and Jacylyn a fucked-up look that made me squirm in my seat. When we was allowed to get off the plane, Smurf's goons handed everybody their suitcases and then we walked to the customs area. It was so crowded with screaming babies, yelling parents, hood rats, businesspeople, O.C. girls with orange tans, and more. Security was deep, too. Every entrance was covered with TSA, police, or military people. Some had big-ass German shepherds with them. Sweat drops poured down my forehead. It was so hot. I fanned myself with the Costa Rica T-shirt I had on.

"Relax," Smurf mumbled before disappearing to a different line.

I let my shirt go and waited in the super-long line with Gorilla Zoe and Green Mile, who was standing in between me and Jacylyn. I looked at her. She seemed just as nervous as I was. She kept pulling her fingers until her knuckles cracked. The security here was much more strict than in Costa Rica. I mean, even with all the terrorism stuff, I never knew it would be this bad. I watched them collect everything. The trash was full of people's stuff like plastic bottles, clippers, and lighters. TSA waved their wands over every inch of the people passing through the metal detectors with the slightest beep. They went through suitcases, taking fruit and food they wasn't supposed to bring back. They even took certain shells and jewelry made from rare animals. I pulled my T-shirt away from my chest again, fanning the heat.

"KiKi, just relax," said Gorilla Zoe in a low voice. "You look like something's wrong."

I glanced over at Smurf, who made a face that let me know he would kill me if something ain't go right. Gorilla Zoe handed me my personal information cuz customs was asking for it from some people. I bit my lip and tried to deal with my feelings. We crept closer toward the customs officials. I thought about that tiny room we stayed in, in that warehouse. The foul smell. The tubes those sick men forced down our throats, and the needles they stuck in our arms to numb us while they did it. I remembered Yenee's warnings and the unnatural sounds of her crying all day after Skinny Man raped her. I thought about Nakeeda and her heartbreaking story about what she did in that Pennsylvania motel room. I thought about how hard she tried to keep the peace and make us believe that we was gonna be okay, when in the end she wasn't. I thought about Rich and Mommy and about being home. I was ashamed of my coke habit, but I was never doing that shit again. Knowing that girls were picked off the street, kept in hidden rooms, starved, and poisoned . . . that they had to actually shit it out of their bodies. I ain't want no part of that.

"I need to use the bathroom," Jacylyn said.

"Fuck that," Green Mile said. "You're gonna stand right here."

Jacylyn rolled her eyes and locked her arms across her chest. We crawled toward the front. The closer we got, the better I was able to see the faces of the officials. There was two people running our line, one black woman and one white man. They seemed like two intense people nobody would ever want to fuck with. I watched them asking questions and going through bags like catching crooks was a competition for them. They batted off small talk, funny vacation stories, and other distractions like they was flies.

And then that's when I noticed the woman with the tapered haircut wore a hearing aid. Not just any hearing aid, but the kind that I knew was for advanced hearing loss. The more I watched her reading lips, the more I knew the woman probably knew sign language. It was my chance to be brave like the other girls was. Jacylyn was brave just by finding the nerve to ask Smurf who planned it. Nakeeda was brave by admitting she made a terrible decision and by confessing what she did to her daughter. Even Yenee was brave, fighting Skinny Man off and for fighting for what she believed.

Now it was my turn. There was three people ahead of me in line. I thought about what I was gonna do over and over. Which words could I sign without making Smurf or his dumb-ass goons conscious of what I was doing? I wanted them to take me seriously right away cuz I might only have one chance. I had to choose my words just right. I knew *help* wasn't enough. With all the thoughts flooding my mind, I couldn't believe how quickly it had become our turn in line. My hands felt sweaty. Jacylyn went first. I glanced over at Smurf, who gave me a stern look, then back to Jacylyn, who was answering questions. Soon she was walking through the other side. Then Green Mile was next, answering the questions they asked and showing his ID. I wiped my forehead nervously as I waited. Then it was my go.

I took a step forward. Before the woman could say anything, I signed, "Drug dealers in line put drugs inside us." I waited to see if she understood. When she just stared at me without an expression on her face, I got scared. I signed, "Help us," but the woman's eyes grew big, like she was confused.

The woman said, "You don't have any luggage?"

"Um...it's right here," I said. I couldn't believe I was wrong. What had I done? She ain't understand me, now Smurf was gonna kill me. I looked over to where he had been in line, and he was gone. The woman asked me several questions about my trip: Where did I stay, what did I buy, and if it was business or pleasure. Then she clicked a few buttons on the computer.

"Did you enjoy your trip?" she asked as she typed.

I nodded, but of course I didn't. I wanted to tell her just how fucked up it was, but Gorilla Zoe was breathing down my neck.

"Good. Happy holidays," she said. "You can go."

I had failed. As soon as I took two steps, I heard a lot of commotion behind me. I looked up and watched the police heading my way, K-9s and all, surrounding me and Gorilla Zoe. Green Mile rushed the customs man who had just handed him his bags. Jacylyn screamed.

"What? What I do?" Gorilla Zoe shouted as the TSA dude pushed him.

I couldn't believe it. The woman had understood me after all. I noticed Smurf walking through glass doors. He looked over his shoulder once before disappearing into the crowd. The surprised look on his face was priceless. I exhaled for the first time in four days. It only lasted a short minute cuz I knew that wasn't the last of Smurf.

26

After hours of questioning from the TSA, the DEA, and even D.C. police, a trip to George Washington Hospital where they X-rayed me and Jacylyn to see the packages inside our bodies, and laxatives, we quickly found out that shitting the packages out was the safest way to be done with it all.

Doctors monitored us, making sure none of them burst. Just in case they did, the doctors had something ready to keep us stabilized. I couldn't believe I actually had to stand in a bathtub and push the bags out. It hurt so bad, and standing in that tub was the most humiliating thing I ever had to do in my life, and I had done a lot of shameful things before. This took the cake. The police stayed there until they recovered all twelve packages. The process was so gross and disgusting. I couldn't believe the street value was worth over a hundred thousand dollars alone. Smurf was looking to bring in half a million dollars using all four of us.

I wanted them to catch Smurf's ass so he could spend the rest of his life in jail. I ain't hold back telling the police everything about what happened to Yenee and Nakeeda and even Elena. I described to them the old tire and car part warehouse in San José that had the name Meliano's on the outside. I ain't have a problem testifying about what happened in that tiny room, but Jacylyn said she ain't want to testify. When they started talking about putting us in witness protection, I got nervous and wanted to back out. I had heard how that works before—that you get a new identity, a new place to live in a random city, that you lose touch with your family and friends. With Smurf still missing and wanting to kill me for snitching, it seemed like something I might have to do.

A couple hours had passed by with the nurses feeding me through a tube before an agent rushed in the room to tell me that Elena had been rescued. It made me feel good that I had the courage to do something on my own. It paid off for me, Jacylyn, and Elena. I was proud of myself for the first time in a long time. When I was finally alone, I called Mommy's house. I ain't care who answered the phone but was relieved and happy that it was Yodi and not Ryan. She told me that the police had already called and told them about me.

"Toya's about to bring us up there," she said.

I smiled. "I can't wait to see y'all." Even Toya.

"Hey, Yodi, ask Mommy to make Christmas dinner for me again since I missed it," I said.

"Okay, I will. Mommy said she love you...Hey, Shakira...um, I love you, too," Yodi said.

Now that was something none of us hardly ever said to each other in my family, and even though I knew they loved me, I felt tears welling up in my eyes.

"I love you, too, Yolonda Scott," I said playfully.

"See you in like an hour. It shouldn't take her long to get here."

After I hung up, I laid down. I was so close yet so far from home. I wanted to call Rich but ain't know what to say to him. Where was I supposed to begin? How did I tell him all the psychotic bullshit that had happened since the day we went our separate ways in Costa Rica? I stared at the phone for a while, then back at the TV where the station was on the local news. I picked up the phone. What was I gonna say to him? Would he even believe me? I hung the phone back up, rolled over, and closed my eyes, wishing that when I opened them, I'd know what to say about what happened to me.

I dreamed about Yenee's bloody wrists and Nakeeda's blank gaze again. Only this time, they was in the same tiny room on that bloody, filthy mattress. I woke up sweating and shaking.

"You all right?" said a nurse, standing over me. She was switching the bag connected to the tube in my arm.

I took a deep breath and tried to erase the thoughts from my head.

"Here, swallow this," she said, holding a tiny paper cup with two pills inside.

I drank some juice and chewed the ice until the nurse left. I ain't wanna fall back to sleep this time. I watched TV and waited for Mommy to come. A few minutes later, I heard Kamau and Chrissie before I saw them, and it was the most beautiful sound I ever heard. Mommy, Yodi, and even Toya walked in the room. They rushed me with hugs, except Toya, who waited until everyone had let go of me, and then she said, "I'm glad you're okay. Here's some clothes and stuff you might need while you're in here."

"Thank you, cuz all I got is a too-small T-shirt from Costa Rica, and it's freezing outside, ain't it?" I asked, giving her a small smile. I knew it was gonna take time to work on our relationship, but I was willing to give it a try.

"Mommy said she's gonna fry another turkey for New Year's," Yodi said.

"Good, cuz I'm starving!" I said. I had lost seven pounds in that short time frame. "Hopefully, I can eat real food by then, too. I'm surprised they let all y'all in here."

"They knew I had to see my baby," Mommy said and kissed my forehead. "I don't cur about dem police people. They better quit playing with me... You gotta tell me what happened!"

I tried to fill them in on everything. Mommy cried as she listened to me remember every detail. Toya shook her head and walked over to the window. It was sick for me to even hear my own voice say the things that happened to me. When I told them about Yenee and Nakeeda, Yodi even teared up a little.

"Well, how long you gotta be here?" Mommy asked.

"I don't know. I'm waiting for the doctor to tell me. Plus, they want me to go testify against the two fools they caught."

"You gon' do it?" Toya asked.

"I think so. I'm just worried about the one who got away," I said in a low voice. "He has my license...with your address, Mommy."

All three of them froze. I knew I had put everybody in danger.

"I don't know what to do," I cried.

Mommy pulled me to her chest and shhhed me the way she used to do when I was little. "We'll figure it out. God has a plan, sweetie."

It was quiet for a while. I guess we all was thinking about what plan God must've had. The doctor came in to check on me and do a quick look over my blood work.

"You seem to be doing well. Everything looks normal, too. You should be able to leave here in another day or two," he said.

"I guess you can come stay with me," Toya said when the doctor left.

As surprised as I was at her offer, I was more concerned about Yodi, the kids, and Mommy.

"Thank you, but if anything, let them stay with you. I don't want nothing to happen to them. I can stay with one of my friends or something."

Toya shook her head. I ain't know if it was cuz of the situation or cuz of something I had said. With her, you never knew.

"How they gon' find this dude? Do they have any clue where he at or where he could be?" Yodi asked.

"I have no idea. I told them everything I knew. I even told them about the house I knew he had in Upper Marlboro," I said, wiping away another tear. This was so fucked up.

"'Kirwuh, look, don't weery about me. I learned a long time ago, what's gonna happen is gonna happen and God will proteck us. Do you understand?"

I nodded even though I ain't feel that way for real. Just as she said it, one of the agents who had been working with me walked in and introduced hisself to my family. He made the offer again for the Witness Protection Program. Mommy told them she ain't wanna be a part of it. Yodi and Toya agreed, too. The detective said they could at least move them to another apartment. Mommy said she'd consider it and let him know. He gave Mommy his card. How could I consider the program if they disagreed with it? I told the agent I was fine and that I would stay with my family.

He said that he would make sure agents and local police was looking out for us until the trial. How certain that was, I wasn't so sure, but after all I'd been through I was willing to take my chances. The agent left us alone.

"Oh, before I forget…Rich called a couple times," Yodi said.

"He did?" I asked, excited. "What did he say?"

"Um, the first time he wanted to know if you was there. And I was like, 'Ain't she with you?' He was like, 'We got into a fight and now all her luggage gone.' I was like, 'Well, she ain't come back here.' Then he was like, 'If she comes, could you please call me.'"

"For real?" I said.

"Yeah," said Yodi. "He called like a couple days later to see if you had showed up, and then that's when we started getting scared cuz you never called and you never came home."

"The next time you leave the country, Shakira, please leave the place you staying, your room number, call somebody to let them know you all right," Toya said. "It's not fair to us to be wondering and worrying every step of the way. Mommy was too scared to even eat the whole time until she finally talked to you today."

Even though I hated to admit it, Toya was right, and I felt selfish for being so careless. I was having too much fun to even think about doing any of that. "I'm sorry" was all I could say.

"Well, you're hur now," Mommy said, squeezing my shoulder. "And the cops and God will proteck us."

"I'm sorry, family, but visiting hours are over," a nurse said, poking her head in the door.

"Are y'all sure you gon' be okay? I can't believe I put y'all in this mess," I said.

"We got Ryan's rockhead ass and his stupid-ass friends to watch us," Yodi said, scooping Kamau up.

Was he any better than Smurf?

"We'll call you in the morning," Toya said, easing out the door.

"Toya?" I called behind her. "I really appreciate what you doing for me. I wanna say . . . I'm real sorry for what happened that day. At the Kennedy Center. I was being a bitch."

A tiny smile crept across Toya's face. "Yes, you was . . . but don't worry about it. It's behind us. Just promise me you're gonna try and take care of yourself for a change."

I closed my eyes and let her words sink in. I knew Toya was talking about everything, not just what I had been through in Costa Rica. I nodded, then said, "I promise."

I felt so ashamed of how what I had been doing was now affecting them. Maybe I should've left everything alone at the airport and my family wouldn't even be in this bind. As soon as I was alone, instead of calling Rich like I really wanted to, I dialed Peaches's number.

She seemed so excited to hear from me. It took

awhile for me to get to the end of my story. I wanted her to hear about all the good parts. The first three days of my trip. I skipped over a lot of the bad parts that happened in the room, except for what Smurf made us do and why I was in the hospital. Peaches went through a roller coaster of emotions in a five-second span. When she finally calmed down, I asked, "Should I call Rich?"

"You haven't called him yet?" Peaches said. "Why not?"

I bit my lip nervously. "I'm worried about what he might say."

"KiKi, after all you went through, you think that nigga not gonna care? He had no idea where you disappeared to, right? Anything could've happened to you. Hell, anything and everything *did* happen! He might be going through a lot of shit worried about your ass. Girl, Rich deserves a phone call."

I thought about what Peaches said long after we got off the phone. Maybe I was overreacting. I felt like such a different person since I left that warehouse room. So much had happened, and I was worried about what Rich might think of me. In a way, Peaches was right. I picked up the phone, then dialed Rich's cell phone number. It rang for a while, then went to voice mail. Listening to his voice on the recording telling me to leave a message made more tears fall down my face. It was the first time I heard his voice in days. Then the beep sounded.

"Um...hey, Rich. It's me. I'm back in D.C. I'm in GW Hospital, though. I should be going home to-morrow," I said, taking a deep breath. "I, um...miss you, and I got so much to tell you. My number is 202-555-7987."

When I hung up, I felt better about calling. I'd figure out what to say to him whenever he did call. I watched TV again and tried not to go back to sleep cuz I was too scared I would have another nightmare. As much as I wanted to forget about what happened less than twenty-four hours ago, I ain't wanna forget about Yenee or the promise I made to Nakeeda. It was easier to watch TV and let my mind drift with whatever was on than to think about the mess I got my whole family into with Smurf.

When the doctor discharged me two days later, I was so happy to be going home with Toya, even if it was blistering cold outside. I stared out the windows, trying to soak in every detail of the city, like I was gonna find something new and out of place. I wanted everything to be just like it was when I left, so I could feel like I hadn't missed anything being away. The people leaned forward against the wind as they rushed down the street and ducked into stores and office buildings to get out of the cold. I couldn't believe it was New Year's Eve and I made it back in time to celebrate the new year with my family. There was still Christmas lights, white wire snowmans, and reindeer decorations up in people's yards and in windows. Once we got to Fourth and W Streets, Ryan's ass was the first person I saw on the corner. He was smoking in front of the apartment building with two other no-life-having dudes from the neighborhood. I saw him flash a smile when he saw us pulling up. I saw Skinny Man's creepy face flash in my head. Ryan walked toward the car. *Please, let him fuck with me today. Please do it.*

"Hey, KiKi! Back from your trip, huh?" he said, smiling. "Heard you had a ball. Bring me something back?"

I rolled my eyes and climbed out the car.

"You can't speak, KiKi?" he said.

I was so hot. I refused to hold my tongue this time. "No, I'm not speaking to your ass, you sick muthafucka!"

"Wait, what's wrong?" Toya asked.

"Yeah, what's your muthafucking problem?" Ryan said, giving me a look that was supposed to make me scared.

I shook my head cuz now wasn't the time. Me and Toya squeezed in the elevator with some other people. I was so heated. As soon as we got off, I could smell fried turkey and all the fixins. When Mommy opened the door, I went straight to the kitchen and opened the tops on the pots.

"It smells delicious, Mommy. Thank you," I said, kissing her cheek.

"See wot you been missing all dese holiday meals you keep skipping," she said, stirring the gravy.

I kissed her cheek again. "I invited Meeka and Peaches, is that cool?"

"Of course. I know they miss you, too."

I wanted to take a real bath and not that mess they had at the hospital. I couldn't get comfortable since nurses and doctors and detectives kept coming in and out. Plus, I couldn't use the stuff I wanted. Never in a million years did I think I would be taking a shower in the same place where Ryan called his home, but things had changed. I wasn't gonna walk on upside-down eggshells around him no more.

As soon as the bathroom got nice and steamy, I locked the bathroom door and cut that nasty lace-front wig off. I climbed in the shower, shampooed my short curly 'fro, then lathered up using some of the Bath & Body Works shower gel I saw in the tub. I wanted to smell like a girl and not like a sick hospital patient. When I was done washing, I used some of the Bath & Body Works lotion, too, and then threw on Yodi's sweater and jeans.

When I came out the bathroom, Mommy was stirring collard greens in one of the pots. Chrissie was sitting in Yodi's lap while her and Toya laughed at something on TV. Ryan was playing with Kamau and some of his Christmas toys on the floor. Mommy's boyfriend, Isaac, was reading the newspaper at the kitchen table. I couldn't believe that just four days ago I was in a

cramped, grimy room with three other girls, chained to
a bed. That just three days ago, I was still shitting coke
out in a bathtub. That just last night I had another terrible nightmare about Nakeeda's baby. It was so odd to
be standing here right now, watching all of them. I felt
that feeling I hadn't felt in a long time. The kind that
made me wish I had some coke to snort, but I shook it
off. I knew that was only a temporary solution to how
uncomfortable I felt. Somebody was knocking on the
door. Ryan went to open it. Peaches stepped in with
Amir, and Meeka stepped in with Quentin. Peaches
looked like she wanted to stab Ryan's ass.

"Damn. Why you looking at me like that?" Ryan
asked.

Peaches took a breath, rolled her eyes, then spoke to
everybody before the two of them gave me a hug. I had
missed my little crew. During dinner, I realized that it
was having good friends like the two of them that made
me get along with the girls in that tiny room. Even
though we was so different, we had a common bond
that made it necessary for us to get along in order for
us to deal with the sick shit that was happening to us.
Peaches and Toya was getting along pretty good over
dinner, talking about the kind of counseling I needed
to get to deal with what I had been through. I was surprised Toya wasn't acting her usual bourgie self. Meeka
was too busy watching her son and Chrissie play together to notice Ryan staring her down like a pervert.

After dinner, I disappeared down the hall to Mommy's room. With all the love in the room, it really made me miss Rich. I was ready to call him again. I picked up the phone and dialed his number.

"Hello?" he answered on the first ring.

"Um...Rich?"

"KiKi?"

I smiled. "Yeah, it's me."

He exhaled a deep breath. "KiKi."

"Rich."

"Man, what the hell happened? You at your mother's, right? Fuck that. I'm on my way. Don't hang up, though. Where the hell you been at? What happened? Why did you leave me?"

He was going a hundred miles a minute. It was too fast. There was so much to tell. Where did I begin? I laid back on Mommy's bed and told him everything that happened from shopping at the market with Caterina, Adriana, and Malia to partying at Castro's. Except for a few "un-huh's" here and there, Rich was quiet mostly. Tears spilled from my eyes when I told him about the ridiculous shit that happened in that room. Suddenly he asked me for the building and the apartment number, and then I heard a knock at the front door. My heart jumped. I ran from the bedroom in time to see Ryan open the door. He took forever to let Rich inside, staring him up and down. As soon as I saw Rich's handsome face, I wrapped my arms around him. He held me long and tight, then kissed me on my forehead, then on my lips.

"Y'all gon' have to take all that shit up outta here!" Ryan yelled from the living room.

"Leave them alone, Rain," Mommy shouted. "Come on in, Rich, make yourself at home."

"How's everybody doing?" he asked, and then he said to me, "You ain't tell me your mother was cooking. I should've stopped and bought something."

Everybody spoke to Rich. I made him a plate and let him eat. Ryan's bum ass kept mugging Rich the whole time, but Rich ain't see him, though I wished he did. I was dying to talk to Rich alone about the trip. I needed to piece the puzzle together for myself, so after everybody said hello, I slipped out the door to sit with Rich in his car. The minute we was in the hallway, Rich hugged me so tight that I felt my whole body stretching.

"I don't wanna let you go, man," he whispered.

I breathed in his scent and closed my eyes. I ain't want the moment to end. I had been holding on to this the whole time I was in that room. I could tell by the way he squeezed and kissed me that he still loved me. When he finally let go, I said, "Rich, what happened when you came back to the room?"

He led me to the elevator and pushed the button.

"Man, the room was tossed upside down, like you just went crazy. All your shit was gone. I kept trying to replay our last conversation over, like...what did I do that made you want to leave. I knew I was pissed at you for that Ty shit, but I was so confused about why you was pissed at me?"

We stepped on the elevator and rode it down to the first floor, and then we walked out to his car. I noticed the silver Impala, the unmarked vehicle at the end of the corner with the detective sitting inside of it. It was so cold outside, I shivered while I waited for Rich to unlock and start his car with his keyless remote. Thank God the heat was already on when I sat inside.

"The first night, I was blown as shit. I mean I drank at the bar all night. I thought maybe you was in one of the other girls' rooms man-bashing and that you'd be all right in the morning. When Ty called, asking if Nakeeda was in my room, we knew something was up. I called Donte and Ed, and their girls was gone, too. Same tossed-up rooms. We went to the police and everything. Told them y'all went shopping in the city and shit and that y'all ain't never come back. At first they thought we all had got robbed, but when we told them our stuff was still there, they was just as confused. And then it was like they thought we had something to do with it. It took them awhile to believe that we ain't do nothing to y'all. Then they showed us the clips of Gorilla Zoe and Green Mile going in and out of all our rooms, leaving out with shit they stole. That's when I knew that dirty nigga Smurf had something to do with it. I wanna kill that nigga, you hear me!"

Rich was so pissed off. I wanted to remind him that I was okay. That I was here with him and safe again.

"I was supposed to protect you, not put you in danger," he said before slamming his fist on the horn. "I wanna kill that crooked muthafucka!"

He shook his head and sat in silence for a minute. Bright lights flashed in Rich's window. It was the detective checking to see if I was okay. I waved my hand to let him know that I was fine.

"When did you come home?" I asked.

He looked down. "Man, after you left that message saying you was in here in a hospital, I called the number you left, but had the wrong number. When I called the front desk, they didn't have you listed in the hospital, not by your last name anyway. I couldn't believe it."

"You was still in Costa Rica all that time?"

He nodded. "When your sister said she never heard from you and that you never came back to D.C., something in my heart told me you was still there in Costa Rica cuz I knew you would've tried to reach your mother if nobody else. I didn't wanna leave without you. I love you."

"I love you, too," I said before kissing him. It was the kiss I had been wanting when we last made love. The kiss that I needed to feel secure that he had forgiven me for betraying his trust. The kiss that I needed to get my mind clear of all the torment that was haunting me every night. I took a deep breath and simply stared at Rich for making me feel so loved.

"There's something else I have to tell you," he said.

I looked up at him confused as he squeezed the steering wheel with both hands. He seemed conflicted as he stared off into the night. A couple cars drove up and down the street before he said, "I haven't been telling you the whole truth, either."

I looked at him strange.

"And I still can't... tell you the truth."

"What are you talking about?" I was totally mixed up.

"All I can say is... I feel fucked up about bringing you down there while I was working. Please forgive me."

"What happened to me wasn't your fault, Rich. I'm here now."

"I was supposed to protect you... and what you went through, just..." He slammed his balled fist against his dashboard and yelled, "Wasn't supposed to happen!"

"It wasn't your fault, Rich."

He shook his head as if there was more he wanted to say, but his eyes told me he wasn't gonna say it.

"We're together now," I said, hoping it was enough to make him forget how he was feeling. Rich picked my hand up to his lips and kissed the back of it. His eyes looked into mine like he was trying to apologize for something, but for the life of me, I couldn't imagine what.

27

Rich and I had just climbed out of his car and was heading back toward the apartment building when Ryan burst through the front door, causing it to make a loud thud against the brick wall.

"The party's over, nigga." His words slurred together. "You can take your ass the fuck home now, slim."

"Ryan, just stop!" I said, trying to avoid his bullshit and walk around him.

"Why your whore ass keep bringing niggas over here for anyway?" Ryan said, getting loud and mugging Rich.

"Hold the fuck up...," Rich said, taking a step closer. I stepped in between them to block whatever was about to go down, but before I knew it, Rich's hand flew up and clamped tight around Ryan's throat.

"What the fuck?!" Ryan struggled for breath and squirmed, fighting to get loose.

"Rich, no!" I shouted. Rage was written all over Rich's face as his grip tightened up. "Rich, he's just a fucking screwup. Let him go!"

The look in Rich's eyes actually scared me. He had no clue about what Ryan had done to me, and I knew by the look in Rich's eyes that if he did, Ryan would be dead.

"Go 'head, slim," Ryan begged, his words spurts of air.

"Rich," I said, looking him deep in his eyes. "Please, stop."

He took a long look at me before he let his grip slack up. "If you ever talk to her like that again, I'll kill your bitch ass."

Rich ain't leave no room for Ryan to doubt his words. Ryan rubbed his throat and breathed in deep. I ain't never seen Rich act that threatening before. I never seen Ryan look that scared before, either. He was still trying to catch his breath when Peaches and Meeka walked out of the building with the kids and take-home plates Mommy must've fixed them. "Hey, there you go," Peaches said. "I was just telling Meeka I'ma treat you to the Red Door tomorrow. What you doing?"

I took a deep breath, glad she and Meeka had interrupted the chaos that was about to erupt between my man and my brother.

"I'm not doing nothing." I loved that spa.

"Damn, I gotta work," Meeka said.

As soon as Peaches used her keyless remote to unlock her truck, gunshots went off. I jumped and screamed even though I thought it was the same usual suspects acting ignorant on New Year's Eve, letting rounds off just because, but when I saw Peaches rock backward on her heels, I knew it was no accident. I screamed again as soon as I saw blood spreading across her lynx fur jacket as she slumped to the ground. Rich made me and Meeka get down with Amir and Quentin. I heard gunshots firing back. It seemed like everything was happening in slow motion. My heart jumped in my chest at the sound of bullets flying. I heard tires pealing down the street, then silence.

"Y'all okay?" Rich asked.

But Peaches was shaking.

I saw Nakeeda all over again on that bed.

I slapped Peaches across her cheeks.

Amir screamed.

"Keep your eyes open, bitch!" I yelled at the top of my lungs. I wasn't gonna let her leave me.

"Tell her to hold on, the ambulance is on its way," I heard the detective saying.

"Hold on, Peaches! Hold the fuck on!" Meeka screamed.

Quentin cried beside her.

I saw Yenee, and I knew I couldn't let Peaches give up her fight. "Amir needs you. I need you. Hold on,

Peaches," I kept repeating as Rich pressed his hands over the wound seeping blood from her coat.

When I heard the ambulance and police sirens, I felt relief calming me. Peaches was still breathing. In all the madness, I ain't realize that Peaches wasn't the only one who had got shot. There was a body laying in the doorway of the apartment building. I could see the bottom of the person's Nike boots. Rich pulled me away when the EMT people took over. I heard women screaming from the building as two more paramedics rushed over to help the person lying in the doorway. It was Mommy and Yodi screaming. Toya was trying to keep them away. *Was that Ryan?* I held on to Rich as I took a few steps toward the building. My heart raced. Mommy ran in place and fanned her hands in front of her. The sounds coming from her throat was too intense. It had to be Ryan. I walked up the steps and looked past the EMTs to see Ryan's wide empty stare. I closed my eyes. Feeling weak, I buried my face in Rich's chest and hid my tears.

"Come on. Give Meeka your car keys so she can take the kids home with her," Rich said.

I did as he said. Then Toya made Yodi and her kids get in her car. Isaac held Mommy as she cried in his arms. I couldn't watch this no more. It was all my fault cuz I ain't follow Smurf's orders. As much as I hated what Ryan did to me, I ain't want him dead. He was still my brother and Mommy's only son. She looked so heartbroken crumpled up in Isaac's arms. Peaches was in an ambulance fighting for her life, and there wasn't nothing I could do about it. This was too much.

Rich said, "We gotta go, KiKi."

"Wait, we wanna ask you some questions," an officer said, but Rich waved him away.

"Not now," he mumbled as I climbed in his car. The detective nodded at Rich and let us go.

Rich's tires squealed as he pealed away from the curb. I looked at my bloody hands and coat. I couldn't believe it was Peaches's blood. Rich's hands was covered in it, too. I shook my head and let the tears fall. All of this was my fault.

"I'ma take you somewhere safe," Rich said, balling out of the neighborhood. "Since Smurf wanna send his sloppy-ass henchmen, I got something for his ass."

What about my family? I kept replaying what had just happened in my head as Rich called Ty to tell him all that went down. Shit was a blur after that. In between tears, I remembered pulling up to his aunt Pat's, her packing up food, then me washing up and changing into some clothes she gave me. I watched Rich throw duffel bags filled with money, guns, and clothes in the back of his Ford F-150, and then he told me to get in the passenger seat. He backed the boat down the driveway and then rode to the highway.

"KiKi, I gotta tell you something I know you might hate me for," he said as we pulled on to the road.

"Don't say that. I could never hate you."

"For this...you could."

I sucked in a huge breath of air and stared at Rich closely. How could that be?

"Aunt Pat ain't really my aunt. Uncle Roy ain't really my uncle, either. He was my mentor."

"Mentor?"

"He was...a detective who got killed about two years ago. He meant a lot to me," Rich said.

I looked at him, confused.

"KiKi," he said, glancing over at me. "I've been working undercover and trying to get with Smurf's Colombian connect for a minute. When I finally did... I never thought what happened to you in Costa Rica would be the price for that."

"Wait a minute," I said, closing my eyes and putting one hand up. What he was saying was too much. His words landed like a ton of bricks in my head. "Back up, Rich."

"That's just it, KiKi. My name ain't even Rich Malloy. It's Rashard Steele."

I covered my face and mouth with two hands before closing them over my face. What had I done? Who was this man? Tears rushed from nowhere. "You played me?"

"KiKi...you wasn't never a part of the plan," he said, squeezing my knee. "You have to believe me. Meeting you was a welcomed distraction from all the shit I was doing. Falling for you was a bonus."

"How can I trust you?" I asked, searching his eyes for an answer.

"KiKi, from the moment I met you, I really just wanted to take you away...let you see something you never seen before. Let you know the world was bigger than all the day in and out drama you see. I could look at you, KiKi, and tell you ain't never dream big in your life. That all you've been used to is setbacks and let-downs. When you was with me, I wanted to make sure you ain't never have to worry. I wanted to make sure you knew that *you* was your beginning. When you first got to Costa Rica, it was like you was dreaming, right?"

As much as I hated to admit it, he was right. I wiped my face with napkins in his glove box.

"I'm sorry for not telling you sooner...but it was too much to chance. My first duty was to the case. You've gotta understand that."

I took a deep breath, desperate to believe what he had shared was the honest-to-God truth. It wasn't like he had known that I ever knew Smurf, and unless he looked me up in some sort of system, he never even knew about my past. "But what about all the businesses you got? The barbershop, the car wash, the Laundromat?"

"It's all just a front. I started cutting hair in college to make extra cash, but the real owners just cooperate with us for situations like this. Favor for a favor, you know?"

"This is a lot. I mean, your name is Rashard. Rashard,

for God's sake?" I said, shaking my head. "What else don't I know about you?"

"KiKi, I'm sorry. I need you to forgive me now."

I looked out the window and replayed everything I thought I knew about him. Where he lived, all the businesses, his friends Donte, Ed, and Ty, the trips out of the country, everything. I felt dizzy. I thought about him waving the detective off a minute ago, him taking me to the shooting range the last time I was down here with him. I thought about how he looked at me those times I craved coke, like he knew I took a hit every now and then, even though he never asked me about it. I thought about everything as we rode into the night.

Finally the marina in Solomons Island came into view along with Ty, Ed, and Donte. Before Rashard opened his car door, I asked, "Are you lying to them, too?"

He sighed and nodded. "Only Ty knows about me because he's undercover, too, but the others don't. If you love me, you'd keep what you know a secret, too. They're still fucked up about what happened in Costa Rica. Remember, they lost people they loved, too."

I bit my lip cuz I did still love him, no matter how upset I was. But how could Ty's foul ass be a cop? Surprise, surprise. I could be forgiving, the same way he forgave me after learning about Ty and my habit.

His boys was waiting with duffel bags, too, looking like soldiers headed on their next mission.

"You all right, shawty?" Ty asked after we climbed aboard the boat.

I nodded even though I wasn't. My brother was dead. I still had no idea what the fuck was going on with Peaches. Mommy was delirious, and I just found out the man that I loved wasn't a hundred percent who I thought he was. I felt a chill crawl over me as I stood in the cold darkness. It was much colder down by the water, and a dense fog filled the air. Ed looked like he was ready to do whatever. He couldn't keep still. Donte looked like he was in deep thought. He never said much of nothing anyway. Rashard had told me before that Donte was a Muslim and that he took everything extra serious. I could only imagine how he felt when he found out what had happened to Yenee in that room. Ty untied the boat when Rashard started it up, and we pulled away from the pier. I sat down and waited to see where we was going and what was about to happen. Rashard seemed too focused to even bother him. Ed lit a cigarette and stared at the water. They all seemed to know what was happening but me. It was quiet on the boat except for the loud hum of the engine. I looked up at the half moon lighting the night sky and wondered how Peaches was doing. Was Yodi and the kids okay over Toya's?

"This nigga gon' catch it," Ty yelled over the engine.

Ed plucked his cigarette in the Chesapeake Bay. I wondered if he felt any of this was karma just like

Nakeeda did. I held on tight to a bar, then walked over to him. In a low voice, I said, "She made me promise to bury your daughter."

He looked alarmed that I knew, but then I hugged him. He stood stiff against the bitter night air and let me squeeze him. I ain't know what else to do.

"I'm so sorry. She was such a sweet girl," I said. When he ain't say nothing, I walked back to where I was sitting and sat back down. By the time I turned around, I saw him wiping a tear away. Donte saw it, too, but looked in the other direction. They both was hurting so much.

I felt like at least an hour had passed by since we first got on the boat. As soon as Rashard docked the boat at another marina that ain't look as up-to-date as the one we had just come from with its raggedy wooden frame, he grabbed one duffel bag and led me off the boat. Ty, Ed, and Donte remained behind.

"What's happening?" I asked, looking back at them. I was scared to death standing in this strange place I ain't know.

"Baby, it's okay," he said, squeezing my hand and leading me up the pier. "Trust me."

I bit my lip and let him take me to another pickup that sat in a parking space. He started the engine and pulled off of the gravel road. We drove for several minutes before we stopped in a wooded area where there was a lone dark cabin. He threw the truck in park and hopped out. My heart thumped in my chest. I knew he ain't plan to leave me here.

When Rashard opened my passenger door, he said, "I can't chance something else happening to you. You gotta stay here until I tell you otherwise."

"What? You gon'..."

He put his finger over my lips to quiet me. "Just trust me, KiKi. I have to handle this shit myself. I brought this shit to you and your family. Now I gotta take care of it."

"But how?"

He took a deep breath. "That nigga must've forgot I know where the fuck he sleep at, too."

I climbed out of the truck, and then I followed him inside the cabin where there was fishing gear in the corner, a fireplace, and three bedrooms. It wasn't a shack or nothing, but it was still scary being here by myself. I watched him light the fireplace, and then he said, "There's a little food in the fridge, and Pat put some food in your bag."

"What is this place?" I asked, opening cabinets and looking around.

"Think of it as a safe house. Look, I don't have much time," he said. "I don't know how long we gon' be, but I'ma call you when I can."

I ain't want him to leave me. "I'm scared. Please don't leave me here by myself."

For the first time, I saw Rashard look like he ain't

know what to say to control the situation. "Shakira, I just need you to be here when I get back. Do you understand? I need you here... when I get back. That's all."

Even though I was scared to death, I sucked it up. There wasn't much he ever asked me to do for him, and I knew this wasn't a time to test his patience or to doubt him. All of us was fucked up and had lost somebody close to us or nearly lost somebody. Rashard seemed on edge just like he was when he confronted Ryan. This was probably how he acted when he saw that tossed-up room back in Costa Rica. I nodded and let him kiss my forehead. I understood.

"Here's a gun just in case," he said, taking the .38 Smith & Wesson from the duffel bag.

I let out hot air.

"It's the same one you used that day we went to the range. Do you remember?"

My hands trembled as he put the lightweight silver-and-black gun in my hand.

"All you have to do is aim and shoot. It's a short-range gun, so if you have to use it, you gotta be close. You understand?"

I nodded and wiped my forehead nervously.

"Double-tap that muthafucka when you use it, too. Just to be sure. You hear me?"

"Yeah," I whispered.

"Okay, KiKi. I'm gone." He pulled me close and

kissed me hard before letting me go. A teardrop landed on his shirt. He wiped it away and said, "I'll call you as soon as I'm in range. Don't be scared. Be brave."

"Where you going, Rashard?"

"Don't worry. I'll be back as soon as I can."

"What if you don't come back?" I asked.

"Then...call Pat. She'll come get you," he said before walking through the door.

I couldn't believe that was his plan. I watched Rashard back the black truck down the gravel road before his headlights disappeared. I had a vision of Dizzle leaving me back in the trailer that time all those years ago. Scared, alone, and in a strange place. At least this time, I had a gun. I checked my cell phone but saw there was no reception. I looked around the cabin and saw that at least there was a landline. I called Meeka to check on Amir and see if she heard any news about Peaches. When she told me Peaches was stable and that she was at Washington Hospital Center, I took a deep breath.

"Where are you?" she asked.

"I don't know, but I gotta go. I'll call you again when I can," I said before hanging up.

I thought about calling Toya to see how Mommy was doing, but that pain was too much. I walked around the cabin trying to take my mind off of everything. Here I was trying to protect her from knowing what Ryan did to me, and instead Ryan is still the cause of her pain. I looked in drawers and closets, hoping I'd find something interesting. I was surprised to see there was a bigger version of the same wallet-size picture Jacylyn had of her and Ty's son sitting in a frame on his night-stand. Guess he used this house, too. Maybe he did have a heart after all.

I went to lay in the biggest bed in the cabin, and the sheets smelled just like Rashard. I was gonna have to get used to calling him Rashard and not Rich. There was probably a lot I was gonna have to get used to, like the fact that he was a cop. It was like we was gonna have to meet each other and start all over again. I put the .38 underneath my pillow and closed my eyes. It took me awhile to fall all the way asleep cuz I was waiting to hear from Rashard. I kept listening to the hum of the fridge. Soon I was knocked out. I woke up a couple hours later cuz the cabin had got so damn cold since the fire had went out in the fireplace.

I sat up and looked at the clock. It was just after five. Rashard had been gone for six hours, and he still hadn't called me. I tried to relight the fireplace with some long matches I found. I rubbed my arms and waited for the room to warm up. I turned the TV on and grabbed a blanket from off the bed to keep me warm on the couch. I cut on an old Mike Epps movie they had sitting in the DVD player since there wasn't no cable.

I was laughing at something funny that had just happened when I heard the front door open.

"Rashard?" I asked, jumping up. Then I smelled the burning cinnamon scent in the air. I only knew one person who smelled like that. Even though I wasn't scared, I ran to Rashard's room. I was gonna have something waiting for Smurf's ass, but he was much faster than I thought.

"Come here, you snitch bitch!" Smurf said, storming toward the room as I slammed and locked the door. His twisted face and heavy accent seemed strange in this safe place. He kicked the door as I fumbled for the gun underneath the pillow. I was too scared to use it, but the more Smurf kicked the door, the more I found the nerve to squeeze the trigger. I fired three rounds at the door. Smurf stopped kicking. I wondered if I had hit him. I waited for another minute, then suddenly Smurf yelled, "You missed, bitch!" Then he kicked the door much harder, and this time it flew off the hinges.

I screamed when I saw his ugly face glaring at me. Smurf was up on me before I could squeeze another round. He slapped me so hard, he knocked me to the ground and the gun fell underneath the bed. Smurf reached the gun before me and slid the nose inside my panties and smiled as I squirmed away. His touch was disgusting.

"All you had to do was play your muthafucking part. You should know how to do that by now!" he yelled over top of me. He unbuckled his pants, and my eyes grew big. "But now I'ma remind you who your ass is."

"No!" I yelled. I wasn't gonna let him rape me. He was crazy if he thought I was gonna let him just use my body again for his own sick pleasure. I thought about Yenee fighting back with Skinny Man, and Nakeeda telling me not to give up. "Get off of me!" I screamed, and then I tried to crawl away backward.

I couldn't let him have me. But then Smurf grabbed me hard by my hair and kept me still with his other hand. I reached around to grab something. Anything. My hand knocked the phone over, and then I reached the lamp cord. I yanked it down hard, making the lamp crash over his head. I hit him in his face and scratched his eyes with my fingernails. I did any and everything to try to keep him the hell away from me. It slowed him enough for me to pull farther away. I flipped over on my knees, feeling for the gun that he had dropped.

"Get back here, you stupid bitch!" He jerked me back toward him, just as my fingers grazed the gun. A few more inches and it would be mine.

"I can fuck you just like this, too," he said, pulling my sweatpants down.

I leaned forward another inch and pulled the gun from under the bed just as Smurf pulled my panties down. I twisted my body around so I could face him with the gun in my hand, but before I could squeeze the trigger, I heard a *poouuf* sound, and then Smurf's heavy body collapsed hard on top of me. Rashard stood over top of Smurf with a gun that had a silencer on it. I was

so happy when I saw Rashard that I cried. My heart
raced with relief.

"I knew that stupid muthafucka was gonna follow us
here. You all right?" he asked, rolling Smurf off of me,
then scooping me up from the floor.

I held on to Rashard tight and tried not to look at the
bullet in the back of Smurf's head as he carried me out
of the room.

"You fought back, baby. You fought back. You're
okay now," he said over my sobs.

He was right. I had fought back, and I survived.
Donte and Ed dragged Smurf's body out to the back of
the cabin where Ty was waiting.

"You're safe now," he said, wiping away my tears and
rocking me in his lap. "I'll never let nothing happen to
you again."

"*I'm* never letting nothing happen to me again," I
said.

Rashard smiled and kissed me. "Yeah, you're definitely a big girl now."

I closed my eyes, relieved that I was safe and that
Rashard was here. I was so proud of myself. I could tell
that I'd grown so much in such a short time. All the
shit I'd been through in my life was only making me
stronger for something else. Even though I ain't know
all of what I was doing with my life, I knew that I was
in control of me and that I had to take care of myself
cuz I was worth it.

"Diamonds are made under pressure," Rashard whispered in my ear.

I guess he had always seen that in me. Seemed like a lot of people seen that in me, except for me. Mommy, Toya, Peaches, Yodi, and Meeka. Even Kareem and Audri saw a light inside of me. I was sorry I hadn't realized it sooner. Yenee said something in that room that still sticks with me—"When there is no enemy within, the enemies outside cannot hurt you"—and she was right. Even though I had Rashard's love and support, there was still much for us to talk about, especially the secrets we both kept. I had to learn to love myself first, though. Flaws and all.

EPİLOGUE

March 2012

I took a deep breath as I leaned forward to look closer at my eyes in the mirror. I was so nervous. My note cards was lying on the bathroom counter, waiting for me to do another practice read. I thumbed through them and took another deep breath.

"Are you one of the speakers?" asked a girl with long braids and big chunk jewelry as she washed her hands in the sink beside me. Her eyes was a dead giveaway for her fifteen or sixteen years, even though her makeup wanted people to think she was much older.

I nodded.

"Oh, which one are you? I'm the mistress of ceremony, Misa Hodges," she said, smiling and shaking her wet hands off before drying them on a towel.

"I'm Shakira Scott."

"Oh, you're the one Ms. N told me to make sure I pay extra attention to," Misa said, smiling.

I smiled because I had finally agreed to talk to Nausy's girls at the annual YELL Foundation Fund-raiser Reception, and it seemed like everyone was here, local politicians and community leaders. My family even got dressed up for the event. Mommy, Toya, and even Yodi came out the house to hear me speak. Peaches and Meeka was everybody's stylists for the evening, making sure we all looked good. Rashard looked hella good in his Michael Kors suit. At the last minute, two girls stumbled in the room looking lost and excited at the same time. One had a real short haircut with cute gold earrings, and the other one, long dark tresses down her back. I couldn't believe my eyes. Camille and Trina Boo had showed up. As happy as I was to see them, my stomach shuddered a little. I was worried about what I was about to say in front of all these people. It wasn't just strangers in the room, but my family and closest friends who was about to learn the truth about me. I had already talked to Mommy about what had happened to me when I was in foster care, about Dizzle, Nut, and even about Ryan. At first she was devastated. She couldn't understand why I didn't tell her or why I never reported Dizzle. I couldn't understand that totally, either. I had just wanted to forget anything bad had ever happened. Telling someone would make it all real. Once I told her that I was okay and that I was doing my best to move on from the pain, she said she'd try her hardest to do the same. Every time I talked to her, I could tell she was getting a little better than the day before and so was I.

"Well, I'll see you out there," Misa said, touching my arm.

"Okay," I said, smiling before putting a second coat of lipstick on. I took another deep breath, then walked out of the bathroom.

The art gallery was filled with beautiful artwork, some from the YELL teenagers and some from well-known artists. I watched Mommy and my sisters eating hors d'oeuvres and talking about some of the sculptures. Just when I was about to move on, I smelled Rashard's soothing cologne beside me.

"Hey, beautiful," he said, placing his hand on the small of my back.

"I'm so nervous, babe," I said, flipping through my note cards.

"Don't be. You got this. Just be you."

Ever since Smurf "disappeared," Rashard's case dried up. He had the Colombian connect, but Salvador didn't make it his business to operate in the States, so there was a big problem. Rashard was assigned to another case, but because he was frustrated with everything that had happened to me and felt somewhat responsible for the deaths of Nakeeda, Yenee, and even Ryan and Peaches's shooting, Rashard had decided to continue his regular detective duties without doing any more undercover work. We had been living in a small house in Chantilly, Virginia, away from all the drama he had become so used to in D.C. The only time I thought about Smurf and what had happened in Costa Rica was when we went to visit Ms. Pat and I saw *Bonita Applebum* parked in the driveway out Calvert County.

"Hey, KiKi... you ready?" Nausy asked, walking up to me. "We're about to get started."

"Okay."

Several minutes later, I listened as Misa shared the purpose for the YELL Foundation to the audience, and then she introduced the speakers. A few of them shared their stories of success, and then Nausy introduced me herself. After she told the audience how reluctant I had been and that she and I knew each other ever since we met at Ms. Val's foster care, she welcomed me to the podium.

I waited for the slight applause to stop, then I said, " 'Just because you have a nightmare, doesn't mean you stop dreaming.' That's a line from a Jill Scott song I heard on the radio on the ride here tonight. From the time I was eight years old, my life was just that... a nightmare," I began, putting the note cards to the side. I thought about what Rashard said. I was just going to be me and say what was in my heart.

By the time I had finished sharing stories from all the muddy roads I traveled down and how I was finally strong enough to talk about it, I had remembered Brianna and her cloudlike dress in that Laundromat all those years ago. I told them that I still had dreams of being a real dancer, that I took dance classes at night, and that when I danced, I felt free. To the young girls in the room, I said, but also signed for my mommy, "No matter what you been through in life, what crazy, dark past you may have, or what sin somebody inflicted upon you, remember to dream. Dream big, too. Know that someone is always there to help you reach your dreams—you. But only if you never, ever give up and always, always love yourself first."

The room erupted into thunderous applause. I wiped away a tear that trickled down my cheek just as a flash from a camera lit up the stage. What I had shared had released me. I took a deep breath and smiled. More flashing lights. Nausynika jumped out of her seat to give me a huge hug. She squeezed both my hands, then said, "Ank thaga ou yaga." *Thank you* in pig latin.

I saw Misa clapping and wiping away a tear from over Nausy's shoulder and knew that I had done the right thing. "No . . . thank you."

READING GROUP GUIDE

reading group guide
discussion questions

1. What role, if any, did KiKi's mother have in what happened to her children being split up across the city? Was she to blame for the discovery Yodi's day care provider made?

2. If KiKi's father was alive, do you think her family would've experienced just as many disappointments?

3. Do you think the relationship KiKi had with Nausy and Dizzle was a result of KiKi's poor self-esteem or something more?

4. Why do you think KiKi decided to work the streets for Nut rather than live with her mother?

5. How do you feel about Peaches not giving KiKi a place to stay when she was at one of her lowest points? Did she owe KiKi considering all she had done to help Peaches get that house?

6. Prostitution is considered the oldest profession in the world. Was KiKi too quick to turn to it every time she was in a bind? If so, what else should she have done for money? Consider her education, experience, and skill set.

7. What was it about Audri that drew KiKi to her? Was Audri right by not getting KiKi some help?

8. How would you describe Toya and KiKi's relationship? Why do you think they never seemed to get along?

9. Do you believe Ryan always had an incestuous attraction toward KiKi? Why or why not? Should she have told her mother sooner about the incident?

10. Why do you think KiKi struggled with the decision to open up about her life to others? Is this something she should've kept to herself? Why or why not?

author q&a

What made you write another book about sexual abuse?

One in four women have been sexually abused in their lifetime. That simple fact says a lot. It's affected people who are very close to me, both friends and family members. I see how their early loss of innocence made them doubt their own self-worth and how it still continues to impact them today. This sort of victimization has long-lasting effects on people and can even impact extended family members. Writing this story made me feel like I'm bringing awareness and compassion to the struggles of the victims.

How did you do your research for this novel?

I am a news lover. Almost every story idea that I have has its roots in a news interview or a documentary. The truth can be so much stranger than fiction. Discussions with friends lead to interviews and more research, including watching documentaries and scouring the Internet for articles.

Who are some of your favorite authors, and what are some of your favorite books?

When I was young I read books by Terry McMillan, Alice Walker, and Omar Tyree. *Mama* by Terry McMillan reminded me so much of my life. I loved *The Women of Brewster Place* because of the many different characters and interconnecting story lines. It was something about the inner struggle of the characters that gave me hope. I was also happy to read books about African Americans where the story didn't involve slavery or oppression. As I got older my range evolved, and I fell in love with contemporary writers who wrote stories about survival in the inner city. Again, these were stories that spoke to me.

When did you realize you wanted to write?

I realized it when I helped write a play about drug prevention when I was in the eighth grade and everybody loved it. After that, I wrote a novel called *Fast Times* about a girl who dropped out of college to live with her boyfriend. What did I know about college? [smile.] I won a twenty-five dollar award for honorable mention from author Marita Golden.

What would you tell aspiring authors?

Someone told me once to first stop calling myself an "aspiring author" and write. Once you write, you're an author. Keep honing your craft, read other people's work, and stay inspired.

Be sure to check out Kia DuPree's other gripping novels now available from Grand Central Publishing!

In the style of urban literary greats Teri Woods and Sister Souljah, Kia DuPree weaves a heart-wrenching story of a young woman living on the streets.

"A knockout of a story...raw, gritty, uncompromising realism, telling like it is honestly and well. DuPree is an author to watch."

—Library Journal

"DuPree displays an excellent ear for the dialogue, thinking, music and world views of her young characters and a talent for setting...far above standard street lit..."

—Publishers Weekly

A woman must deal with the trials and tribulations of urban life and protect her children from the tough streets of Washington, D.C.

"DuPree's knack for dialogue and her insight and compassion for her characters inspire the reader's empathy—an outstanding achievement."

—Publishers Weekly

"This novel is the real deal. Folks seeking a title for an urban book club need look no further. Its inner city realism compares favorably with Sister Souljah's *The Coldest Winter Ever* and Sapphire's *Push*. This is easily one of my top-five fiction books of 2011. Buy it...promote it."

—LibraryJournal.com